DANCING WITH DEATH

Recent Titles by Amy Myers from Severn House

The Nell Drury Mysteries

DANCING WITH DEATH

The Jack Colby, Car Detective, Series

CLASSIC IN THE BARN
CLASSIC CALLS THE SHOTS
CLASSIC IN THE CLOUDS
CLASSIC MISTAKE
CLASSIC IN THE PITS
CLASSIC CASHES IN
CLASSIC IN THE DOCK
CLASSIC AT BAY

The Marsh and Daughter Mysteries

THE WICKENHAM MURDERS
MURDER IN FRIDAY STREET
MURDER IN HELL'S CORNER
MURDER AND THE GOLDEN GOBLET
MURDER IN THE MIST
MURDER TAKES THE STAGE
MURDER ON THE OLD ROAD
MURDER IN ABBOT'S FOLLY

DANCING WITH DEATH

A Nell Drury Mystery

Amy Myers

Severn House Large Print
London & New York

This first large print edition published 2018
in Great Britain and the USA by
SEVERN HOUSE PUBLISHERS LTD of
Eardley House, 4 Uxbridge Street, London W8 7SY.
First world regular print edition published 2017 by
Severn House Publishers Ltd.

British Library Cataloguing in Publication Data
A CIP catalogue record for this title is available from the British Library.

ISBN-13: 9780727893772

Severn House Publishers support the Forest Stewardship Council™
[FSC™], the leading international forest certification organisation. All
our titles that are printed on FSC certified paper carry the FSC logo.

MIX
Paper from
responsible sources
FSC
www.fsc.org   FSC® C013056

Typeset by Palimpsest Book Production Ltd.,
Falkirk, Stirlingshire, Scotland.
Printed and bound in Great Britain by
T J International, Padstow, Cornwall.

Author's Note

There are many magnificent stately homes in Kent where Wychbourne Court is located, but Wychbourne is fictitious, as is the Ansley family. Nell Drury and her team also belong entirely to the world of fiction – unfortunately, as it would be handy to call upon their expertise at times of domestic stress. That Nell and Wychbourne sprang into fictional life is entirely due to my agent, Sara Keane of Keane Kataria Literary Agency, and to my publishers, Severn House. To both, my deep gratitude. I leapt at their suggestion that I delve back into the twenties for inspiration. It was an extraordinary age, very understandable in our own – a time of eager hope overshadowing but not forgetting the war which was not far behind it and from which so many were still suffering. My gratitude also to Steve Finnis of the Royal West Kent Museum and to my husband, James, who has encouraged me every step of the way. As they would have said back in the twenties in his native America, he's a real doozy.

Wychbourne Court

Members of the Ansley family appearing in Dancing with Death

Lord (Gerald) Ansley, 8th Marquess Ansley
Lady (Gertrude) Ansley, Marchioness
  Ansley
Lord Richard Ansley, one of their three
  sons
Lady Helen Ansley, their elder daughter
Lady Sophy Ansley, their younger daughter
The Dowager Lady Ansley (known as Lady
  Enid)
Lady Clarice Ansley, sister to Lord Ansley

The Upper Servants

Nell Drury, chef
Frederick Peters, butler
Florence Fielding, housekeeper
Mr Briggs, Lord Ansley's valet
Miss Jane Checkam, Lady Ansley's maid

Guests, other residents, and visitors

Arthur Fontenoy, former lover of the
  7th Marquess
The Honourable Elise Harlington, guest
Charles Parkyn-Wright, guest

Lady Warminster, guest
Rex Beringer, guest
Guy Ellimore, bandleader
William Foster, under-gardener at
  Stalisbrook Place
and
Detective Inspector Alexander Melbray
  of Scotland Yard

One

'Galloping codfish, Kitty! What the dickens do you call that?' Nell Drury peered at the apricot mousse wobbling in fright at the thought of presenting itself for consumption by high society at Wychbourne Court.

'A disaster, Miss Drury,' Kitty answered dolefully, even though they both knew no one would ever notice the slight blemish where it had caught on the mould as it emerged from its shelter.

Nell laughed. 'Garnish, that's the ticket! The cook's chum.'

In her view, temperatures rose high enough in a kitchen without the chef adding to it. Her predecessor had run this kitchen like a prison before he stormed out in a fury because the soufflés sank. That wasn't going to happen now she was chef, Nell had vowed. She'd been in charge for six months and so far all had run relatively smoothly. Soufflés had risen, pies had been raised and tempers had retreated.

Here she was at the top of her profession and only twenty-nine years old, although tonight was her biggest challenge yet. Dinner for forty guests at seven o'clock, followed by dancing into the small hours, during which a late supper would be served both for them and the additional guests who were coming for the dance only. It was going to be fun, especially as many would be in fancy dress.

As with the mousse, however, all was not quite perfect. Nell made a determined effort to dismiss her misgivings and concentrate on checking the menu for the dinner, which was currently performing a chaotic dance of its own in her mind. First the band struck up with the hors d'oeuvres, then the twists and turns of the tango brought the fish into her mental checklist, then came the heart of the dance with the waltz of the entrées and roasts, then the artistic pleasure of the desserts foxtrotted and quickstepped through her head, and finally a last waltz appeared with fruit and savouries. And, of course, there were the exciting unexpected dishes – sorbets, salads, ices. They were like these new dances coming in from America, including one called the Charleston which sounded like fun.

'Miss Drury, you do know it's already four o'clock?' Mrs Fielding snapped. 'Lady Clarice will be waiting for you in the boot room.'

Trust Mrs Fielding to throw a fly in the soup. Nell knew all too well that the formidable house-keeper waited eagerly for her slightest slip-up in the hope of regaining her own lost authority. A mere cook would be under her jurisdiction, but as a chef Nell held equal ranking, controlling her own domain and staff.

'A clock five minutes in advance/Allows the chef a very last chance,' she sang out, waving a hand at the kitchen clock as she hastily improvised.

It was amazing that in this year of 1925 the old rigid hierarchy still prevailed for some, Nell thought. After the war, it had looked set to crumble, but the Mrs Fieldings of this world still clung to it like limpets to their rock. Mrs Fielding must be well into her forties now and no longer the bustling, sturdy power she once was, so who could blame her? Mrs Fielding was, as Nell's father would have said, a 'fine figure of a woman' and every inch of it was brought into play when she stormed in like Boadicea if she thought her territory was being invaded. The still-room was her chief weapon and gave her any excuse she needed for a complaint. Preserves and distillations were Mrs Fielding's domain and that of the still-room maid, but that left a grey area which she exploited to the full.

Ah, well, if you set your mind to it, life's troubles could melt away like isinglass. Onward, girl, onward, Nell tried to instruct herself when an obstacle reared up before her. Don't waste time blaming an underchef like Kitty or the Mrs Fieldings of this world, just get on and solve the problem, small or large. Get rid of the whey in life, deal with the best of the remaining curds and you'll produce the cheese.

Nell was all too well aware of the ticking clock, however, and had one last look around. In the scullery, the two maids were working on pans and mixing bowls, two kitchenmaids were busy preparing vegetables and Mrs Squires, Nell's plain cook, was looking after the servants' hall meals with one eye while the other was tackling the melon. Pretty little Kitty and Nell's other underchef, anxious young Michel, were busy preparing other hors d'oeuvres, *foie gras* and garnish for the main course.

'I see you've Soufflé Helen on the menu again,'

Mrs Fielding sniffed as Nell whipped off her apron to go through to the main house. 'No use expecting any raspberry preserve from me.'

'We've fresh fruit, thanks to Mr Fairweather,' Nell replied, rushing past her. He was the aptly named vegetable gardener and she cherished her good relationship with him, loving the colours and sheer excitement of the range of herbs, vegetables and fruit that he produced. This June Saturday evening was going to be a one hundred per cent triumph for Wychbourne Court and the Ansley family, Nell vowed, and every inch of her would be concentrating on making that happen, despite the nagging blot on the horizon that refused to disappear.

The ghost hunt.

Wychbourne, like old houses everywhere, had its secrets and some of them in the long-distant past had been dark ones. Lady Clarice, Lord Ansley's sister, was bent on reviving them through her devotion to the many ghosts that haunted it – at least, according to her. But even so, what could go wrong with a ghost hunt?

The Ansley family had been at Wychbourne Court, set deep in the Kentish countryside between Sevenoaks and Tonbridge, since time immemorial. No coming over with an upstart conqueror for the Ansleys. Wychbourne Court oozed history and that's what Nell loved about it. She had been fascinated by stories of kings and queens right from the time her father had taken her to the Tower of London and she'd seen those Beefeaters and been told they were the queen's soldiers.

The way of life at Wychbourne Court fascinated her. Every so often the present marquess, the eighth, would toddle off to the House of Lords and every so often the new prime minister, Stanley Baldwin, would toddle down to Wychbourne. It seemed to Nell, however, that on such occasions the affairs of state were rather less important than billiards and entertainment. Most days she would see His Lordship setting off to walk round the estate – that was where his heart lay. Politics seemed mostly to fly over his head.

They flew over the head of his sister, Lady Clarice, too. Her one preoccupation was those ghosts. She had never married and now, in her early fifties, was devoted to their welfare. She was rather ghostlike herself, Nell thought, with her thin, tall figure and perpetual anxious expression. Eccentric she might be, but Nell was fond of her.

She found Lady Clarice already installed in the boot room near the main entrance to Wychbourne Court, looking lost amid the piles around her, some in boxes, some just in heaps. Some of the boxes were in the open doorway to the adjacent and usually locked gunroom and Nell had to resist asking whether she intended to chase the ghosts with guns. Instead, she asked politely, 'You wanted to see me, Lady Clarice?'

Lady Clarice looked astonished. 'Of course, as you're leading the second group on the ghost hunt.'

'Am I?' This was the first Nell had heard of it.

'Did Lady Ansley not tell you? We are to divide

5

into two groups so as not to frighten our ghostly visitors. You are able to commune with them.'

Was she? This too was news to Nell. She groaned inwardly. Fond though she was of Lady Clarice, she suspected she was as much of a burden to Lord and Lady Ansley as she could be to the servants. 'What would you like me to do now?' she asked.

'Check this equipment for the hunt. And I do want to run through the ghosts with you.'

Running through ghosts? That sounded like a challenge. Nell managed to keep a straight face as Lady Clarice continued, 'I want you to be particularly careful not to upset dear Hubert.'

Nell was at a loss. 'Is he one of the guests?' she asked cautiously.

'Don't be foolish,' Lady Clarice said impatiently. 'You must have met him. He was the Lord Ansley who died during the Civil War when he was abandoned in the Priest's Hole by mistake. However, Simon – who appears very rarely – told me the other day that it was actually his wife who shut him in. There's no proof she murdered him, of course, and Simon is such a fibber.'

'Simon?' Nell queried faintly.

'Really, Nell.' Lady Clarice sighed. 'The fifth marquess. Do take care of poor Hubert. He does seem very scared of women. Perhaps understandably if his wife *did* murder him.'

'I'll be very careful,' Nell promised gently. 'But I'll need a list of the ghosts and where they haunt.'

'If you wish, but there are only nineteen of them known to be active, including the baby and the dog.'

This was getting worse. 'A list would be *very* helpful,' Nell said firmly. 'Shall I begin checking the equipment boxes?'

On her knees – and grateful that she still had her afternoon working skirt and jumper blouse on, not her evening wear – she pulled the first box to her and began counting.

'Torches and lanterns, ten,' she informed Lady Clarice.

'I asked for fifteen,' she moaned.

'I could ask Jimmy – he's the lampboy – to bring candles—' Too late, Nell realized she had put a foot wrong.

'On no account.' Lady Clarice was appalled. 'Ghosts lose their power by candlelight.'

It was going to be a long business, Nell could see, mentally listing the work still awaiting her in the kitchen. She would speed up. 'Pads and pencils,' she said briskly. 'Twenty of each. Magnifying glasses, ten.' What on earth were they to do with these? she wondered. Crawl after the ghosts like Sherlock Holmes? 'Measuring tape, three—'

'Far too few.'

'Chalk,' Nell pressed on, skimming boxes one after the other at high speed. 'Two barometers, two thermometers, two phonographs for recording, two cameras, two dark cloths for focusing, two bags of flour.' What the dancing dickens was that for? Don't ask, just get on with it, she advised herself. 'Four mirrors.' Those really did puzzle her. 'What are these for, Lady Clarice? I thought ghosts couldn't be seen in mirrors?'

Lady Clarice beamed. 'Anything that does

appear in them will therefore be automatically excluded from the list of ghosts sensed. This is a scientifically conducted experiment, Nell. I expect you promptly at a quarter to twelve in the great hall. My nephew Richard will be moving this equipment out there.' A pause. 'Do you really need a list?' she asked doubtfully.

'I do,' Nell assured her earnestly. 'I don't want to offend any ghosts by addressing them wrongly.' That, however, was the least of her qualms about the ghost hunt.

The story of Wychbourne Court was an amazing one to Nell. Before William the Conqueror strode into England this site had been a humble farm. The family and its farm had survived and under Good Queen Bess the current Ansley, Sir William, had become a baron and acquired the means to rebuild on a much grander scale. A seventeenth-century red-brick frontage had later been added and in the eighteenth century the house had taken flight with the addition of two huge wings, resulting in the whole sprawling, elegant mass it was today. That had been thanks to William's descendant, Philip, who had rendered services during the Seven Years' War that resulted in his becoming the first Marquess Ansley. The family's future was assured.

When war struck in 1914 its financial position rocked but recovered. There were far fewer servants here now than there had been twenty years earlier but, as Nell knew, that was the case everywhere. The Ansleys' great loss had been a hammer blow. The second son of the present

Lord and Lady Ansley, Noel, had died at the Battle of Ypres. The eldest of their five children, Kenelm, was married and working abroad for the Colonial Service, but the other three still lived at Wychbourne Court. The gap that Noel had left was still there. Nell knew that even though she had worked here only a year, and for only half of that had she been on familiar terms with Lord and Lady Ansley and their children – the latter not always a pleasure.

She had come a long way from Spitalfields, where her dad had been a costermonger. He had taught her so much about vegetables and fruit that she could spot a rotten orange a mile off. He had wanted her to join him on the barrow but by that time she had fallen in love with the bright lights of London and become a chambermaid at the luxurious Carlton Hotel on the corner of London's Haymarket. There she had ploughed on until she came to the notice of its chef, Monsieur Escoffier, who had spotted her interest in the kitchens. Interest turned out to be talent and he had trained her – a unique privilege as not one of his fifty or so staff had been a woman until she joined it.

Hard though that had been, she had watched, learned and cooked, and by the time Monsieur Escoffier had retired five years ago she had become one of his underchefs. She hadn't married – why should she? Why marry to be dominated by someone else's life? She wanted her own and after four years as a chef at a manor house north of London, here she was at Wychbourne Court, busy appreciating the difference of operating in the countryside. Oh, the bliss of having an orchard and vegetable garden at one's disposal!

Why should she have misgivings about the evening ahead? Ghosts belonged to the past and this was a new age. A dancing age for everybody, both literally and metaphorically. The bright future lay ahead and tonight's festivities were a mark of that, although war and its tragedies lay deep and not forgotten. How could war be forgotten when so many soldiers had come home to no jobs and no hope? How could it be forgotten during the slump of 1921? Tonight it would be put aside, however. Tonight, Nell vowed, Wychbourne would be shouting welcome to the future – and not worrying about ghosts.

Sophy Ansley watched her brother and sister warily. They had great plans for tonight and had summoned her to the Blue Drawing Room to join them, although she wasn't sure she agreed with them. She had to appear to do so, however. She had too much to hide not to. She had little in common with her big sister Helen and big brother Richard. They were the bright young things of the family but she preferred books. That was what was important in life, even if she had made a mess of her coming-out last year, ending it not only without a potential husband but without a flock of admirers.

After all, Sophy consoled herself, she was only nineteen and neither Richard nor Helen was married yet at twenty-five and twenty-three respectively, even though Helen was famous for her golden-haired beauty and Richard was almost another Rudolph Valentino. Women swooned over him, which was cuckoo.

Nevertheless, Sophy had had to face the humiliating thought that she had no eager admirers attending the party tonight. Half of her wanted to be one of the new flappers; the other half thought they were all off their rockers. And Mother's insistence on her wearing that black and pink chiffon dancing dress wasn't going to help. Designed by Chanel or not, her figure was too short for it and had too many bumps. Her breasts refused to disappear to fit under tight bodices in order to meet the current boyish fashion craze. She often envied Helen's languid elegance and Richard's sporty hail-fellow-well-met charm, but tonight she didn't. She was Sophy and had her own plans for the evening. She *would* have a partner – and a very special one. Meanwhile, she must show some interest in their stupid jokes.

'You have asked Charlie, haven't you?' Helen asked Richard accusingly. There she was, Sophy thought, looking like a goddess sprawled on the daybed in her fashionable silk house pyjamas.

'Of course I've asked him, sister mine,' Richard said smugly. He would smoke those awful gaspers. Sophy knew everyone did it nowadays, even girls, but they looked silly and smelt horrible.

'Will he do it?' Helen demanded.

'Charlie's a good sort,' he answered. 'Of course he'll do it. Can't wait.' A languid wave of the cigarette in its elegant holder.

Sophy wasn't so sure that Charlie Parkyn-Wright was a good sort, even though everyone seemed to adore him. She prided herself on

11

noticing things, such as the way his jolly grin disappeared every now and then and how some people seemed nervous of him, which suggested they didn't like him at all. When in a rare, sisterly moment she had voiced these thoughts to Helen, however, her sister had been furious.

'Charlie's a dish. Can it be you're jealous?' she snapped.

No, it couldn't. And that confirmed Sophy's suspicion that Helen had her eye on Charlie, a thought that appalled her, especially as that nice Rex Beringer was so stuck on Helen.

The London season was in full flow, but as their London house was let – for economic reasons, Father had explained – this year they would remain in Kent at Wychbourne Court and entertain here. Tonight's ball was surely designed in the hope of marrying Helen off – and probably herself too, Sophy thought dismally. Neighbours from the Sevenoaks and Ightham area would be coming, together with some driving over from Sussex and others from London, including Charlie Parkyn-Wright. He seemed so much in demand as a ladykiller that he could pick and choose which parties he attended during the London season. Helen and Richard had been thrilled that Charlie had chosen to accept the invitation to Wychbourne, but Sophy had not. She thought he was a rotter. *And*, as usual, he was among the guests staying for the weekend in the west wing.

Charlie was Richard's best friend so he never noticed anything amiss with him – although that could be due to the fact that Richard was too busy ogling Elise. The Honourable Elise Harlington was the toast of the town, the ideal model for Lanvin's fashionable creations. Sophy didn't care for her either. When Elise sashayed into a room all eyes were on her, especially Richard's and Charlie's – and she knew it. One of the advantages of not being a bright young thing, Sophy thought, was that one had time to see what was going on – but no one else did. That's what she was counting on tonight, even if she had to play along with Richard and Helen for their silly game. She wasn't happy about that, but after all, Aunt Clarice deserved it. Her and her ghosts.

'We're going to give Aunt Clarice the night of her dreams,' Richard drawled. 'Anyway, Charlie's a good egg. At Harrow everyone agreed he was the tops. It will make the evening, you'll see.'

Aunt Clarice's soulful insistence that every corner of Wychbourne Court boasted a ghost of Ansleys past was a running joke that was getting tedious. There was the dairymaid in the mid-nineteenth century whom the fourth Marquess Ansley failed to marry; Lady Henrietta, who'd been cut off in her prime by her unloving husband; Sir Thomas, who had been away on a crusade and returned to find his beloved wife Eleanora had seduced, or been seduced by, a minstrel; and the first marquess, who returned from time to time to see how the builders were getting on with the two new wings at Wychbourne. They were just a sample of the many with whom Aunt Clarice claimed to be on friendly terms.

Nothing excited Aunt Clarice more than discovering an ancient tome in the library that confirmed her hopes that there might be another ghost

13

lingering around. Now that ghost hunting was all the rage, Helen and Richard had dreamed up this idea of a midnight hunt with the entire party (or those who wished to leave the dance floor and supper room) prowling darkened corridors led by Aunt Clarice in search of her ghosts. Aunt Clarice had seized on the plan with great enthusiasm.

'It's going to be fun,' Richard added, 'especially with some of us, at least, in fancy dress.'

Fancy dress was another thing that Sophy didn't like and she had flatly refused to become St Joan of Arc for the evening, even if that did mean that she was stuck with the black and pink chiffon concoction her mother had foisted on her.

Nell hurried back from the boot room through the great hall, aware of that ticking clock. Perhaps the ghost hunt wouldn't be such a nightmare as she had feared, she thought optimistically. Through the open doors to the dining room and drawing room she could see the conservatory and the far-off lights twinkling in the gardens beyond it. Wychbourne would be ablaze tonight, a fantasy world of gleaming lanterns and lights, conjuring up all the riches of the world with the bright glowing colours and costumes of the fancy dress, the band playing in the ballroom and all the exciting smells and tastes of the banquet to crown it all. The best food – she liked to think *her* food – aroused all five senses: taste, touch, sight, smell and even hearing – the anticipation of the sound of the gong, the clatter of plates, the gas burner pops, the champagne corks or even the rustle of greaseproof paper round sandwiches at a picnic.

14

Tonight was something special, though – a magnificent party right here in Kent. There'd be dancing in the ballroom and perhaps in the conservatory too, where a gramophone and records were ready. Probably some of the dancers would whirl their way to the terrace or even sneak down to the gardens below. Whether she was cooking or watching from the serving room, or later, the supper room, Nell was going to enjoy every minute of it. Even the ghost hunt.

Peters, as he thought of himself during working hours – the Freddie was kept for his private life and his memories of a childhood long past – was luxuriating in his task of greeting the new arrivals at the main door. As butler, he felt part of things and heard things without getting involved himself. It was like being back in the army when he was batman to the late Lord Noel Ansley, or rather Major Ansley as His Lordship had been during the war. Peters never thought he'd get another job after the war because of his record, but he did, thanks to poor Lord Noel. Even though he knew he didn't look imposing either in height or appearance, he'd quickly learned how to be a butler and relished it, despite the fact that there was only one permanent footman under his command, and of course young Jimmy, who helped him with the Wychbourne Service plates and other jobs as well as seeing to the lights. Only the ground floor needed attention, still lit with oil, although elsewhere electric lighting was installed. Excellent, as long as the generator didn't break down.

It was after six o'clock now and guests had been arriving for the last hour. Some of those staying for the weekend were still not here, and the guests who were only coming for the evening dinner and dance were also due. He thought with pleasure of the ball to come. There'd be dancing in the servants' hall too – they had a gramophone there. Mrs Fielding – his Florence – would be present, splendidly regal in her blue satin evening dress, and he thought with happy anticipation of the warmth of her sturdy body next to his as they waltzed together. None of this ragtime stuff for them. Nor rumbas and congas and whatnot, though the tango held possibilities for a bit of fun. The new chef was a lively one too, Peters thought, for all she was not as cuddly as Florence. He didn't approve of women chefs as a rule, though. Cooks were what women were, no matter how fancy the food.

There was Lady Warminster's Delage sweeping to a halt in the forecourt. No driving round to the motor car park by the stables for her. And here she came.

'Good evening, Peters.' She gave a sweet smile as she swept up to him in her fur-collared cape, handing the Delage keys to his footman, Robert. She hadn't deigned to wear fancy dress, he noted, even though she was only here for the evening. She thought she was fancy enough already with her diamonds and sapphires.

At least she had acknowledged him, Peters thought. Some things were changing in this world, at last. Servants were no longer below notice, even though the world of the servants'

16

wing usually remained untrodden territory to the families for whom they worked.

He bowed to her as she passed. 'Lady Warminster,' he murmured deferentially. Not that he felt deferential towards her. A jumped-up person, in his opinion. Husband something high up in the army in Persia before it was thrown out of there, he was now advising the RAF in neighbouring Mesopotamia. Where the general had found his wife, Peters wouldn't like to speculate, and Stalisbrook Place over Tonbridge way wasn't a patch on Wychbourne.

Now Mr Rex Beringer pulled up in his Bentley Tourer – another motor car to swoon over. He was a gentleman you couldn't fault. Delicate heart, they said. That's why he'd missed the war and looked frail now. But he always had a polite word. It was said he was keen on Lady Helen but she had her eyes elsewhere.

'Shall I drive it round to the stables?' Mr Beringer asked.

'Our pleasure, sir. Robert will take your baggage and park the motor car for you.'

Ten minutes later came two more weekend guests. Charles Parkyn-Wright was a gentleman who always put a smile on one's face. He'd been coming here for years as he was an old school-friend of Lord Richard's. He was leaping out of his Hispano-Suiza sports car to assist his passenger. Down stepped the Honourable Elise Harlington. She wore a cape too, this one in glittering silver. But it wasn't too large to hide her tall, slim, graceful figure, the black hair, the smoky dark eyes, the black Egyptian fancy dress and jewels

17

flashing everywhere. Cleopatra was on her way to dazzle the entire assembly.

Mr Parkyn-Wright wasn't yet changed for dinner and no doubt the flannels and striped blazer would quickly turn into fancy dress or evening attire. He was hatless, Peters noted disapprovingly, but that was an increasing tendency among the young thanks to the example set by the Prince of Wales.

The Honourable Elise bestowed a gracious smile on Peters as she languidly strolled past him. She was a wild one, he had heard. Every night club in London knew her. Lord Richard was sweet on her but he didn't stand a chance. Not with Mr Parkyn-Wright around. Peters signalled to Robert as he returned from his earlier mission to take the luggage.

Meanwhile, Mr Parkyn-Wright was beaming at Peters as though he had spotted his best buddy. 'Keeping well, Peters? Heard you had a spot of trouble with your leg recently.'

'Thank you, sir. I am quite recovered.'

'Excellent. The old place wouldn't be the same without you.'

Peters glowed. 'Thank you, sir. May I say how delighted we are to see you at Wychbourne again.'

'You may, old sport. You may. Quite like the old days, isn't it? We'll have a chat about *them* while I'm here.' Charlie chuckled as he continued on his way in the wake of Cleopatra.

Peters' glow faded. What did Mr Parkyn-Wright mean by having a chat? Surely it couldn't mean he'd heard the old story?

Two

The last half hour before dinner was served might be the worst, Nell thought, but it was the most exciting. Their familiar *Alice in Wonderland* caucus race was in progress. Everyone had to be winners tonight. Dishes were lined up on the central kitchen table and a procession of footmen seized them, completed the circular route round the table and disappeared into the corridor to head for the serving room in the main house. They then reappeared a few moments later for another delivery. No one actually ran – they just moved so quickly it seemed as though they did.

Poor devils. Many of these footmen hired for the occasion were probably ex-soldiers who couldn't find other work. The aftermath of the war and the following slump had hit men at all levels of society. Nell had bought matches in the street from men she had seen dining at the Carlton in earlier years; she had bought them from men who had been seriously injured either physically or mentally; she'd bought them from men who in a pre-war world would have been labourers or office clerks and could find no work now.

'Take that back, Michel.'

Nell spotted a small dish of marigold eggs that failed to please. On the menu the dish was *oeufs d'or*, Lady Ansley having reluctantly decided that the menu had to be French tonight even if the occasional English dish such as this slipped in under a French name. Monsieur Escoffier would have nodded approvingly, Nell thought. He was all for simplicity and so was she. Thankfully that style of cooking was now becoming more fashionable. Using English recipes with all their colours and smells and tastes thrilled her. They enabled her to use Mr Fairweather's wonderful array of herbs and fruits in the vegetable garden and orchards, together with the spices in which England had once revelled and which were beginning once again to delight diners. In the Wychbourne library she had discovered a treasure trove of Ansley family recipes harking back to earlier centuries, but tonight's guests would be expecting French dishes. Mousses, not tansies. Fruit soufflés, not fools and whim-whams.

Mrs Fielding couldn't bear to be left out of the proceedings. 'Those raspberries don't look ripe to me,' she said with great satisfaction. For a moment, Nell thought she was right – but she wasn't. The Soufflé Helen had cooled nicely and the raspberry purée was ruby red.

'Perfection,' Nell assured her.

'Don't say I haven't warned you.' Mrs Fielding glared. 'You should have used my preserve.'

When the dinner began, Nell would begin the cooking of the *noisettes* of lamb. Frying pans were ready, as was the butter, on her trusty Golden Eagle range. She knew where she was with that. The new electric stoves were splendid, if you didn't mind your food being either burnt or uncooked, as the ovens offered one heat only. Mrs Fielding had one in her still-room and indeed

Nell had one here in the main kitchen, but you couldn't beat her Eagle for reliability.

It wouldn't be long before the gong went now. They couldn't hear it in the kitchen but Nell could tell the time was coming because Miss Checkam, ladies' maid to Lady Ansley and her daughter Lady Helen, had appeared, and in her wake came her counterpart, Mr Briggs, Lord Ansley's valet. That signalled that the Ansleys must be present at the gathering in the great hall where Peters would be superintending Robert and his hired team as they maintained the flow of champagne cocktails, juleps, love's revivers and horse's necks. It wouldn't be easy to keep to the set time for dining as some of the guests might have wandered through the drawing room and conservatory out on to the terrace outside on such a fine June evening.

'Tell us the worst, Miss Checkam,' Nell said cheerfully. There was often some titbit of doom to be teased out of her and, provided it didn't stop the flow of work in the kitchen, her arrival was a useful guide to what was going on beyond what was once a green baize door between the servants' wing and the main house.

'There's something afoot,' Miss Checkam said darkly. 'Lady Sophy's up to some mischief.'

'Perhaps they all are,' Nell joked. 'After all, this ghost hunt is asking for trouble. You should see all the equipment Lady Clarice has been gathering.'

Mrs Fielding snorted. 'How do you hunt a ghost? There are no such things.'

'Lady Clarice says there are lots of them here,' Miss Checkam retorted.

21

She too had problems with Mrs Fielding and was on equal footing with her, as were Mr Peters and Mr Briggs. Mr Briggs had no problems with Mrs Fielding or with anyone. He just smiled and lived in his own world, which consisted of his work for Lord Ansley, eating, sleeping and going into the gardens to watch birds – 'it was something in the war' was the whisper.

'She's off her trolley,' Mrs Fielding contributed.

'Just daffy,' Nell said mildly, moving towards the range and tweaking a mint leaf for the garnish of the *pommes de terre*.

Mrs Fielding's eyes gleamed. 'You ever seen a ghost, Cook?' she demanded.

'Far too busy.' Nell ignored the jibe and beckoned to Michel to bring her the meat.

'I did once,' Kitty whispered. 'I heard that one who sings in the corridors – Calliope.'

'I met one too, Miss Checkam,' said Mrs Squires. 'Jeremiah, the smuggler what haunts the cellars.' Mrs Squires was a sturdy lady from the village who seldom took part in communal discussions, being more devoted to her pastry, so her talk of Jeremiah had credibility.

'Is he the ghost who murdered—?' Michel began.

'No,' Nell interrupted. 'That'll be me if you don't get a move on. Ghosts aren't on the menu until midnight. Dinner is in five minutes. Fish and vegetables, everyone!'

A moment's appalled silence and then everyone sprang into place. A crispy slice of artichoke fell off a plate, the *sauce normande* was lost but quickly found, to be rushed to the serving room

22

for the Dover sole fish course (or *sole de la Manche*, as it was tonight), and the truffles, *foie gras* and *pommes de terre* to accompany the *noisettes* of lamb were behind schedule for delivery in their appropriate dishes.

'Suppose Lady Clarice is right, Miss Drury?' Kitty whispered when they'd recovered their breath. 'Suppose there really are ghosts around?'

'All adds spice to life,' Nell replied. 'And the ghost hunt won't be hunting in our wing.'

'Why will they not?' Michel demanded. 'This is old too.'

'Because all those old Ansleys never put foot in the servants' wing,' Nell pointed out. 'And our ghosts never go outside four walls – not the aristocratic ones, anyway. You get highwaymen and the like prancing around the countryside as ghosts, but not here. Ansley ghosts like to keep themselves warm. There's said to be a cook haunting the old kitchens just for the warmth.'

Michel thought this over. 'You told us about a dairymaid ghost and the dairy is cold.'

'The marquess of the time liked to be comfortable when he seduced dairymaids,' Nell quickly improvised, 'so he got her to climb up the ivy. She haunts the boot room now.'

'Miss Drury,' Michel said after he had thought this through, 'you are being funny with us.'

'Just a little.'

It was better to laugh. Then she would forget the ghost hunt that awaited her later tonight.

Time to check the serving room, Nell realized. The *noisettes* were ready to be cooked to their delicious

23

pinky-grey best and the hors d'oeuvres and the fish course were under control, as were the vegetables. That left the salad, the soufflé and the final bowls of fruit. Once they were done, Nell could begin to relax – save for the thought of the ghost hunt ahead. At least the ghost list had arrived, courtesy of Jimmy.

On her way to the serving room, however, she collided with the members of the band to whom Mrs Squires had arranged supper to be served in the servants' hall. Nell stood aside while they went in but then she saw who was bringing up their rear, clarinet case in hand. The shock hit her like a tidal wave from the past. Tonight of all nights. Why the blazes hadn't it occurred to her that this might happen some day? Shock or not, though, she almost laughed when she saw the thunderstruck look of recognition on his face.

'We've met before,' he said, recovering some of his all too familiar poise.

'At the Carlton,' she agreed.

'As if I'd forget.' He smiled at her. 'Can't stop, Nell. We'll talk later.'

Would we indeed? she thought mutinously.

Guy Ellimore had served as an officer in the Royal Flying Corps and then the Royal Air Force during the war; he had been decorated with the DFM too, but somehow after the war ended he hadn't fitted in. Maybe he couldn't get a job, but she thought it was more than that. He'd told her that he preferred to roam and running a band let him do that. 'Music, dancing, they keep me going,' he had told her once. 'And being on the move.'

24

Nell had understood then and she did now. There had been a restlessness in him as there had been in her. She had settled hers but he had not. He'd always be travelling on, would Guy. 'It's the jazz inside me,' he'd explained. He was still overcoming the horror of the war, though. 'Dead friends dance before my eyes,' he had told her in a rare moment of outspokenness. Music helped. He'd talked of the Dixieland Jazz Band who had come over from America in 1919. 'Jazz is all the rage there now and it will be here as well soon. You don't even need to read music. You just play. That's freedom, Nell.'

Freedom. That's what the twenties were all about. Not the same old poetry and music with set rules, but new ways, new rhythms for the new world, like Edith Sitwell's *Façade*. Fun, the unexpected. Nell didn't regret not having thrown in her lot with Guy, though it had been hard to part at the time. She had done the right thing, though. A man in her life would stop her doing what she was born to do. After all, some day she might want to move on from Wychbourne Court, perhaps to Paris, where everything seemed to be spinning even faster than in London. How could she do that if she had a husband and children?

'Later,' she answered him now. 'I'm running one of the groups on the ghost hunt, so after that.'

He grinned. 'We've just heard about the ghost hunt. Ghosts of the past, Nell. I can't miss that.'

Making a determined effort to put Guy out of her mind, she checked that nothing was amiss in the serving room then ran upstairs to her bedroom

25

in the servants' wing to find something suitable to change into later for the ghost hunt. Left to herself, she would have worn red or bright blue or pink, but ghosts (in the form of their mouth-piece, Lady Clarice) would not like that, so she laid out a grey sleeveless dress of voile over a slip of the same colour. It would do. Her stockings would have to remain as they were and fortunately they hadn't so far laddered today. Black beads around the neck – no, red beads. They went better with her light brown hair. Right, add a touch of face cream and lip rouge and yes, she would be presentable.

'Come on, ghosts, I'll be ready for you,' she announced to her mirror as she held the dress up in front of her to see how it looked. (Even though one can't see ghosts in a mirror, she might as well be polite to them, just in case they were there.)

Clothes laid out on her bed in readiness, she gave a sigh of relief. Now she could concentrate on the dinner ahead again. And that too held its problems. During her final check of the dining room, she had come to the conclusion that Lady Ansley must have been in one of her 'let's have fun' moods when she planned the seating for this dinner. It was extraordinary considering the feud between the Dowager Lady Ansley, who lived in the Dower House, and Mr Arthur Fontenoy, who lived a stone's throw away in Wychbourne Court Cottage. They never spoke or even acknowledged the other's existence, but this evening they would be sitting next to each other. What a recipe for disaster! In addition to the family and neighbours of all ages, a bevy of bright young things was motoring down from London, so the guest list was already a heady mix. Add a dose of Lady Clarice and her ghosts and there could be trouble.

'We should dine, Gerald,' Lady Ansley murmured to her husband. Peters had sounded the gong some minutes earlier but the party was so dispersed that Gerald had to lead the way to the dining room.

Here we go, Gertie, she told herself. It was performance time again. She mentally rearranged her face from this brief excursion into her Gaiety Girl past to today's gracious hostess. She played that role expertly by now and still had the same quickening of excitement as the curtain went up on another spectacular Wychbourne Court party.

'Certainly, my dear.' Gerald, the eighth Marquess Ansley, extended his arm to his mother, the Dowager Lady Ansley – Lady Enid, as she liked to be addressed – while Gertrude decorously took the arm of the highest-ranking gentleman at the rear of the procession.

These old rules of precedence were on the way out now that the world had moved on at such a pace, but Gerald never seemed to notice that. Gertrude still loved some of the ritual, fortunately, although what she did not love was the endless decisions that had to be taken for such events. Nell – Miss Drury, as she must think of her tonight – was a tower of strength. She hadn't taken to her at first. Nell had seemed such a determined young woman. Then Gertrude had realized that was what she liked about her. She was modern, just doing what Gertie would have done at her age – *had* done, in fact, for actresses were hardly highly ranked in society back in the nineties. That's when she had met darling Gerald, who hadn't even seemed to notice the social distance between them.

Gertrude's practised eye surveyed the room as guests were conducted to their seats. All seemed well, but then . . .

'Peters!' She beckoned him to her side, almost frozen with horror, as she saw that all the ladies were now seated.

'Your Ladyship?' He was there in an instant.

'Lady Enid – the dowager.' She could hardly choke the name out. How in the name of Hades had this happened? How could she have made this mistake? Her mother-in-law was seated to Gerald's right, as regal in her long, purple evening dress as Queen Mary herself. About to take his seat next to her, however, was Arthur Fontenoy, who not unnaturally looked flabbergasted. For one terrible moment, as Peters looked poised for instructions, Gertrude feared the unthinkable would happen: that the dowager would rise to her feet and walk in slow and stately fashion out of the room.

Instead, her mother-in-law chose to bring the battle to the enemy. Her voice rang out throughout the entire room. 'Good evening, Mr Fontenoy. Indeed, it is so good it makes one eagerly anticipate the coming of good night.'

Arthur, with most of the forty diners spellbound as to what would happen next, bowed his head. 'Good evening, Lady Enid.' With great courage, he took his seat.

For all his seventy-odd years, he was no match for her mother-in-law, Gertrude thought pityingly. He had already lost the first round.

'What happened?' Gertrude hissed at Peters, whose usual imperturbable control seemed to have deserted him.

'The seating order. Someone must have changed it,' he babbled.

Gertrude believed him. Her eye fell on Sophy, who was looking appalled. Surely she wouldn't have done this? It was more likely the work of Richard or Helen, or even of the great Charlie Parkyn-Wright. Delightful and popular as Charlie was, he was renowned for his little jests. What else, she wondered, might he have in mind?

Really, the young of today were so unpredictable. She had sensed this evening might be like going on stage – somehow one knew that this would be a performance when one forgot one's lines or tripped over one's petticoats. Perhaps she should have joined the young folk and worn fancy dress.

Her children were a puzzle to her. Kenelm, currently posted abroad, was so stiff and unbending, although with a wife like Honoria she supposed that was inevitable. As for poor Richard, he looked so out of place tonight as an eighteenth-century soldier, despite his good looks. Or perhaps he was looking despondent because of that wretched Elise. Cleopatra, indeed. Did the young of today wear *any* underclothing? she wondered, looking at Elise's seemingly impossible slender form. Richard was seated next to her, at his insistence, and yet owing to the way Elise-cum-Cleopatra was so animatedly talking to Charlie Parkyn-Wright on her right, he didn't look happy. Charlie, on the other hand, did. His Tutankhamun costume rather suited him.

And then there was Helen, dressed as Helen of Troy. Oh dear. Not that she didn't live up to the costume. Her blonde beauty came from Gerald's side of the family, not hers. Helen must have some goal in life but what was it? Her elder daughter was a mystery to her. Up one moment and down the next. There was something wrong with the girl, but what?

Sophy was another problem. Perhaps her daughter had been right. That dress didn't suit her. This evening would be an ordeal for her, although she was looking more content now. Her dinner partner was someone Gertrude didn't know – Hugh Beaumont. He wasn't in fancy dress and he did not look at all content. At least Sophy looked happier, though.

Everyone else, in fact, also seemed happy – even her mother-in-law after her little victory. No, Gertrude realized, not everyone else. Lady Warminster was certainly not looking at all content. She looked extremely annoyed, gazing at someone else further down the table.

Gradually Gertrude felt herself relaxing, however. Once they all began to eat Miss Drury's superb banquet, all would be well. How could it not be?

'What a scream!' Nell laughed.

The story of what had happened between the dowager and Mr Fontenoy had quickly reached them, courtesy of footman Robert. The drama of

30

the situation had of course escaped the hired staff. There had been no time to savour it while dinner was still in full flow but now that the Wychbourne Service plates and dishes were mostly in the scullery with the boiler doing its utmost to keep up the flow of hot water, Nell had breathing space. Thank goodness the silver plates and glasses were still looked after in the butler's pantry. Apart from the soufflé lacking a few raspberries to garnish the dish as perfectly as Nell would have liked, all had gone well.

Mostly the servants just accepted that Lady Enid did not like Mr Fontenoy, but Nell knew the whole delightful story from Lady Ansley herself. Sometimes Her Ladyship longed for a shoulder to cry on or just to share a good laugh, and Nell provided it. She liked Lady Ansley. Despite the dowagers and Mrs Fieldings of this world, the rigid wall between the family and servants was gradually eroding and sometimes even had a gateway, such as the one that had led to Lady Ansley talking to Nell about the rift between her mother-in-law and poor Mr Fontenoy.

'I fear this feud between them is all down to my husband's late father, Hugo, the seventh marquess,' Lady Ansley had lamented. 'How could he have done it? His will included a legacy to his wife and one to his *friend* with whom he had been *friendly* for many years,' Lady Ansley had emphasized meaningfully.

Nell had seen the problem. The word 'friend' was one even the broad-minded Lady Ansley didn't care to explore more fully. 'So Lady Enid

31

and Mr Fontenoy don't like each other because they see each other as rivals?'

'Far worse than that,' Lady Ansley had told her. 'The immediate legacy to each of them was comparatively tiny. The major part of the legacy was left in trust for whichever of them survived the other. Unfortunately my father-in-law died at a relatively young age, forty-nine.'

Nell had gasped. 'Joker, was he?'

'I fear so,' Lady Ansley had blurted out. 'I never met him as my husband had just inherited the title when we met. I would have got on well with my father-in-law, I think. More perhaps than with . . .'

She had stopped there, but it had given Nell great amusement. So Lady Ansley suffered difficulties with the dowager too and also no doubt from the two antagonists, who refused not only to speak to each other but to recognize each other's presence. Tonight had indeed been a battlefield but Nell doubted whether it would end in a peace treaty or even an armistice.

There was very little left for her to do towards the late supper. She had supervised the preparation of the cold buffet but its management would be largely left to Kitty and Michel, subject to her own last-minute check. Mr Peters also liked to be involved in such matters since it was to be served not in the dining room but in the supper room adjacent to the ballroom.

It was time, Nell thought thankfully, for her to change into her evening wear and then perhaps join the servants' hall dancing for a time – once she was sure that the band was safely in the ballroom. She wasn't yet ready to meet Guy Ellimore again.

Sophy was cross with herself. Here she was clasped in her partner's arms dancing the foxtrot to 'Toot, Toot, Tootsie' and she ought to have been on top of the world, even if she did look like Koko the Clown in this dress. She was sorry about her slip-up in changing the table plan that had resulted in her grandmother being next to her arch enemy, but at least she had succeeded in keeping Hugh Beaumont well away from Lady Warminster.

Her plan had worked wonderfully well (barring one little slip-up) and no one queried who 'Hugh Beaumont' was. It just went to show what a farce all these rules were. 'Hugh' was looking splendid in his tailcoat and absolutely right for the evening, although he seemed ridiculously worried. Of course, it was a nuisance that Lady Warminster was here at all and that she had not noticed Her Ladyship's name on the guest list until too late. Lady Warminster hadn't looked at all happy at dinner, and 'Hugh' was sure she had recognized him. She hadn't said anything, though, and so that was all right, Sophy thought. Now she wanted to enjoy the rest of the dance, but 'Hugh' kept twisting his head all the time to see if Lady Warminster was staring at him.

'What's worrying you, Hugh?' she asked, as the jerk of his arms didn't seem entirely due to the foxtrot.

'I shouldn't be here, Lady Sophy,' he muttered

in her ear. 'She didn't tell me she was coming here.'

'Call me Sophy,' she hissed. 'Remember?'

Eventually, as he continued to look hunted, she had a brainwave. 'Let's go into the gardens,' she said. 'You won't keep seeing her there.' That would be fun, she thought. He might even kiss her. She didn't care much either way, but it would be an interesting experience.

'Hugh' brightened up.

'We must be back for the ghost hunt, though,' Sophy added firmly.

Helen Ansley was also upset. It was all very well being dressed as Helen of Troy but she wasn't doing well as a magnet as far as partners were concerned – thanks of course to the magnificent Elise, who as Cleopatra seemed to be attracting all the Mark Antonys she wanted. In particular, she was attracting Charlie. Rex Beringer was a good standby but so dull. He was always *there*. He danced well, he looked well and talked well but there was no excitement with him. Not as there was with Charlie.

She craned her neck to see where he was – sure enough, he was whizzing around with Elise. He looked so splendid too in his Tutankhamun costume, though the headdress seemed rather odd. Elise looked a tramp as Cleopatra. When will it be my turn? Helen thought anxiously. My turn for Charlie's dance.

'Sweetheart,' Rex murmured in a rare protest, 'don't keep looking over my shoulder.'

Helen tried to pull herself together. 'Darling, you're imagining things.'

'It's Charlie, isn't it?' he said quite conversationally. 'That's whom you're staring at all the time.'

'Nonsense. Why would I?' she responded with as much affection as she could summon up.

'It could be because he's been dancing with Elise all night,' he replied, sharply for him.

This had to be stopped. Helen realized she was beginning to tremble. 'And that, darling Rex, is only because I'm dancing with you – much more fun than with horrid Charlie.' She managed a happy laugh.

But Rex didn't laugh back. 'I wouldn't be too sure of that, Helen. He was at Ma Meyrick's Forty-Three Club with her the other evening.'

The tremble became worse. She must dance with Charlie tonight, she really *must*. 'He was only with her because I wasn't in London. Why do you think he came down here this weekend instead? Besides, brother Richard is keen on Elise so Charlie wouldn't dare try and take her away.'

'I wouldn't be too sure of that either.'

Nor was she. Helen knew just why Charlie had come this weekend. *And* Elise. And several others here too. They couldn't do without Charlie or his dance, and he'd promised to see them during or after the ghost hunt this evening. After the joke on Aunt Clarice, of course.

The band was playing 'It Had To Be You' and at last Richard had managed to secure Elise as a partner. He'd managed to despatch Charlie temporarily to the library to check all was well with the you-know-what, and with luck he wouldn't be back before the dancing stopped in time to rally for the ghost hunt. And then, thankfully, Charlie would be well out of the way as arranged.

'Cleopatra dancing with an eighteenth-century soldier. A good mix, isn't it?' Richard tried to joke. He was a good dancer but Elise was better and was apt to make her partner's mistakes all too publicly known. 'Seventh heaven,' he added.

'So glad you think so, my sweet.' Elise replied automatically. 'Dancing with Charlie was becoming the most awful bore. And so is this music. Ask for a Charleston, darling.'

Thrilled though he was that Charlie had blotted his copybook, Richard was thrown into confusion. There was talk of this Charleston dance about to reach England and that it would even take over from jazz, but so far he hadn't learned how to do it. And then there was some joke about Charlie's dance too, which he didn't understand. He'd had plenty of dances with her.

He tried to brazen it out. 'The band won't know the music. How about the King Porter Stomp or the Black Bottom?'

'You're so sweetly out of tune,' she sighed. 'You poor things, living in the country. The Charleston really is the coming thing.'

'Nothing can be better than dancing anything with you, Elise.'

She laughed. 'Dear, sweet Richard. You'll be asking me to do the cake-walk next.'

Richard did not reply. He didn't want to be her sweet anything. He wanted to be masterful, like Rudolph Valentino or Charlie, come to that, to sweep Elise off her feet. But somehow that wasn't easy. When they were married, it would all be different. At least Charlie wouldn't be around.

Elise broke away from him, ran up to the band, had a word with the leader and then gaily beckoned to him.

'They *can* play the Charleston,' she cried triumphantly. 'So let's have fun!'

Richard tried his best but he had no idea what he was doing and soon Elise was dancing alone, the wonderful, beautiful, sultry Elise, whose legs were flying in all directions, kicking with stocking tops on show as she hitched up the Cleopatra skirt. Nothing stopped Elise. Richard was intoxicated with watching her flying feet and arms. During the ghost hunt he could kiss her in the dark because Charlie would be out of the way. As soon as she whirled past him again he would seize her in his arms and spin her round masterfully.

But as he did so Charlie came back. 'I've had a look at the you-know-what. Still time for a whirl before I creep away, so you won't mind, old chap, will you, if I take Cleopatra off your hands?'

Richard did mind. Very much. And, even worse, Elise didn't object.

No avoiding it now, Nell thought in resignation. It was eleven forty-five and time to take up her responsibilities for the ghost hunt. She had been swotting up on the ghosts and felt as ready as she ever would for the hunt. When she arrived in the great hall Mr Peters had already taken up his post. He had decided, he told her, that this should be

37

close to the door on a corner of the corridor linking the grand staircase hall to the breakfast room, a good spot for keeping an eye on what was happening. The great hall was a hive of activity. Lady Clarice, Lord Richard, Lady Helen and Lady Sophy were busy handing out equipment to the guests already gathering for the hunt. The phonograph was in place and the cameras and their paraphernalia were ready to capture images of the great hall ghosts.

Thankfully Nell realized that few of the guests would be participating in the hunt; the others must have sensibly preferred to walk and talk in the ballroom or gardens, accompanied by champagne and not ghosts. At least there was full lighting in the ballroom, as there was in the two wings to the house. Roll on the day that Wychbourne Court would be blessed with a better electrical supply. Meanwhile, the faithful oil lamps still did their duty in much of the main house. The ghost hunt would see them turned to their very lowest and the electric lighting elsewhere turned off. Much of the route therefore would be in the semi-dark, lit only with their lanterns. In Nell's opinion, these ghosts were far too choosy about what they required in order to make an appearance.

'We shall be twenty in all,' Lady Clarice announced, her eyes sparkling. She was wearing a soldier's helmet for some reason, although she was not otherwise in fancy dress. Did she think the ghosts were going to conk her on the head? Nell wondered. Her affection for Lady Clarice grew. 'I shall lead the first group and Miss Drury

38

will escort the second,' Lady Clarice continued. 'You all have your route plans?'

It appeared they all did, but what use would they be in the semi-dark? Nell would be taking her group into the west wing, save for the ballroom and supper room, and returning through the library to the great hall, where they would be meeting Lady Clarice's group returning from hunting through the main house. They would then change routes and Nell would be beginning – as Lady Clarice would now do – with the great hall and minstrels' gallery, where a total of five ghosts spent their haunting time.

'We shall not be visiting the servants' east wing,' Lady Clarice continued, presumably, Nell thought, on the grounds that no self-respecting ghosts would so demean themselves as to haunt that. Even the cook ghost pre-dated the east wing. 'The two groups will exchange information at twelve thirty here in the great hall,' Lady Clarice explained, 'in order not to put our ghosts under stress. Be gentle with our friends, everyone. They only want their case to be heard. Justice!' she bellowed in conclusion.

'What if we do see a ghost?' Elise asked languidly. 'Do we ask him to dance?'

She was fixed with a stern look by Lady Clarice. 'Be polite to him, that is all. Listen if he sends a message.'

'Over the wireless?' Elise drawled.

'No. Record it on the phonograph.'

Match point to Lady Clarice, Nell thought with pleasure. She had been given her set of equipment by Lady Sophy, but had a sudden panic.

Who had actually been deputed to take photographs in the great hall? No one, as far as she knew. Too late now, and anyway, ghosts weren't going to hang around to have their photographs taken.

Here we go, she thought, summoning her courage. Holding her feeble lantern light before her, she led her group to the main staircase. Lady Clarice's group included Lord Richard, Lady Helen, Lady Sophy, Miss Harlington, Mr Beringer, Lady Warminster and other familiar faces, but in her own party Nell recognized nobody, although Mr Fontenoy had said he might join it later.

Fortunately the dowager had not joined either group. Lady Sophy had confided in Nell that her grandmother had departed the drawing room after coffee with a second unprecedented comment to her arch enemy – on this occasion a pointed reference to the bone of contention between them.

'Do not fear, Mr Fontenoy. I shall not be accompanying you on this expedition. I have no plans to become a ghost in the near future.'

In the semi-darkness everything felt out of proportion, the familiar disappeared and the imagination took over. Nonsense, Nell, she told herself. Even so, the same mood seemed to have fallen on her party because the laughing and joking had greatly diminished by the time they reached the new chapel on the first floor of the west wing. Calliope was a ghostly singer in the corridor of this wing; Adelaide, a Victorian lady, appeared from time to time (according to Lady Clarice's notes), and so did a former butler who had displeased an earlier marquess in the eighteenth century and met an unfortunate end while running for his life. He was, Lady Clarice had noted, sometimes to be seen at the place of his death, but at others in the great hall where he was still trying to serve drinks and answer the bell.

Tonight there was nothing – no noise, no atmosphere – just the sound of breathing: unsteady breaths as though unease had replaced the early jollity. Nell did her best to enliven the proceedings with the ghosts' stories, although she was guiltily aware that the laughter they evoked would, in Lady Clarice's view, scare any potential manifestations away. Perhaps the original chapel in the main house, which no longer existed, might have produced more positive results. As the group made its way back to the great hall neither the morning room nor the billiards room revealed any ghosts, however, and nor did the library, although much of that seemed to be curtained off. Nell almost felt responsible for this failure as Lady Clarice was going to be disappointed.

On the contrary. Lady Clarice could barely wait for Nell to finish her account of the ghostless journey before conveying her exciting news.

'There is a presence here. A groan was heard. Here in this hall. It was just after you left. I believe it came from the minstrels' gallery, in which case it was undoubtedly the wronged Sir Thomas killed by that traitorous minstrel. The phonograph was not yet switched on so that remarkable opportunity was squandered. But, nevertheless, we all heard it. That we could be so fortunate! If you are similarly blessed this will be such a night, such a night indeed.'

Lady Clarice called her flock to her and they departed in great anticipation of what might await them next. It seemed to Nell there weren't quite as many in Her Ladyship's group as there had been before, and having heard the three young Ansleys trying hard not to giggle she wondered if there had been deserters. Who could blame them? Her own group seemed to be intact, although Nell hadn't even produced a groan for them so far, and Arthur Fontenoy was now joining her as well.

The great hall was in almost complete darkness and had enough atmosphere of its own without adding ghosts, in Nell's view. She quickly gave her followers a brief introduction to the ghosts of the great hall, thinking longingly of the kitchen, with its leftovers from the banquet and a cup of hot chocolate followed by a welcoming bed. Not yet, though. She steeled herself for the task ahead.

'Onward, troops,' she encouraged her flock. 'Up the staircase to the minstrels' gallery. If you're lucky, that medieval minstrel who serenaded Her Ladyship in bed in the twelfth century will pop out and give us a tune.' That raised a general titter, but the *joie de vivre* had vanished. Then she jumped as she felt someone clutch her arm. A ghost? No, it was Guy, of all people.

'This tour, dear Nell, is ridiculous,' he whispered.

Where had he sprung from? 'Of course,' she hissed defensively. 'But this is the nineteen twenties. We *can* be ridiculous. What are you doing here?'

'I came to protect you from your ghosts. Are there any?'

'I think the other party heard a moan or two.'

'You're joking, of course.'

'That's what Lady Clarice told me.'

'In that case I shall definitely remain behind you and you can protect *me*.'

Nell had only been up to the minstrels' gallery once before but remembered thinking that she pitied any minstrels (or their ghosts) who used it. The narrow spiral staircase to the gallery was just through the open door where Mr Peters was standing, and the corridor by which it stood ran past the far end of the gallery, to which a twin staircase also gave access. There was little room on the gallery itself because a dividing screen, half panelled, half latticed, ran its full length, giving a narrow space behind it and a wider passageway in front looking down over the great hall. Even so, it was only single file and Nell had to edge her way along it with her faithful followers behind her.

She could smell the old woodwork which gave the gallery a creepy atmosphere, as though those minstrel songs could still be heard if one listened hard enough, although there was another sweeter smell mingled with it. The scent of a ghost? She heard no moans or groans, but nevertheless, she would be glad when they were down those stairs again. Perhaps Sir Thomas really was here . . .

She waved the lantern in front of her just in case, and its light picked up something she couldn't see clearly.

Something was oozing out under the screen's central door.

43

What the flaming fritters was it? There was nothing but that empty narrow space behind the screen. Without thinking, she reached out and pulled the doorknob and the door shot open in front of her – not because of the pressure she had applied but because of the force of something behind it.

The something fell out, falling half this side of the door and the rest lying inside. It was wrapped in cloth – no, more than that. Nell leapt back in horror as even the dim light revealed what it was. It was a body, now lying half in, half out of the screen door, clad in fancy dress. Alive? Dead?

Instinctively she fell to her knees to find out and be sure that in this dim light she wasn't imagining things. She wasn't. There was blood on her hand and no movement. Swinging the lantern, she moved closer to see the face and froze with shock.

It was Charles Parkyn-Wright.

Three

Get moving, girl. As she knelt at Mr Parkyn-
Wright's side, images raced through her mind:
her father shaking her awake in the small hours
when it was time to leave for Spitalfields and the
barrow; the day she had woken up at the Carlton
to hear the news that the country was at war; the
terrible feeling in the pit of her stomach on the
day her mother had died. Nell knew she had to
force herself into action. What action, though?
How could death strike in so ugly a fashion during
a dance? This had nothing to do with ghosts and
the ghost hunt. The blood was all too real and
some was on her. Automatically she felt for a
pulse, but there was none and the hand fell away
as she dropped it.

Someone was shouting, 'Doctor, police . . .'
and she saw Mr Fontenoy leaning over the balus-
trade. Lamps were already being turned up in the
great hall and she could hear Mr Peters' voice
below.

Police? It was only then that she took in the
significance of the thing sticking out of the chest
in front of her. Pull it out? No, leave it in, despite
the fact that it looked so horrific. Nothing could
hurt Mr Parkyn-Wright now. Was it a knife? No,
the handle was too ornate. There was blood on
his clothes as well as on the floor. He seemed
– she forced herself to look again at the

45

bloodstained Tutankhamun costume – to have been stabbed more than once. And that thing must be a dagger. She was aware that Mr Fontenoy was at her side again, peering down at the body. Not since the Zep had flown over the Carlton during the war dropping its bombs had she felt so helpless.

Who would want to kill someone in this terrible way? Mr Parkyn-Wright had been visiting Wychbourne for many years and was of course well known in the servants' hall, so much so that most of them talked of him as Mr Charles. She longed to rush downstairs as many of the guests on the balcony with her had already done, but someone had to stay here. Mr Charles had been the life and soul of the party, but now the party was over.

Then she felt a hand on her shoulder. Mr Fontenoy? No, it was Guy Ellimore, who was helping her to her feet and no one else was left in the narrow gallery but he and Mr Fontenoy.

'There's nothing you can do, Nell,' Guy said.

'Who would want to murder him?' she blurted out.

'That's for the police to find out, Nell. You go down. We'll stay.'

'No. I'll have to stay here. It's my job.'

'As leader of the ghost hunt?' he said, perhaps teasingly.

She couldn't cope with that. 'No.' She looked down and shuddered again at what she saw. 'Because this has happened *here*,' she tried to explain. 'At Wychbourne Court.'

* * *

46

Gerald, Eighth Marquess Ansley, hung up the receiver as Gertrude came hurrying to join him in his office near the morning room. 'I've heard this terrible news, Gerald,' she cried. 'I was in the ballroom when Peters found me. Is it true?'

'I'm afraid so, my dear,' he said gravely. 'Our party is over. Peters has sent for the doctor and the police. We can expect a chief inspector here, several constables and a photographer. But there is more,' he added gently. 'I have made a telephone call to the assistant commissioner.'

'Of Scotland Yard?' Gertrude was aghast. 'But surely this is some local matter. An accident. It can be dealt with—'

'I fear not. I have asked Peters to relieve Miss Drury and her companions in the gallery. It is no place for a woman, or a stranger, or an elderly man like Arthur. It seems likely to be a case of murder.'

Gertrude gave a cry of horror. Murder belonged to the world of Dr Crippen and that madman who had killed William Terriss at his own stage door. Not to Wychbourne Court.

'We need this affair to be handled carefully, Gertie,' Gerald told her. 'The local police are most agreeable to Scotland Yard's involvement, especially as so many of our guests have come from London tonight. The local police would not welcome the responsibility.'

'But the killer will surely be found quickly?' Gertrude was appalled. 'Perhaps it was a tramp – one of the hired footmen.' She grasped eagerly at this theory.

'And what if he is not found quickly, my dear? What if this madman is to be found among our

47

own guests?' He paused. 'Or worse? That is a risk we cannot take.'

Gertrude was even more shaken. What was Gerald hinting at? 'A *risk*?' she repeated faintly.

The look on his face filled her with even more fear. 'My love, whoever this killer proves to be, not only our guests but our home and family must be investigated. We need the expertise of Scotland Yard.'

'Family, Gerald? You cannot think one of us murdered this man?' Even as she said it she realized that the suspicions she had harboured for some time were shared with her husband, and that therefore the even worse possibility of their involvement in this murder existed. She had tried to spare Gerald from her fears but perhaps he had been trying to spare her.

'Of course not,' he replied, but without conviction, she thought. 'Nevertheless, we must face the fact that the police will look into *everything*. I fear the commissioner was not pleased to be woken but he understood our position. A superintendent is coming immediately by motor car with their best officer and sergeant, together with their own photographer. They will be here before dawn and I'm sure matters will then move smoothly. You may have no fear of that.'

Needn't I? thought Gertrude despairingly. It was all very well for Gerald to put his faith in Scotland Yard, but suppose they discovered that her sudden fear about Charlie's dance might be true, although it probably had nothing to do with the murder. Guilty and innocent would be *investigated* together and there could be many false trails trodden before the culprit was discovered. And what about Charlie's family? There would be parents to consult. Should she offer them hospitality here? No, surely that would not be appropriate in the very house where their son had met his death? But on the other hand, if she did not make this offer they might consider the Ansleys uncaring or that they had something to hide. As indeed they might have. What should she do? The answer came to her. She would ask Nell. Nell would know.

Curtain up, Gertie, she told herself. But this time it was on a tragedy, not a Gaiety Girls' musical comedy. Tonight's performance had brought not only death but might bring ruin and disgrace to the Ansley name.

The lights were going out all over Europe, so the foreign secretary had said on the outbreak of war, Nell recalled, but on this catastrophe the lights were going up. They were blazing now and whatever ghosts Lady Clarice might have hoped to have seen would long since have retreated. The doctor had attended to confirm the death, and Nell had been free to leave the gallery after the arrival of first Mr Peters then the village constable to guard the body. Where should she go? She could not go back to her own room in the east wing until the Sevenoaks police had talked to her.

She had washed the blood from her hands but how could she wash it from her mind? Then she remembered the supper room. What was happening to the buffet? With great relief at having a mission, however spurious, she left the great hall

49

and made her way there. There it was – the array of mousses, jellies, sandwiches and savouries that she, Kitty and Michel had looked on with such pride earlier this evening. Those who had not attended the ghost hunt had, from the look of it, already sampled the supper, and no one was present now save for the hired footmen who must be agog to know what was going on but were unable to leave their posts.

In the adjacent ballroom she could hear piano music, perhaps from one of Guy's men, perhaps being played by Guy himself. The sound was muted and by the lack of conversation when she went in to listen it was having a calming effect. There were quite a few people in there but some, she thought, must have left, either with or without police sanction.

When she returned to the supper room Mr Peters was there, which was a relief as she liked him and he was usually undemanding company. He didn't look like the average butler. He wasn't tall or particularly imposing – indeed, he was on the skinny side – only of medium height and sharp-featured. He was jolly good at his job, although tonight he looked as stricken as she felt after his vigil in the minstrels' gallery.

'That was a nasty shock for you, Miss Drury,' he said. 'Why don't you take some supper? You'll feel better.'

'Just at the moment, I feel I'll never want to eat again.'

'Brandy then or coffee. It'll buck you up.'

That was an idea. 'It might buck everyone up,' Nell suggested. 'Let's take both round to everyone.'

With the prospect of another mission, she felt better. She'd consult Lord and Lady Ansley immediately. She found them in the drawing room. No sign of the dowager thankfully, but Mr Fontenoy was with them. Surprisingly – but then convention had no place here tonight – Miss Checkam was sitting primly to one side. No Mr Briggs, of course. The noise and disturbance in the house this evening would have sent him out to listen to nightingales or watch the owls.

'Coffee.' Lady Ansley grasped the idea like a lifeline. 'That would be splendid.'

'For everyone,' her husband confirmed.

'Let's take the garden route, Mr Peters,' Nell suggested. To walk over the terrace and gardens to the kitchens would avoid her having to take the service corridor past the great hall where the gallery might still shelter its terrible burden.

It was calmer outside. The stars looked like the sky's lanterns, she thought, far away from the nightmare in progress in the great hall.

'It was like this in the war,' Mr Peters said, sharing her mood. 'Didn't seem right that the stars went on looking so peaceful up there even though hell was taking place down on earth. You'd be thinking of the Germans and how the same stars were looking down on them but we'd be going out to kill each other the next day. I ask you, Miss Drury, who'd want to kill Mr Charles? Must have been a mistake.'

'No,' Nell said dully. 'No one would be up there with that dagger just by chance or use it by accident.'

A silence, then at last Mr Peters replied as they

51

reached the servants' wing, 'That dagger, Miss Drury. Lord Ansley identified it. It's the one that hangs below the portrait of the first marquess. If you ask me, I'd say it was some practical joke went wrong. Why else would Mr Charles be up behind that screen? He couldn't have been pushed in there dead. Too heavy. I should know. Handled enough dead bodies in the war.'

Nell stared at him. 'A joke? You mean set up by the family? Guests wouldn't play one on their own.' Then she realized with a sinking heart that he was right. It was far more likely to have been thought up by Lord Richard and his sisters. The joke must have been something to do with the ghost hunt.

He hesitated then lowered his voice. 'Speaking confidentially, Miss Drury, there was some joke or other set up in the library too. I was told by Lord Richard that it was part of a plot for the hunt.'

'Probably to upset Lady Clarice,' Nell said. 'There was a groan heard in the hall when her group set off. That must have come from Mr Charles who would already have been behind the screen.'

Mr Peters nodded. 'To encourage her, no doubt.'

'Unless,' Nell said, her heart thumping, 'he was crying out in agony.' That was a terrible thought. Had the group misinterpreted the cry of a dying man?

'No, Miss Drury,' Mr Peters said comfortingly, 'I heard that groan and it wasn't the kind you're thinking of.'

Nell breathed more easily. It had been a joke,

but one that had gone terribly wrong. The newspapers would make a fine story out of this. *The Times* might keep it discreet but others would be thrilled at the thought of a body found in the minstrels' gallery of one of the finest homes in England.

'What's going on?' Mrs Fielding, still fully dressed, came bustling into the kitchen where Nell was busy putting kettles on the ranges, still warm from the supper preparations. 'What are you two doing here at this hour?' she asked sharply.

Mr Peters swelled with importance. 'One of the guests has been found dead, my dear,' he told her with great solicitude. The endearment was a sign that he was off duty, Nell recognized. Never would he have the temerity to address Mrs Fielding thus during working hours. But then at a time like this how could working hours be defined? 'Murdered,' Mr Peters added lugubriously.

Mrs Fielding gaped. 'In Wychbourne Court?' she screeched. 'You're having me on, Freddie.'

'Miss Drury found him,' Mr Peters added. 'We're here for refreshments required in the house.'

Mrs Fielding swung round to stare at her, as though suspecting Nell was up to no good by such a move. She did not deliver one of her usual blasts, though, merely an: 'Into my still-room, both of you. We'll organize it from there and use the cups from the breakfast-room servery.' That settled, 'Who was it?' she asked as they followed her to her sanctum. 'You're sure it wasn't one of the family?'

'No,' Nell reassured her, intrigued by Mrs Fielding's use of 'Freddie'. Such informality suggested rather more than a working arrangement. 'It was Mr Parkyn-Wright.'

Mrs Fielding was aghast. 'Mr Charles? He's Lord Richard's friend and Lady Helen's had her eye on him.'

'You wouldn't think so tonight,' Mr Peters contributed. 'Our Mr Charles was dancing with that Miss Elise Harlington. Lord Richard couldn't get a leg in edgewise. Nor Lady Helen.'

'I said he was a so-and-so,' Mrs Fielding declared triumphantly.

Mr Peters disappeared to his pantry to organize glasses and brandy and, following Mrs Fielding's orders, Nell made her way to the breakfast room to prepare trolleys for serving coffee. Passing the open door to the great hall, she glimpsed two police constables on duty inside and another up on the gallery, together with a policeman with a camera. They looked like alien intruders into the world of Wychbourne Court, as alien as murder itself. She hadn't known Mr Charles well as she'd only been here for a year, but he couldn't have deserved this fate.

When the trolleys were ready, Nell made her way to the drawing room with Mrs Fielding, determined not to be left out, following in her footsteps. Mr Peters was already there with brandy for those who wanted it. Lord Richard and his sisters had now joined their parents, the fancy dress costumes looking woefully out of place. All three seemed dazed with shock. The dowager was now with Lord and Lady Ansley, but thankfully Mr Fontenoy had moved to the far end of the room to comfort Lady Clarice.

54

Precedence should have sent Nell to Lord and Lady Ansley first, but tonight, Nell decided, Lady Clarice was in more urgent need of coffee.

Mr Fontenoy took a cup for her. 'You'll feel better with this, Clarice.'

'I won't.' Lady Clarice was weeping. 'That poor man. But what was he doing hiding behind the screen? Didn't he realize that he would scare the ghosts? They took their revenge.'

Mr Fontenoy cleared his throat. 'He might,' he ventured, 'have been responsible for the groan we heard.'

Lady Clarice stared at him. 'What *do* you mean, Arthur? That was Sir Thomas moaning.'

Mr Fontenoy did not reply and Nell hastily poured coffee and handed him a cup. 'Mr Peters told me that the groan could not have been one of pain,' she whispered to him as she pushed the trolley away, hoping that Lady Clarice was too preoccupied with Sir Thomas to hear.

Mr Fontenoy immediately rose to follow her. 'I agree,' he said gravely. 'The groan was definitely one of a young man intent on pretending to be a ghost. There were cadences in it, a true moan rather than one of pain and fear.'

She swallowed. 'Thank you, Mr Fontenoy.'

When she reached Lord and Lady Ansley, Lord Richard and his sisters had moved to the window seat and there was a stranger with their parents, a burly, comfortable-looking man who wasn't clad in evening dress.

'It was Miss Drury who found the body, Chief Inspector,' Lord Ansley said as Nell handed his coffee to him.

Of course. He wouldn't be wearing uniform – he was a detective from the local police, Nell realized. He looked almost reassuring in his very ordinariness, if anything could be so termed tonight.

He smiled at her. 'Thank you, Miss Drury. We'll need a word with you later.'

How much later? she wondered despairingly. 'Are any of us allowed to leave?' she asked boldly.

'Everyone's to stay for the moment.' Comfortable looking he might be, but his words brought home to her that he was here with a job to do.

She was about to turn away when Lady Ansley rose to her feet. 'Miss Drury, there are one or two household matters to discuss.' Her voice was trembling. 'Shall we go into the conservatory?'

What the devilled onions was all this about? Nell thought wearily. Her Ladyship looked as exhausted as Nell felt. 'It's the guests, Nell,' she burst out when they had left the drawing room. 'They'll have to stay, won't they? How can we manage?'

All of them? was Nell's immediate thought. That just wasn't possible. Then reason came back. 'Guests from London who aren't here for the weekend can either return there once the police have seen them or stay here if there's special need.' She gulped. 'I'll ask Mrs Fielding to look after it.' A momentary guess at Mrs Fielding's reply flashed by her.

'Oh, would you, Nell? And then' – Lady Ansley looked utterly despairing – 'there are Charlie's parents to consider.'

'Tomorrow,' Nell said firmly. 'They'll come then.'

'Yes,' Lady Ansley said thankfully. 'And they might not want to stay *here*. But there's something else, Nell. Something that might affect this terrible affair. It's in the library.'

That curtain, again, Nell thought as she followed Lady Ansley out of the conservatory and across to the west wing. She could see the ballroom was fully lit again now, but when they reached the library it was in almost complete darkness. Some moonlight penetrated through the windows, just enough to see the mysterious curtained-off area of the room.

'It's hiding a sheet of glass in front of the balcony and a large mirror and some kind of light below,' Lady Ansley told her unhappily, tweaking the curtain aside to let Nell see at least the mirror propped up at an odd angle.

'Do you know what it's for?' Nell was beginning to feel too tired to cope.

'I'm afraid it might have been a joke thought up by my son and daughters. It was for a Pepper's Ghost illusion – you remember there was a craze for it?'

Nell had heard of it and had a dim recollection of having seen one at a fair years ago.

'This would be nearly at the end of the ghost hunt for Lady Clarice's group.' Lady Ansley sighed. 'I suppose the plan would have been to create a ghost up there on the balcony.' She pointed to the narrow balcony running along the length of the library wall to give access to the higher bookshelves. 'Richard with his military uniform would have been the ghost, I imagine, with his mirror image reflected up there,' she added unhappily.

'It didn't happen, though,' Nell said in the hope of comforting her. 'Our group just walked through the library and the real target, Lady Clarice's group, didn't reach that point. But I think that the other part of the joke – the groans – was to be carried out by Mr Parkyn-Wright and that's why he was behind the screen.'

'Oh, Nell.' Lady Ansley began to cry. 'Isn't it terrible? That means that at least Richard and probably all three of my children knew Charlie was up there, you see. No one else did.'

She broke off but she had no need to go further. 'They could have told many other guests where he was,' Nell comforted her. 'You don't have to worry,' she added gently. 'Just tell the police everything you know. They won't suspect Lord Richard as he was Charlie's great friend, nor Lady Helen, who was very fond of him.'

Lady Ansley did not reply for a moment or two but then said bravely, 'Of course not. But just in case, Nell,' she added hopefully, 'can't *you* find out what really happened so we can be sure the police don't get it wrong?'

Nell reeled in horror. 'Me? But it's the police's job.'

'You know us, though,' Lady Ansley pleaded. 'They don't. You're so good at solving problems. It might have been anyone – the guests, neighbours, servants perhaps.'

Easy to blame the servants, Nell thought wryly. But then Lady Ansley could be right, she supposed, even though some of the servants had never set foot in the main part of the house and would hardly have rushed in to kill someone

58

behind a screen they didn't know existed. Nevertheless, Mr Peters knew about the jokes being played on Lady Clarice and some of the servants did have access to the main house.

Including her – and she had found the body.

'Will you do it, Nell?' Lady Ansley asked. 'You notice things, you put things together, and,' she hesitated, 'you do care what happens to us just a little? Will you?'

Nell surrendered. 'I'll try.' She had pushed away her instant fear: suppose it *was* one of the family?

Time, which had passed so quickly earlier in the day, now dragged by. Nell couldn't go to bed until the police had interviewed her but there had been no sign of their doing so, although it was nearly three o'clock in the morning. She sank down in the conservatory, which she seemed to have to herself. Remaining guests and family must be dozing elsewhere, she supposed. She had told Mrs Fielding what might lie in store for them, and surprisingly instead of blaming Nell she had rallied to the challenge of readying rooms for possible unexpected guests at short notice in the middle of the night. Whether she had finished the task or fallen asleep in her room in the east wing, Nell neither knew nor cared. Mr Peters must be at Lord Ansley's side, Mr Briggs was not to be seen and Miss Checkam was last seen assisting Mrs Fielding.

Nell felt herself beginning to doze. It seemed to her she was in a far-off land, over the hills and far away, where none of the usual rules of her trade or job applied. Perhaps a ghost or two would come and cheer her up, she thought grimly . . . and then surprisingly it was Sir Thomas who was visiting her, questioning her closely about the recipe she had used for the geranium jelly. She told him it had been an old one she had found in the library, handed down by generations of ghosts . . .

In thanks, Sir Thomas had the nerve to shake her shoulder.

No, someone *was* shaking her shoulder.

'Are you the cook?' the someone was demanding to know before she could even clear the sleep from her eyes and mind.

'Chef,' she murmured automatically.

'Same thing.'

'*Not* the same thing,' she whipped back.

Regarding her was a man she hadn't seen before. Steely blue eyes, medium height, probably in his mid-thirties, fair hair, suit, waistcoat. He wasn't dressed for a party, so, macerated mushrooms, who was this?

'Miss Drury?' The voice was pleasant enough but those eyes weren't building any bridges between them. No apologies for waking her.

'Who wants to know?'

'Melbray. Detective Inspector Alexander, Scotland Yard. I'm told you found the body.'

Four

Nell struggled to sit upright and rub the sleep from her eyes. While she had lain huddled in the armchair the skirts of the grey dress had risen uncomfortably high and her hair seemed to be all over her face. It annoyed her that she even worried about this. That blankety-blank man waiting in the armchair opposite her, brown-covered notebook lying on the table between them, wouldn't care two hoots about her legs.

'I need you to come with me,' Inspector Melbray informed her.

She pulled herself together, defences to the fore. 'That was quick. Are you arresting me?'

He didn't even smile, which annoyed her even more.

'I didn't have that in mind – not yet,' he replied. 'We're going to the minstrels' gallery.'

Nell froze. 'Is—?'

'No,' he interrupted. 'The body has gone and the photographers and my sergeant have finished up there.'

'Fingerprints,' she retorted automatically. 'Well, of course, mine would be there.' Fingerprints were all important nowadays – much too late for her to remember that now.

'No doubt. Did you touch the dagger?'

Unwillingly she forced herself to think back to that terrible moment. 'I had blood on my hands so

61

I may have done,' she blurted out. Had she? She scrabbled through her memory without success.

The eyes remained speculatively on her. Already she was beginning to feel guilty. *Had* she touched the dagger, driven it in further and so killed Charlie? No, of course not. She was half asleep. She couldn't have done.

'I'm still dozy,' she said crossly. 'I don't know what I'm saying.'

To which he said nothing but merely waited for her to continue. That made her feel even guiltier. 'I didn't kill him. Plenty of folk can swear to that.'

'Good.'

She glared at him. What on earth was this *inspector* trying to do to her? Where was that nice, kind, plump, comfortable-looking policeman she'd seen earlier? Not here, anyway. She rose to her feet. 'Let's get it over with.'

'Thank you, Miss Drury. If you'll follow me.'

Follow? She gritted her teeth. 'Keep your fires burning down below in the range,' one old chef had said to her. No sense sending for the Merryweathers before they're called for. They'd been the old fire engines she remembered from her youth. She stalked after Inspector Melbray through the now-empty drawing room and into the great hall. It was beginning to get light outside now but the lamps were still burning within with their soft, comforting glow.

There were other strange faces milling around in the hall too. These must be the Scotland Yard sergeant and the photographers. The local police were there as well, some in uniform, some not, but not one of the guests or the family was to be seen.

'Where are Lord and Lady Ansley?' she called out to the inspector.

'Taking some rest,' he threw back over his shoulder to her.

'And everyone else? Have you begun inter-viewing the guests yet?'

He stopped and turned to face her. 'We'll look after that side of things, Miss Drury. That is not on your menu.'

He made it sound an insult, she fumed, and be blowed if it would stop her asking reasonable questions. She had a right to know, especially – as she remembered uneasily – after that rash promise she had made to Lady Ansley. 'And the band?' she persisted.

This time he relented. 'Departed to the Coach and Horses Inn in the village,' he told her. 'To which once we have accomplished all we urgently need here, I, my sergeant and photographer will also go. My superintendent has already returned to London and the case is in my hands. If I might continue my job, however . . .'

'What would you like me to do?'

He looked at her in surprise at the note of cooperation in her voice, purposely placed there. 'I want you to retrace exactly what you did from the moment you began to climb this stair-case to the gallery.'

'Wouldn't that destroy evidence on the stairs? Cigarette stubs, strands of fibre, bus tickets, the odd farthing – that sort of thing?' she asked innocently.

He came straight back at her. 'Fortunately, Miss Drury, my men have already removed any such useful items, together with a black bloodstained cloth found in the inner passageway which was probably used by the victim's attacker to protect him from any blood when he struck Mr Parkyn-Wright. With so many people around that would be essential. Lady Clarice identified the cloth as part of her photographic equipment.'

Nell decided that discretion was the better part of valour and so said no more. Instead she braced herself to walk up the stairs again. 'If you want me to replay exactly what happened shouldn't we be in the dark? The oil lamps are full on now but the darkness would have affected the way we walked and how slowly. I had a lantern too.'

Inspector Melbray took the point. 'You're right, Miss Drury.' He gave her a keen look but didn't seem to be bearing any animosity towards her. It was a modest victory for her, she thought, as one of the men dimmed the lights below and another handed her a lantern. It wasn't lit but there was a little daylight reaching the gallery now. She needed to concentrate in order to face this ordeal and tried to push the annoying inspector from her mind.

'I had ten people behind me – no, twelve.' Guy had joined in as well. 'Mr Arthur Fontenoy was behind me. He and Mr Ellimore joined us halfway through.' She tried to convince herself that Mr Fontenoy was following her now and *not* the arrogant inspector. At the top, she hesitated.

'Did you halt like this when you came up before?' came the voice behind her.

Nell was startled because she wasn't sure why she had halted. *Had* she done so the first time? 'Yes,' she remembered, 'I did. I don't think I had a particular reason – yes, there was one. Nothing important, though.'

'Everything's important at this stage.'

'There was a faint smell.'

'Cigarette smoke.'

'I couldn't tell. Perhaps it was just the woodwork or something that floated up from the hall.'

A sigh from behind – unless she was just imagining it. 'So it could be. Advance, Miss Drury.'

Her stomach churned but she couldn't refuse. She couldn't let him see how sick she felt at what lay before her. There's nothing there, she told herself as she walked forward. Nothing.

Even without the lamplight it was much lighter now than it had been the first time she made this journey, and that made it easier, less creepy. It also revealed white powder on the woodwork which made her hesitate.

'Go on,' the voice said, 'we've taken what fingerprints we want from here. You may touch it if you wish.'

She didn't wish. It was almost as if by touching this nightmare would become more real and she had to distance herself as much as she could. When she reached the central door, she stopped. 'Here,' she said unnecessarily. Nothing could make her touch that. 'I caught hold of the doorknob,' she said.

'What made you do that?' he asked. 'You were on a ghost hunt, I gather. Did you see a ghost?' He came up close behind her.

65

'I thought I saw this blood on the floor.' She could see it still there, or at least traces of it, but it had dried now. She willed herself to keep as detached as he was.

'How could you have seen it? It was dark – your lantern would have been too high to pick it up.'

He was right. 'I did see it, though,' she said stubbornly. 'Perhaps it was still flowing.' Nausea threatened her again but she wasn't going to let him suspect that. 'I had the lantern in my left hand and my right hand was on the doorknob. I must have pulled at it and it opened.'

'Why did you do that?'

'To see whether the blood was coming from behind the door, I suppose,' she retorted. The whole horrible episode was back with her now. 'And then I felt the door move of its own accord and—' She choked slightly but he still said nothing. 'I saw this weight falling out. I didn't realize what it was at first, and then we saw it was a body. He must have been sitting propped or wedged against the door.' Surely she had told him enough. It seemed not.

'The dagger has gone as well as the body,' he told her matter-of-factly. 'The butler recognized it as one taken from the great hall, as was the dark camera cloth. As for fingerprints on that dagger, whoever killed him might have been careful enough to wear gloves or more likely to have wrapped something round the handle. Were you wearing gloves?'

'No.'

'Then if you touched the dagger your prints

might well be on it. My sergeant will take your fingerprints when we've finished here,' he added. 'Would you show me what happened next? I'll open the door myself if you prefer.'

No, she would do it. She was conscious of the inspector's breathing close behind her as she pulled the doorknob and was instantly back in the nightmare. Would something fall out this time? Had the body really gone or was this a trick being played by Inspector Melbray?

Nothing fell out, thank the blessed heavens. Nell let out a small whimper of relief, which he must have taken as fear.

'There's nothing here but us two, Miss Drury. I won't keep you much longer. What happened next?'

'I knelt down beside him.'

'Humour me, please. Do it again.'

She obeyed without a word.

'Now are you sure whether or not you touched the dagger?' he asked her.

'I'm still not sure. I thought I might pull it out. That it might help him. Then I remembered that might make the situation worse. He was bleeding anyway, from one of the wounds—' She stopped. The nausea was rising again now. 'I'm sorry. I can't go on.'

'Just a few more questions. You used the word "we" earlier. Was that you and Mr Fontenoy? It's only single file here.'

'Yes. He was shouting for help and everyone seemed to disappear apart from him and someone else.'

'Who was that?'

'The bandleader, Mr Ellimore. He joined my group at the last moment.'

'Why?'

'He heard about the ghost hunt and thought it would be fun.'

'Was it?'

'It should have been.'

'It wasn't a serious Harry Price or Society for Psychical Research investigation then?'

'It was only serious for Lady Clarice, Lord Ansley's sister. She believes fervently in ghosts.' Should she tell him about the planned hoaxes, the moaning . . .? No, that wasn't on her menu, as he had put it. 'That's why Mr Parkyn-Wright was behind the screen,' she then added stupidly.

A moment's silence. 'Thank you. I hoped someone would enlighten me on that point.'

She could have kicked herself. He would have to know but why did it have to be her who told him and why now?

'Some kind of hoax then,' he continued. 'Did you *know* about this, Miss Drury?'

She was getting into deep waters here, she realized with terror. 'Not then.' Please, please, no more questions, she silently begged him. She was already beginning to feel like a traitor. 'But why does all this matter?' she burst out. 'My group couldn't have murdered Mr Parkyn-Wright; he was already dead when we reached him.'

'I'll be talking to the family tomorrow,' he told her as if reading her mind. Perhaps he was, she thought. There were such methods. 'Lack of sleep does not become you, Miss Drury. We'll take your fingerprints and then you can get some rest,' he said calmly.

That did it. Whether he meant it as an insult or not, she would choose to take it as one. 'I hadn't realized an unbecoming face was evidence,' she shot back at him.

He wasn't in the least thrown. 'It's not, but sleep does smooth the path for both interviewer and interviewed. I too am tired.'

She was still smarting as he conducted her to the morning room, where not only his sergeant awaited her but, it seemed, half the Sevenoaks police force. All eyes followed her as she placed her fingertips on the white paper, duly removed them and watched as the sergeant covered it with black powder and her prints appeared. They were now police evidence. Such a small thing yet it seemed to link her closer to the murder than anything that had gone before. She was involved. She was part of it.

Then, mercifully, she was allowed to return to her own bedroom high up in the servants' wing, where she could sleep and sleep and sleep. She was well aware that it wouldn't help that she had been first to find the body *and* that she might well have known Mr Charles was behind that screen. That was tomorrow's problem – no, later today's, she realized. Dawn had broken at Wychbourne Court.

The kitchen, to Nell's relief, looked close to normal when she came down five hours later, and she thanked her lucky stars that she was not responsible for breakfasts and that luncheon was still some hours away. Mrs Squires was busy with rolling pastry and Nell could see that vegetable preparation was well under way in the scullery. The only drawback was that Mrs Fielding was in her element, determined to show how indispensable she was in the absence of the chef.

'Good morning, Miss Drury,' she declared, exuding importance. 'I shall be leaving for church now but everything is in hand for luncheon and dinner. I've discussed all the household arrangements with Lady Ansley.'

I bet she has, Nell thought, but she wasn't going to fight that battle today. 'How kind of you,' she said warmly. 'If you'll give me the menus I'll take it from here. I assume we have more visitors than originally planned?'

Mrs Fielding swelled with pride. 'The exact numbers are not yet known, of course – just as I foresaw. Mrs Squires will run through the arrangements we've made.'

Nell summoned up yet another warm smile. 'Thank you. How is Mr Peters this morning?'

'Coping splendidly.' The implication was that Nell was failing to do the same. 'He's in the steward's room, at hand for Lord Ansley and the family whenever needed.'

The steward's room was an outmoded name as the estate no longer had a steward. Lord Ansley and his son, Lord Richard, looked after the estate between them, and the room, being next to Lord Ansley's, was a convenient office for Mr Peters when discussing the wine lists and so on.

'Have the police come here to question you or summoned you to the house?' Nell asked.

70

'Not yet.' Mrs Fielding looked disappointed, as though Nell were taking an unfair advantage.

She doesn't know what she's in for, Nell thought. 'Perhaps it would be wise, Mrs Fielding, to list those in this wing who were in the servants' hall last night, irrespective of whether they could have played any part in the events that took place.'

'A good idea, Miss Drury. I shall do so, *if* so requested by Lady Ansley.'

Normal relations were restored, Nell thought. 'The menus then, Mrs Fielding.'

'Mrs Squires will inform you of those.'

Victory to Mrs Fielding then. This morning Nell couldn't have cared less. She had to begin thinking about the best way to follow up her promise to Lady Ansley.

The steward's room was a haven, and Peters was relieved to be there and not in the servants' wing where he would be bothered by question after question. Nor was he being ordered off to be interviewed by the police as though he were being hauled up before the beak. He'd thought about sneaking off to church as if this were a normal Sunday but decided it would be in his interests to stay and know what was going on. He mustn't look as though he had anything to hide. Here he was in command, no matter what this police inspector had in store for him. It couldn't be worse than trying to cope with a dozen or so guests making free with the house. The morning room was now solely police territory, Lord Ansley had explained. At least they hadn't demanded to stay in the house overnight. The village inn was quite good enough for them and they hadn't left here until six a.m. so they wouldn't be returning yet.

He was wrong. There was a knock on the door and in came that Inspector Melbray he'd seen last night.

'Mr Peters? May I have a word with you, if you please?'

It didn't seem to matter whether he was pleased or not, as the inspector didn't wait for an answer. No idea of etiquette, these police. A smart-looking fellow, though. That suit wasn't Savile Row but near enough.

'You're the butler here? On duty last night?'

'Correct,' Peters answered.

'Formerly batman to Lord Noel Ansley during the war?'

Peters froze. Where was this leading? 'Yes, sir. He died for his country at Ypres.'

'As did so many. Was it through his recommendation that you're butler here?'

Peters breathed a little more easily now. 'Yes, sir. His Lordship was good enough to employ me after I'd done my bit.'

The inspector had seated himself and was looking around the room as though there were clues in every corner. Thankfully, as this was the steward's office photographs and mementoes were strictly of the Ansley family and their famous guests.

'Is that our prime minister?' Inspector Melbray asked curiously.

'It is, sir. Mr Baldwin values Wychbourne for

its peace and quiet.' Too late, it occurred to him that these weren't the best words to use in view of what had just happened, but the inspector did not comment. Instead he turned his attention to another photograph.

'As does His Majesty too, I see.'

'More rarely, but we are sometimes honoured with a visit from King George and Queen Mary.'

'Did you know Charles Parkyn-Wright?' The inspector switched subjects in the same casual manner.

'Yes, sir. Not,' Peters added hastily, 'exactly knew. But he had been a guest at Wychbourne on many occasions and also at the London house.'

'In Eaton Square, I understand.'

'Correct, sir.' Peters was growing uneasy again. Why all these questions, which had nothing to do with the sort he had expected, such as 'Where were you last night?'

'How often had he come here?'

'I really can't be sure, sir.' Peters decided some stiffness would be appropriate in order to show his solidarity with Wychbourne and its family. No telltale servant, he. Hear no evil, see no evil, speak no evil – that's what a butler should do. He'd keep gossip to himself. 'Perhaps half a dozen times a year,' he finished.

'For dances or just to stay with the family?'

'Both, sir.'

'Were you at the door to greet him on his arrival yesterday?'

'Yes, sir. He drove his Hispano-Suiza down from London and Miss Elise Harlington was with him.'

'She is still a guest in the house, I'm told, as was Mr Parkyn-Wright.'

'She is.' Peters hesitated. Perhaps he had been too stiff, which wouldn't do at all in his position. He might draw attention to himself. In the circumstances he would venture a little further, therefore. 'Miss Elise is not altogether popular' – too late, he remembered that Lord Richard was sweet on her and solidarity with the Ansley family required reticence – 'and nor was Mr Parkyn-Wright, although I cannot understand why. He always seemed to me a most charming young man. He was Lord Richard's best friend.'

'So I've heard. You like Miss Harlington too?'

He tried to repair the damage. 'She is always very polite to me, sir.' A touch of woodenness might help.

'You kindly provided a list of the guests to the party for me, as well as of the guests who are staying in the house. The local police also gave me one that they had compiled as soon as they arrived here. Did all the guests on your list arrive?'

'Yes, sir,' Peters answered.

'Including a Mr Hugh Beaumont?'

'Yes, sir. One of Lady Sophy's friends from London, so she told me.'

'He wasn't on the list compiled by the police on their arrival. Nor was another guest, a Lady Warminster.'

'She was on the ghost hunt, sir. I saw her.' Peters decided it was time to be anxious. 'I believe one or two motor cars left before the local police arrived.'

'Whose?'

'Regrettably, I cannot say. I am not responsible for matters outside the house itself. You should speak to Mr Ramsay who manages our stables and garages. You'll find them beyond the east wing. You'll see a line of high bushes shielding the kitchen yard, and the stables and garages are beyond that.'

'Were all the motor cars parked there?'

'Some were left in the forecourt, sir. Against Lord Ansley's wishes, but youth will be youth.'

Peters metaphorically mopped his brow when the inspector left. On the whole, he thought he had done fairly well. After all, it would be the guests on the ghost hunt on whom the inspector would be concentrating, not the servants. He was relieved to be considered one of the latter.

Luncheon had passed surprisingly well, Nell thought, especially considering Mrs Fielding had a hand in choosing it. The roasts had been ample enough to satisfy the additional dozen or so guests as well as the family and a visit to the vegetable garden had produced enough to provide ample sustenance; the meal had been crowned with ice creams and desserts left over from the night before. It was basic food but no one's mind would have been on haute cuisine – including her own. Nell's usual eagle eye had wavered from time to time. As the dinner menu too was already chosen and in hand, Nell decided she could relax in her chef's room – her own retreat.

She would read a novel to take her mind off the murder, but the one she chose, Mrs Christie's

Murder on the Links, took her straight back to the world of murder and detection, which was but a small step to worrying about the task hanging over her and what she could effectively do to help the Ansleys. The police, she reasoned, would find all the tangible clues which should lead them to the person who had killed Mr Charles. Without knowing whom they suspected, however, how could she explore the full story of what had happened?

Perhaps, she thought, she could come to the puzzle from the other direction. *Why* had he been murdered? For money? Sexual reasons? Through jealousy? Or fear?

Before she could explore this angle further there was a knock at the door. It was probably Miss Checkam calling her to Lady Ansley's side. Or was it that inspector again or his sergeant?

It was none of these. It was the dapper Mr Fontenoy. Amazed at this departure from normal procedure, she leapt up to greet him.

'Pray do sit down, Miss Drury,' he said. 'I propose to do the same if you have no objection.'

'I didn't expect to see you the wrong side of the green baize door,' she said lightly, wondering what on earth had brought him here.

'One doesn't expect murders at Wychbourne Court either, yet they happen,' he pointed out. 'Besides, barriers are fast vanishing in these modern times and I am here on a mission.'

This sounded ominous. 'For what?' Nell asked cautiously.

'I was told confidentially by Lady Ansley that you're trying to ensure that the police collar the right fellow for this murder and that they don't tread on too many toes while doing so.'

She was very cautious now. 'I'd like to help – and I won't get in anyone's way. Nor will I throw in any red herrings. Is that what's worrying you?'

'It is not and I thoroughly approve of Gertrude's suggestion. However, every Sherlock needs a Watson, Miss Drury. Have you considered myself from that angle?'

She had not and it had not occurred to her that she should do so. 'Were you planning to be Watson or Sherlock?' she asked carefully. She couldn't have her movements tracked, checked or changed by someone who might have his own axe to grind. Was this a plan by Lady Ansley to put someone on her tail, a double check?

'Watson, my dear Miss Drury. I'm far too old and far too unpopular with some members of the family to be a Sherlock.'

'That inspector is Sherlock,' Nell pointed out.

'No, no, *no*. He's Lestrade. It is we outsiders who see most of the game.'

'I wouldn't be too sure,' Nell said firmly. 'He's not only a dark horse but a clever one.'

'All the more reason that you need assistance in your role. I do not jest, Miss Drury. Nor has Lady Ansley requested me to check your movements. This is my own idea since I have a great affection for the Ansley family and wish to see justice done with no harm coming to it. I believe I have a role to play by working with you.'

'Go ahead.' She eyed him carefully, though. She had always liked Mr Fontenoy. Not only was he invariably polite to her and seemingly tolerant of the dowager's unrelenting antipathy to him, but she had noticed how careful he was to support the family without seeming to intrude.

'Society,' he observed, 'is becoming more equal, although hardly heading for communism. This is England. However, barriers still exist. You are a most discreet lady, Miss Drury, and therefore the family may undoubtedly confide in you with safety. Nevertheless, some members might not take kindly to your questioning them over private matters. On the other hand, you are admirably placed to have both an objective view of Wychbourne and the family and of the servants' hall. It seems to me I might be a useful adjunct in your quest. For instance, have you heard of Charlie's dance or dancing?'

'No. What's so special about that?'

'I cannot tell. It's merely a whisper that I overheard but one that you might not have come across.'

Nell thought fast. Could he have his own reasons for offering his services? Only scoring a point against Lady Enid, perhaps. Could he have had a grudge against Mr Charles or know who had killed him? Could *he* have killed him?

'Before you condemn me, Miss Drury,' he continued, clearly amused, 'I was not the perpetrator of this dreadful deed. Much as I believe I have a duty to protect the family – even Lady Enid – it would not extend to murder on its behalf. In any case, I was for the entire duration of the ghost hunt partaking of supper with a most delightful young gentleman who had elected not to go on the hunt. Several footmen also observed my presence and my rapt attention to this guest. How do you view the matter now?'

Increasingly favourably. Mr Fontenoy had a point, Nell realized. He might indeed have access to some people who would not speak freely to her.

'What would you be looking for?' she asked.

'Tell me first what *you* would be looking for, Miss Drury.'

She liked that approach. 'The reason for his death.'

'Would you agree that more than one person might have had cause to kill him even if they did not pursue it?'

'Yes, although he seemed very popular both with his friends and with the servants here and I never heard anything bad about him.'

'At least one person, you would agree, kept their dislike well hidden.'

She followed his line of thought immediately. 'And where there is one secret, there might be more?'

'Correct. Wychbourne, as Lady Clarice can testify, has over the centuries hidden many secrets from the world and doubtless the twentieth century is no exception.'

'There were a lot of guests here last night,' she pointed out.

'But only a limited number who could have committed this crime *and* knew this house well enough to commit murder.'

'And,' Nell added, 'knew that Charlie was behind that screen.'

'I agree. Shall we work together on the exchange of information then? I should consider it an honour.'

She took the plunge. 'I should like that.'

'Then to you I am not Mr Fontenoy but Arthur, and I hope a friend. My dear, I have but little entertainment in my old age. My small role in assisting you in your efforts will not lessen the horrific nature of this murder, but I trust it might lighten the journey to its solution.'

He was right. Already the path before her seemed less daunting than it had earlier. 'We shall need to meet – Arthur,' she said, struggling with the informality of using his Christian name. 'Anywhere in this house or even your home might be too conspicuous. What about the old dairy? It's sufficiently hidden from the house not to attract notice.'

'Perhaps too,' he suggested, 'we have need of a Baker Street Irregular to pass messages. Telephone calls are too public. I hesitate to suggest the lamp boy but he is well acquainted with both of us and with both houses – and you have no need to fear for his well-being as far as I am concerned. The late Mr Oscar Wilde did a great service to drama but a sad disservice to us poor lesser mortals.'

Nell laughed. Using Jimmy was a good idea. 'Agreed, Arthur.' It came more easily now. 'For the moment, you could concentrate on the family and remaining guests and I on those from the servants' wing who had access to the main house?'

'The upper servants, as they are traditionally termed?'

'Yes. Mr Peters, Mrs Fielding, Miss Checkam – and Mr Briggs.'

'That dear man.' Arthur sighed.

'And Robert the footman.' She frowned, thinking this through. 'It won't just be a case of talking to those we think had reason and opportunity to kill Charlie, but anyone who was there that night or who knew him. Even the guests who were here for just that one night.'

'There was that bandleader,' Arthur observed. 'The one who joined us on the balcony when we discovered the body.'

She was grateful for the 'we'. 'Mr Ellimore,' she said. 'I used to know him. He wouldn't have known about that screen.'

'Unless he was told – news about the impending joke on poor Lady Clarice could have travelled very quickly during the dance.'

'That broadens the picture,' Nell said. 'Anyone could have joined either group in the darkness. And no one would have noticed if someone had switched groups temporarily.'

'That, unfortunately, is true. How relieved I am that I am only Watson.' A pause. 'Do you have a secret plan, Nell? I do hope so. It does seem a rather difficult task we've taken on.'

She pulled a face at him. 'Sizzling swordfish, Arthur, you can't give up now. We haven't even started. What would Lady Enid say?'

Five

'The maître d' sees the best of the banquet; the diner only sees what's before him.' That's what someone had once remarked cheerfully to her at the Carlton. That, Nell thought, was her role in this murder and she wasn't sure she was suited to it. Or was it reluctance on her part, bearing in mind that there was a murderer at large whose aim would be to avoid discovery and would probably go to any lengths to do so?

If she ignored that aspect and went ahead, she had to struggle with the same questions: why would anyone want to kill Mr Charles *here* at Wychbourne Court and who had done so? Even after a whole night's sleep, Monday morning had so far thrown no more light on the puzzle. The likelihood was, Nell reasoned, that the murderer was on the ghost hunt. There had been far too many people around in the great hall after eleven forty-five to have killed him before the hunt actually began, and in any case the groan from above after it started ruled that out. Mr Charles must have gone up to the gallery before the hunt equipment was handed out from a quarter to twelve onwards, and during the time that Lord Richard and Lady Helen were bringing in the equipment from the boot room.

Next thought: Mr Charles's killer would probably have been in the first group led by Lady

Clarice but wouldn't Mr Peters, who must have been in the great hall throughout this period, have seen if anyone had doubled back to attack Mr Charles or if anyone else had gone up those stairs? There were two spiral staircases to the gallery, of course, one at each end; the one at the near end would be right under Mr Peters' eye as he stood inside the open door to the great hall and the staircase rose from the corridor just beyond it. What about the far end? Still surely too much of a risk of being seen by Mr Peters.

Where did that take her?

First get your barrow and then set off to market to gather the goods, she told herself. She recalled the sound of her father's barrow scraping along the cobbles, the only noise in the quiet of the darkness, and then the growing racket as they reached the bedlam of the market itself – people jostling, jesting, shouting, excited, angry. Once inside they had a part to play. It was the first step that was so daunting. As now.

Get into that market, Nell, she told herself. Where better to begin on a Monday morning than the servants' hall lunch? Everyone had been quiet at dinner last night, both in the servants' hall and in the main dining room. The police presence at Wychbourne Court had been all but invisible, but nevertheless it was casting a shadow. Meanwhile, there was luncheon for the Ansley family and guests to think of.

'Turbot à la Tartare,' Nell decreed. 'You take care of the sauce, Kitty, and you, Michel, the fish. Sorrel and potatoes with black butter sauce.' Nell paused. 'Have the police been here to interview you?'

'The sergeant, Miss Drury,' Kitty told her. 'He wanted to know where everyone was on Saturday night.'

'Did you know Mr Charles except by sight?' she asked cautiously. 'He seems to have been a popular chap.'

Michel hesitated. 'Some liked him, some did not.'

'He was not nice at all,' Kitty said. 'He thought he was the cat's whiskers and he tried to tumble Polly. He locked her into his bedroom – it was only because someone heard her screaming that he let her go. And she wasn't the only one.'

Nell was horrified. Polly was one of the chambermaids and not the sort of girl to make this up, so if this was Mr Charles's standard behaviour pattern it showed a vastly different side to him than the one Lady Helen and Lord Richard knew.

There was no sign of either Mr Peters or Mrs Fielding in the butler's pantry where the upper servants sometimes took lunch together, but she was in luck because Miss Checkam was there. Miss Checkam often took lunch in Lady Ansley's dressing room if she was busy with laundry or clothes repairs. Mr Briggs was also present today but was eating his meal in silence, as was his habit. Whatever she had to say to Miss Checkam would probably pass right over his head.

In all the twelve months that Nell had been at Wychbourne Court, she had never sized up Miss Checkam. She couldn't be much older than Nell – in her early thirties, perhaps – but with her long, dark brown hair severely drawn back into a bun and her mid-calf-length skirts in a dowdy brown that didn't suit her, she seemed to stem from a different age even though her face was quite attractive. Despite her willingness to impart gossip, Miss Checkam was, it always seemed to Nell, at one remove and sometimes it was hard going.

'You must be very upset. You're so close to the family,' Nell sympathized with her.

'Thank you, Miss Drury.' Miss Checkam hesitated, then continued in a flurry of words, 'To tell you the truth, I'm worried about Her Ladyship.'

Nell leapt at this opening. 'Just what I wanted your advice on. I'm concerned about her too,' she said to Miss Checkam tentatively, hoping this wasn't a step too far. The servants' hall wasn't used to exchanging confidences. Miss Checkam's face grew rather pink but she did not comment or retreat, Nell noted with relief.

'There's something wrong, I know there is. It's not just the murder. It's all this *dancing* and so on,' she said.

'Dancing?' Nell was puzzled. 'The new Charleston dance?' Surely Lady Ansley was too sensible to be worried by that on her children's behalf? She'd been a dancer herself in her youth.

Miss Checkam waved this aside impatiently. 'No. It's the way Lady Helen talks sometimes and behaves – not only to me but to young lady visitors. Sometimes I'm called on to dress their hair, as well as Lady Helen's. Sometimes they're all giggling and dancing around, as though they're in some conspiracy. I think it worries Lady Ansley too. She's not herself nowadays.' Too late, she cast a glance at Mr Briggs, but he was placidly working his way through Mrs Squires's steak and kidney pie.

'What about Lady Sophy?' Nell asked.

'No. She isn't one of them, if you know what I mean.'

Good. Nell did. 'Charlie's dancing,' she said, remembering that odd thing Arthur had mentioned. Could this have any relevance to his murder?

Miss Checkam looked startled. 'I've heard Lady Helen and that Miss Harlington talk about that, not that she's a friend of Lady Helen's exactly.'

'Did you ask Lady Helen about it?'

'I did presume to once. She wasn't very pleased. She told me that it was nothing to do with me because I was only there to do her hair. I was very upset.'

'She didn't mean it,' Nell comforted her. 'Lady Helen's up and down like a yo-yo. She was keen on Mr Charles – and you must have come to know him through his visits here. Did you like him?'

Miss Checkam stiffened. 'He was always very polite to me.'

She'd moved too quickly and put her foot in it, Nell realized, but her reply was forestalled.

'Not good man.' Mr Briggs startled them both as he leapt to his feet, shouting out: 'G/26420 Corporal Briggs, *sir.*'

This occasionally happened when Mr Briggs was upset and reverted to his wartime memories, but it was odd that he had been so agitated by Mr Charles's name. 'You knew Mr Charles, Mr Briggs?' Nell gently enquired. 'Did you see him on Saturday evening?'

His face went blank. 'Panama,' he said.

'Mr Charles wore one?' Nell asked, mystified.

'No, it's Lord Ansley's hat,' Miss Checkam explained. 'You must have seen him in it. He loves wearing it round the estate although it's so unfashionable now. Mr Briggs likes it, don't you?' she asked him.

Back in the familiar territory of Lord Ansley's wardrobe, Mr Briggs was calmer now. He nodded and carefully put down his knife and fork. 'Thank you,' he said simply. 'Goodbye.'

With that he rose to his feet and left. Nell watched him through the window as he walked past on his way to the gardens. Had it been the mere mention of Mr Charles's name that had upset him or was it that he now associated it with death and had blotted it out? It was hard to tell. He was just Mr Briggs. He must have a Christian name but she'd never heard it or seen it used.

'Do you know where Mr Briggs was on Saturday night, Miss Checkam?'

'No. I didn't see him. Out watching for owls, I expect. He said he heard a nightjar a few days ago but that's very unlikely.'

'He had no reason to dislike Mr Charles, did he?'

Miss Checkam glanced at her. 'Who knows what goes through his head? Whatever it is, I don't see him killing anyone, do you?'

'No, but he might have seen something?'

'Such as what?' Miss Checkam asked sharply.

'All five of us,' Nell pointed out mildly, 'spend our time between the servants' hall and the main house, so we're in a position to see what goes on in both places. We might pick up some reason why someone wanted to kill him.'

87

'He was a lovely man,' Miss Checkam said firmly.

Too firmly? Nell wondered.

'I never heard any of the family say anything against him either,' Miss Checkam continued.

She was very flushed and it was clear that Nell was going to hear no more. If, Nell pondered, Mr Charles had regarded it as his right to force his attentions on women who were unlikely to be able to fight back, could Miss Checkam have been one of them?

'Did you know about the joke he was going to take part in?' Nell asked.

Miss Checkam was hostile now. 'Of course I didn't. How would I have known?' she snapped.

In for a penny, in for a pound. 'I thought Lady Helen might have mentioned it to you and that you might have been in the great hall when Mr Charles provided a groan or two from the other side of that screen.'

'I wasn't, and she didn't.'

'I merely thought you might have been helping Lady Helen move the equipment,' Nell said hastily.

Miss Checkam calmed down. 'No. I went to the servants' hall dance briefly and then to my room. The next thing I knew there was a lot of noise and that must have been when the police came. That's what I told the nice inspector.' She looked at Nell defiantly.

Nice inspector? If the inspector had a *nice* side she had yet to see it, Nell thought crossly. She must put all thoughts of Inspector Melbray out

88

of her mind, however, and consider how to tackle Mr Peters. Of all of them he was, as butler, the most likely to have seen what was happening on Saturday evening *and* to have any interesting information on Mr Charles. Mr Peters was the most obliging and helpful butler she had ever known. That was understandable, as he'd been through the war and like so many must have found it hard to get a job afterwards. She knew he hadn't been in service before the war, so he was fortunate indeed to be at Wychbourne Court and must still be anxious not to put a foot wrong. He had been on her side when the former chef had tried to get her dismissed and even reasoned with Mrs Fielding when she'd informed Lady Ansley that she wouldn't work with a female. That was good of him because he was fond of Mrs Fielding. He must be over forty now, and Mrs Fielding couldn't be much older, so she might be right in thinking there was a closer link between them than met the eye of the servants' hall.

Guessing he would be in the steward's room, she forced herself to walk through the great hall, schooling herself to think happy thoughts and not about what had happened on Saturday night. She thought of all the banquets that had been held here over the years. In Elizabethan days there had been a separate banqueting hall in the grounds where the desserts were served but today it lay in ruins while the great hall remained a tribute to the Ansley family over the ages. Portraits looked down benignly (or sometimes not so benignly) on their successors. Just one solitary police constable stood beneath the minstrels' gallery, nodding politely as she passed. On the far side of the hall she could see the entrance to the morning room where she supposed the police must now be gathered – including that *nice* inspector.

Mr Peters was indeed in the steward's room and fortunately alone. He was looking somewhat forlorn, she thought.

'I'm glad you're here, Miss Drury,' he greeted her.

She was instantly alarmed. It wasn't like him to make such an informal comment – except when they all got tiddly at the servants' New Year dance.

'You look as drained as a pan of boiled spuds.' She had hoped to raise a smile, although she was concerned at how ill he looked.

'Too many late nights,' he said. 'What brings you here?'

'I wish I was over the hills and far away,' she said lightly, 'but that's not possible, so I thought I'd escape from the east wing for a while.'

'There's no escaping murder,' he said gloomily.

How to reply to that? 'We can keep a watchful eye.'

He stiffened. 'On what?'

'The family,' Nell said. 'All those guests and so on. All these police. The family will want to be polite but they have their own worries. Have the police interviewed you yet?'

'I felt like a fried onion after it,' he replied, again unexpectedly human.

'Me too. And I was finely chopped first.'

'How long are those fellows going to be here?' he asked plaintively after he had managed a laugh. 'Everyone's upset, every*thing's* upset. I ought to be managing the lot, Miss Drury, but I'm not. Not doing my job.'

'None of us is,' Nell said. 'We've just got to *look* as though we are. Keep on butlering, keep on cooking, that's us.' She was relieved that he showed signs of perking up. 'Are there any more guests arriving?' she asked. 'Mr Charles's family, perhaps.'

'They live in Derbyshire. They're coming down today for the inquest on Wednesday. The son lived in a London flat most of the time.'

Inquest! She hadn't even thought about that. Of course there would be an inquest and she might even have to give evidence. 'Where will it be?' she asked. 'Here?' That would be *too* much to cope with.

'The Coach and Horses in the village. They always use that upper room for inquests. Used to be a ballroom in the old days and then they did music hall there. Still do, sometimes.'

And hold village dances there, Nell knew. She'd been to one once. 'Are the parents staying here?'

'Over at Stalisbrook Place with Lady Warminster.'

She'd been on the ghost hunt, Nell remembered. Stalisbrook Place was a sizeable Georgian mansion closer to Ightham and Tonbridge than Wychbourne. 'One less thing for the Ansleys to put up with,' she observed.

'Plenty to take its place.'

'There seem to be mixed views about Mr Charles. You liked him, didn't you, Mr Peters?'

91

Another defensive answer. 'He was pleasant enough.'

'Someone didn't think so. He doesn't seem very popular in the servants' hall.'

Mr Peters looked trapped. 'Mere tittle-tattle. He was a most pleasant gentleman. It must have been one of the guests on the ghost hunt who lagged behind and killed him. I was down below in the hall all the time and I'd have seen if anyone else had gone up those stairs other than ghost hunters.'

'Even though there are two staircases and neither of them leads up from the hall itself? I suppose someone could have gone up at the far end and edged along behind the screen.'

'Don't see how. I'd either have seen or heard them,' Mr Peters said defensively again. 'I told the inspector that and he saw my point.'

Ambiguous, Nell thought, if those were the *nice* inspector's exact words. 'Mr Charles must have slipped away from the dancing some time before the groups gathered. Did you see him go up to the gallery? You must have known about the joke being played on Lady Clarice.'

Mr Peters was growing restless. 'Lord Richard told me about it earlier that day and Mr Charles must have gone up while I was briefly in the boot room giving a helping hand with the equipment.' He paused and then added, 'I've read a lot of detective stories, Miss Drury, and it's my belief that all those brilliant sleuths would have to conclude someone killed him during the ghost hunt, not before or after.'

'That moan you heard rules out that happening

before the group got up there,' Nell agreed. 'Unless the moan came from one of Lady Clarice's ghosts,' she ended lightly.

Mr Peters managed a laugh. 'How delighted Lady Clarice would be if that were true. No, I am quite sure that it was someone on the hunt itself.'

He was very obstinate on that point, Nell thought, but she still wondered whether anyone could have stolen up that far staircase in the darkness.

'Why do you think he was killed, Mr Peters? You think he was a very pleasant man, but it wasn't very pleasant of him to have danced with Miss Harlington all evening when he must have known Lord Richard wanted so much to do so, *and* that Lady Helen was longing to dance with him.'

'Minor matters, Miss Drury. They're young. They tease each other.' But he did not look her in the eye.

'Do the words "Charlie's dancing" mean anything to you?' Nell asked at random.

He shook his head, but he hadn't asked her the reason for the question, she noted. On the contrary, he seemed all too anxious to get rid of her.

At Lady Ansley's request Nell had postponed her usual morning meeting with her, and when she rang on the house telephone to see if it was convenient to come now even though it was usually her teatime, Lady Ansley sounded relieved.

'Yes, Nell, do come,' she replied loudly. 'My visitor is just leaving. *Now* is most convenient.'

Nell took the heavy hint and hurried to the

Velvet Room or parlour as Lady Ansley called it fondly. If she took the grand staircase she might even catch a glimpse of the departing visitor and satisfy her curiosity. Not a welcome visitor clearly, but why not? Perhaps, she thought, she was beginning to develop a taste for detective work. Was it any more complicated than disentangling what lay behind some of the old recipes she used? If you took some of them at face value you could be floundering around with culinary disasters. There was an old eighteenth-century recipe 'to disguise a leg of veal' that had caused her a few problems, not to mention the fourteenth-century one for Brewet of Almony which she'd found in the library.

To her disappointment she passed no one on her way to the Velvet Room. The small parlour, tucked away from the grander rooms, was the only one where Her Ladyship displayed mementoes of her former life. Here, clad in wonderful Edwardian skirts and hats, Gaiety Girls kicked their feet modestly in photographs and posters. There was Gertie Millar who became the Countess of Dudley. There was George Edwardes himself, owner and manager. There too were Lady Ansley's family photos – gentlemen, ladies and children looking earnest with Victorian scowls as they waited motionless for the picture to be taken – and Nell's favourite, the much-loved dog Napoleon that had belonged to the late marquess. According to Lady Clarice, Napoleon still haunted the boot room waiting for his master's return.

'Come in, Miss Drury,' Lady Ansley called when Nell knocked. She could tell from the tone of her voice that the visitor was still present. Who could it be? It took a lot to drive Lady Ansley dotty.

It was the Honourable Elise Harlington, draped half sitting, half lying on a daybed, her striped, full-sleeved afternoon frock clinging to every inch of her long, snaky body. She looked most elegant and Nell mentally smoothed the wrinkles from her own humble pleated skirt and over-blouse. At least she had removed her apron and chef's hat.

The Honourable Elise looked her studiedly up and down and smiled at her through the cupid's bow of her heavily rouged lips. Nell realized that she was now the target. 'Such exquisite food,' Miss Harlington drawled. 'Wychbourne Court is so fortunate to have your services, Miss Drury, at such a terrible time for us all. I'm quite envious, Lady Ansley. It was simply gorgeous.'

'Thank you, Miss Harlington,' Nell said meekly, hoping that Lady Ansley would not pick up the sarcasm in her voice.

She didn't seem to notice. She had a fixed smile on her face, although her eyes suggested a different emotion. Fear? But why? Nell wondered.

'Dear Lady Ansley, I really must depart. Do consider my suggestion.' A note of steel had entered Miss Harlington's voice. What, Nell wondered, was that about?

'You don't look well, Lady Ansley,' Nell said in concern once they were alone.

'Lack of sleep, Nell,' she replied hastily. 'The strain of the last two days. That's all. It's all been quite terrible.'

'What can I do to help?'

'Try to find out – you know what we talked about. And hurry. How is the servants' hall. How are they taking it?'

'Those who aren't involved find it exciting,' Nell said frankly. 'The rest of us are in the same position as you. We're possible suspects for Mr Parkyn-Wright's murder.'

Lady Ansley shuddered. 'How and why? Why should any of us have wished to kill him? Why should anyone here?'

'He was not as popular as he seemed, Lady Ansley – at least not in the servants' hall.'

When Lady Ansley did not reply, Nell wondered where she could delicately tread next. 'He attacked one of the chambermaids,' she added. 'And he liked teasing people and upset people at the dance.'

Still Lady Ansley said nothing, just stared at her.

'Charlie's dancing, Lady Ansley,' Nell continued in desperation. 'Do you know about that?'

There was real fear in Lady Ansley's eyes now. 'It means absolutely nothing, Nell,' she managed to say at last. 'Only that Charlie was leading everyone a dance, I'm afraid. You were right. He teased poor Richard *and* poor Helen by dancing with Elise. That must be what's meant by his dancing. Now what did you want to see me about?'

Nell had been shut out. She was going to learn no more. 'The menus, Lady Ansley.'

The arrangement over using Jimmy's services seemed to work well, as when Nell arrived at the old dairy that evening Arthur was already there.

96

Certainly it was a bleak place and with the light fading it seemed forbidding. It was an old eighteenth-century building classically designed with portico and rotunda. Some of the old equipment was left inside and the fountain still worked. But the dairymaids had long gone and the ceramic tiles were grimy and broken.

Arthur looked around and sighed. 'I'm sure Clarice must love this place, home perhaps to at least one dairymaid ghost, but it's been sadly neglected. Perhaps I'll bring champagne next time in order that we may see it with rose-coloured spectacles. How have you progressed, Nell?'

'Only by inches. Mr Parkyn-Wright seems to have had a penchant for chambermaids, however likeable he is at his own social level.'

'That is interesting.'

'And the words Charlie's dancing or dance brought reactions but no explanation.'

'Even more interesting.'

'Miss Checkam and Mr Briggs apparently weren't present in the main house during the evening but Mr Peters was. He says he saw no one, though. I do get the impression that he and Miss Checkam are holding something back.'

'I too have that impression from my own humble efforts,' Arthur said. 'I have spoken with my nephew, Richard – that is how I like to consider him, not altogether to Gerald's approval as he is Hugo's son. Richard is torn between sorrow at his friend's death and bewilderment as to Charlie's behaviour in keeping him away from his beloved Miss Harlington. That seems to be

97

all he has against Charlie or all he is willing to tell me. Lady Helen is even more muted on the subject. She is not at all well, and no mention of Charlie must be made, according to Lord and Lady Ansley.

'Lady Sophy is much more forthcoming,' he continued. 'She was not an admirer of Charles Parkyn-Wright. On the other hand, she definitely does not wish to discuss what happened on Saturday evening. Rex Beringer is more outspoken. He disliked Charlie and extends that to Miss Harlington, based on their behaviour to Lady Helen, he says. There may be more. The ghost hunt, Nell. It comes back to that. Not everyone knew the design of the gallery. Not everyone knew that Charlie would hide there. Those who did were almost certainly in that first group and therefore the reason why he died seems to me to take second place to who killed him. Would you not agree?'

'Up to a point,' she conceded, 'but you can't have the gravy without the meat. There's nothing so far that gives anyone a real motive for killing him. That first group might indeed hold the answer but it does include three of the Ansleys – four if you include Lady Clarice.'

'Indeed it does, but I take it that we do not consider her as a suspect?'

'I think not,' Nell agreed solemnly. 'Lady Clarice was leading her group and if she had designs on Mr Charles then she would have taken a less conspicuous role in it.'

'I admit I am most relieved. I do not see dear Clarice wielding a dagger. Even if she mistook a live man for a ghost as he was clad in Egyptian costume, I fail to see why she would have taken a dagger as part of her equipment.'

Nell smiled. 'Let's assume then that whoever killed Mr Charles had good reason to do so in their opinion. They would need to know how *long* the ghost hunt would take. My group took half an hour to go round the west wing and return to the great hall, and when we arrived the other group was already there so their tour took a little less time. We set off together in our different directions.'

'Had the first group returned long before?'

'I don't know, but they were all there. Lady Clarice would have noticed if any of them had vanished.'

'Not necessarily. But they would have had to have known about Charlie's whereabouts, which unfortunately brings us back to Helen, Richard and Sophy.'

'And whomever they told,' Nell said.

'Would that include chambermaids?' Arthur asked mildly.

'No,' Nell said wearily. 'We're back at the beginning, Arthur. There has to be a lot more to learn about Mr Charles than his attacking one chambermaid.'

Six

The upper floor of the Coach and Horses Inn, which stood by the entrance gate to Wychbourne Court, did indeed look transformed since Nell's last visit there for the Wychbourne village dance. That had been wizard fun – a mix of folk dances and inexpertly performed modern dances, together with some jigging about to ragtime. It bore no relation at all to the dancing she had seen at the Carlton or at Wychbourne Court and was much closer to her childhood memories of wild jumping around to music hall songs being belted out in local East End pubs.

On this Wednesday morning, the Wychbourne village dance was also consigned to memory. The platform where the band had played was now occupied by a large table, at which the coroner would no doubt soon take his place. To one side was a seat, probably for the coroner's officer or his clerk; the latter's job so far was as a sheepdog herding people into their rightful positions for the inquest. There was a lectern – presumably the witness stand – and chairs ranged along part of both walls. Nell had been conducted to the witness rows, and the jury would presumably file in to the opposite row. The rest of the hall was packed full of the very eager press and public.

'I feel like a pea in a pod waiting to be shelled,'

Nell whispered to Lady Clarice, who was sitting next to her.

Among her other fellow peas were Miss Harlington, dressed as if for Ascot with the largest brimmed hat Nell had seen for many a long year. Trust her to wear a brim among a forest of cloche hats. She was languidly talking to Lord Richard, who was sitting with obvious pleasure at her side and looking more cheerful than of late. Perhaps Mr Charles's behaviour last Saturday had opened his eyes to his so-called best friend. Best friends were all very well, Nell reflected, but as with pork, garlic and rosemary, best friends could still fall out if they had too much of each other.

She could see Inspector Melbray further along the row, sitting next to the local doctor. On Lady Clarice's far side was Lady Helen with Lady Sophy next to her. The press was occupying the front row of the public seating and behind them was a row that seemed to be reserved by unspoken assent for the Ansley family, including the dowager. Nell craned her neck to see whether Arthur was present too and picked him out two or three rows back, between Mr Beringer and Guy Ellimore. Typically for Guy, he was next to Lady Warminster. Was this by accident or design? Nell wondered, and if the latter, was it by Guy's or hers? Guy was a great ladykiller but surely he wouldn't have had a yen for Lady Warminster. Not his style at all.

'Nell,' whispered Lady Clarice, 'can you sense him?'

'Sense who?' Nell asked blankly.

'Charles Parkyn-Wright. He is with us, I am sure. He is the most vibrant person here.'

Fortunately the jury and then the coroner chose to enter at that point. He wasn't from Wychbourne so perhaps with a death at the prestigious Wychbourne Court to investigate he had come from Sevenoaks or Tonbridge.

'In a way, Lady Clarice, I do agree with you.' Their entry had given Nell time to reply diplomatically. 'Absent but present in our minds.'

'He is waiting to join our family,' Lady Clarice told her proudly.

It took a moment for Nell to tumble to what Lady Clarice meant. 'He's becoming one of the ghosts of Wychbourne Court?'

'He is about to do so,' Lady Clarice said gravely. 'He will be joining Sir Thomas with whom he has an affinity.'

'When will that be?'

'Who knows, but soon, I believe. It is not for us to meddle. Once justice has been done and his killer discovered, then Charles may choose to leave us again, of course. It is his decision.'

'It is indeed,' Nell said gently. The tension in her stomach grew as the coroner opened the proceedings and evidence of identification of the victim was given to the jury, including that of Mr Charles's father. Would she be next? She was so busy preparing herself for that that she wasn't prepared for the coroner's next pronouncement. The cake then well and truly sank in the middle as he announced that the inquest had been adjourned until Tuesday, 7 July at the request of the police.

102

What the dithering dumplings was the reason for that? She had nerved herself up to give evidence, only to have to do so again in just under two weeks' time.

She glanced along the row but Inspector Melbray's face was, as usual, impassive. Common sense told her that he couldn't have revealed news of this adjournment earlier, but her irritation was exacerbated just because she knew it was irrational. A worse thought struck her. If there was to be an adjournment, didn't that mean the inspector must know who the killer was? If so, she needed to work quickly if she was to be any use to Lady Ansley. What would happen to the guests at Wychbourne Court? Would they stay or return home? What would happen next?

That, at least, was answered. Upon the coroner's departure, the Honourable Elise Harlington climbed on to her chair with her flimsy chiffon skirt fashionably flaring around her elegant legs.

'Let's party!' she cried, throwing her arms up in ecstasy.

Party? Where? Was she crazy? Nell trembled for the reputation of Wychbourne Court. Lady Helen burst into tears, Lord Richard looked dumbfounded, and from the public seats Lady Ansley was hurrying towards her daughter. The press were crowding round with interest and those about to leave stopped gathering jackets and belongings to stare at the spectacle. Someone then caught the mood – or Miss Harlington's mood, at least. 'Let's do it!' he roared.

Oblivious of this distraction, Lady Clarice began to make her way out. Should she go with her? Nell wondered. No, she might be needed here. 'Why don't you stay, Lady Clarice?' she urged her as the shouting continued. 'Mr Parkyn-Wright might welcome that.'

Lady Clarice stared at her. 'Very well, but they simply don't understand, do they?'

Did anyone understand anything in this bedlam? A few people were yelling approval, some disapproval, others just staring. The clerk of the court seemed to consider his role over and was making a speedy exit. She noted that fortunately Inspector Melbray was keeping an eye on the proceedings, as the Honourable Elise was still dancing on her chair.

'I'm going to party with the peasants!' she shouted, clapping her hands in glee.

At that the said peasants revolted with an outburst of protests.

'Let's do Charlie's dance!' Miss Harlington shouted over the noise, ignoring the fact that the 'peasants' had opted to stomp out of the room. 'Ye old village green,' she continued, not a whit perturbed. 'Under the spreading chestnut tree. Fiddle. You!' She pointed at Guy Ellimore. 'You're the fiddler.'

'I play the clarinet,' he called back to her.

'Then find the fiddler for me,' she ordered in grand style. 'We must celebrate the end of Charlie's dance as he would have wanted.'

She began to sway and Inspector Melbray helped her down from the chair without a word. He didn't even object, Nell noticed, when the Honourable Elise Harlington swooned in his arms. Or *appeared* to do so.

'Mulligatawny mussels,' Nell muttered to herself. 'What's that woman going to do next?'

She didn't have to wait long to find out. Inspector Melbray deposited his burden – somewhat ungently, to Nell's pleasure – on to the nearest seat, upon which she came to her senses and pointed at Nell. 'You,' she said grandly, 'prepare us a picnic. Serve it on the green.'

Nell declined this unwelcome offer, and was about to guide Lady Clarice to the protection of Lord and Lady Ansley when Lady Sophy came over to them.

'Miss Drury, I think everyone here has gone cuckoo,' Lady Sophy announced, 'but if Elise is really going to do this Charlie's dance, whatever it is, I should be here, if you wouldn't mind escorting my aunt home.'

'Certainly not,' Lady Clarice informed her niece with asperity. 'If Charles is dancing then I must be present. He will expect to see me here.'

'I'll take you home, Clarice.' Arthur must have spotted what was going on and came over to them. 'Charlie will want to speak to you confidentially, not at a party. Miss Drury, I believe you might find the village fiddler most entertaining. Do stay.'

His heavy hint was endorsed by Guy Ellimore, who seized the moment to join them. 'Do stay, Nell,' he urged her, taking her arm.

She removed it. 'I suppose I should. I'll arrange the picnic with the inn. Not much is going to happen otherwise.'

At least Inspector Melbray wasn't clamouring to join the party.

* * *

It should have been idyllic, Nell thought. Grouped around the village green were half-timbered cottages. There were other cottages whose beams had been covered with weatherboard and plaster but which had wisteria and roses climbing over them. There were one or two Georgian homes among them and several of the cottages served as shops on their ground floors. On the opposite corner to the inn was St Mary's Church with its rectory tucked behind it. All a glorious sight and a splendid place for a picnic – on a normal day, which this was not.

The chestnut tree that Miss Harlington had been glorifying to the courtroom was actually an oak tree which spread its majestic branches regally, ignoring the excesses of the interlopers beneath them. No village smithy stood here as in Longfellow's poem, however, though there was a blacksmith-cum-garage out on the Hildenborough road. Even if Longfellow's smith had been present, his attitude of 'Something attempted, something done, has earned a night's repose' would be doomed to failure today. She hoped for his sake that his nights had been uninterrupted by ghosts or murders – or his days by idiotic bright young things like Miss Harlington.

The required picnic had challenged the innkeeper's wife. Not only was she unaccustomed to providing lunch for passers-by, but the thought of pleasing not only the guests from Wychbourne Court but Miss Drury herself overwhelmed her. Nell solved the problem. Pip, the young son of the inn, was despatched on his bicycle to the baker's for bread, his sister to the grocer's for ham, the dairy for cream and cheese, and to Mr Barney, the greengrocer, for cucumber, lettuce and strawberries. All bills to go to Wychbourne Court.

Once they had arrived, Nell rolled up her sleeves. 'Right,' she said to the innkeeper's wife, 'tell me what you want doing.' Somewhat dazed, the lady found she could cope after all with Nell's help.

Cider and beer were flowing by the time Nell rejoined the party outside. To her amusement, she could see that the village fiddler, who must have been pulled off his seat at the bar to rush home for his fiddle, was now playing for the Honourable Elise Harlington and Lady Helen, who were performing the Dashing White Sergeant all by themselves.

Guy strolled up to meet her. 'Is it usual for village inquests to end up like this?'

'I doubt it, but if it keeps Madam Elise quiet it's worth it, whether the village approves or not.' Nell couldn't see Lord and Lady Ansley or the dowager, although Arthur and Lady Clarice were still here – the latter probably waiting for Mr Charles's ghost. Altogether between twenty and thirty people were gathered.

The sandwiches were being brought out now and by the time Nell had helped with their distribution Guy had returned to Lady Warminster, to Nell's relief. She needed time to get her breath back. Instead, the minute she began to tackle her own plate of sandwiches, Lady Sophy came over to her. 'Can I sit with you?' she asked wistfully. 'You're sensible,' she added as Nell waved her down on the grass beside her.

'Thank you,' Nell said.

'It's Richard and Helen who aren't,' their sister said gloomily.

'Ah. Careful, Lady Sophy.'

'I'm always having to be careful. Careful about getting in Richard and Helen's way. Careful about not upsetting Mother, careful not to bother Father with matters he won't understand. People aren't his stock-in-trade. He's good at buildings, though.'

'I wouldn't be too sure about his not understanding people.'

Lady Sophy ignored this. 'My brother and sister have both been acting oddly since Charlie died. I just want to be sure . . .'

'That they don't know anything about his death,' Nell finished for her when she came to a halt.

'Well, they did plan it – not his death, of course, but the moans and groans and Pepper's Ghost and all that.'

'They weren't to do with his death. It was just a joke and the police know that.'

'Do they?' Lady Sophy didn't seem convinced.

'Did you talk to anyone else about the joke beforehand?' Nell asked. 'Or did Mr Parkyn-Wright?'

'Oh, yes. To Queen Elise for one, and lots of people giggled when we heard the groan just after we set off, so they must have guessed. After all, Charlie was dancing with Elise right up to the time he left to go and play the stupid joke.'

'That would be not long after eleven thirty?'

'Yes.' Lady Sophy gave her a curious look. 'You've got a very enquiring mind, Nell. Is that

108

because those cooking recipes of yours need careful timing?'

'Perhaps,' Nell said cautiously. 'But I did find the body. I suppose because of that I feel some responsibility. Why did someone want to kill him? He seemed popular in his own set.'

'Seemed,' Lady Sophy said darkly. 'But he was one of those people whom one feels one *ought* to like. Does that make sense?' When Nell nodded, she continued, 'So many people were busy saying how nice he was that everyone else thought they must be wrong if they didn't agree.'

'Is that how your sister felt?' Nell tried not to sound too interested and helped herself to another sandwich. Not bad for a hurried job.

'I don't know,' Lady Sophy said simply. 'Richard flies off the handle so easily nowadays you can't talk to him about things. He was furious with Charlie for dancing with Elise all evening. And Helen – well, she was upset but I can't believe she really loved Charlie. He was fun but no more. Just a bit swept off her feet, and at the dance she found herself stuck with poor old Rex Beringer.'

'Why poor old? Just because his affection isn't returned?'

'Yes. I like Rex. He's a real person. As I hope I am. He's not at all like all those debs and flappers and jolly young men. Stage-door johnnies, Mother still calls them. Rex doesn't live in one of those balloons floating through the sky until someone pricks it. He does love Helen, though she's in a balloon most of the time and doesn't even notice him. She used to like real people, not people like Charlie or Elise or Lady Warminster. I say, *she* could have killed Charlie, couldn't she?' she added in sudden excitement. 'She was on the ghost hunt.'

'Why would Lady Warminster want to kill him, though?' Nell asked practically.

'She's ageing for a flapper,' Sophy said eagerly, 'but she could have had her eye on Charlie.'

Nell decided to ignore the fact that Lady Warminster must be roughly the same age as she was. 'Lady Warminster is married,' she pointed out. Not that that seemed to matter overmuch nowadays.

'To some old army general who's away in Mesopotamia most of the time. She gets bored.'

'How do you know that?'

It was an idle question but Lady Sophy went pink. 'It's common knowledge,' she said almost defiantly. 'Anyway, she could have killed Charlie. She was in the first group and she rushed away before or as soon as you found the body and all the brouhaha began. Perhaps she had blood on her.'

Nell's attention quickened. 'Did she come by motor car?'

'Yes, she drove herself. The Warminsters don't have *a* motor car – they have to have several. She has a chauffeur and someone else who usually drives her when she comes to Wychbourne. Her Ladyship fancies herself as another Gertrude Jekyll, so she comes here to cross-examine Mr Fairweather and the other gardeners about what they're doing in our gardens.' She hesitated. 'That's her Delage.' Lady Sophy pointed to a

110

motor car parked in the roadside. 'She likes driving herself sometimes, though, because people won't know where she's going.'

'*You* seem to have noticed,' Nell said mildly.

'That's only because she was here and could have killed Charlie,' Lady Sophy muttered defensively.

'Did she know him? Had she met him at Wychbourne before or does she visit London clubs?' That was a thought. Was she one of Mr Charles's cast-offs and killed him in revenge? Nell wondered.

'No, she might have met him here before but I don't think so, and she wouldn't dare go to London clubs in case her husband found out. He's old school. He'd cut her allowance off and maybe divorce her, and she isn't silly enough to risk that.'

'Is this common gossip,' Nell enquired, 'or are you guessing?' Blithering beetroot, she noticed, the girl's gone bright red again.

'Yes, just gossip,' Lady Sophy muttered, scrambling to her feet. 'I must go. Helen isn't looking well.'

Nell agreed with that. Miss Harlington looked as though she was the Queen of the Night with her kohl-lined eyes and dark blue chiffon frock, but Lady Helen seemed to have lost several nights' sleep. Emotions could get muddled at such times. Some people can't help laughing at funerals, some cry at weddings. Was it the murder itself upsetting her or was there something more?

Just as Lady Sophy was leaving, Mr Beringer came up to greet her then he turned to Nell. 'Miss

Drury, I've admired your cuisine greatly, so now I can thank you personally.'

'That's nice of you, Rex,' Lady Sophy replied before Nell could answer from her disadvantaged position on the ground. 'If you were like Charlie, though, you'd have said something crass like "and now I can admire *you*".'

'Fortunately,' he replied gravely, 'I'm not like Charlie.'

'I was going to see if Helen's all right,' Lady Sophy said to him. 'You should go instead, though, Rex.'

'I've just tried. She doesn't want me around,' he said gloomily.

'No, but she needs you. Have another go.'

Thus reassured, he set off again, and Lady Warminster was the next to greet Lady Sophy while pointedly ignoring Nell. 'Dear child,' she cooed.

'I'm nineteen,' Lady Sophy pointed out crossly.

'So young, with the future stretching out before you. Unlike dear Charlie.' A lace handkerchief was extracted from her silk handbag and briefly touched her face. Not the carefully pencilled-in eyebrows, though, Nell noticed as she reluctantly got to her feet.

'My condolences,' she continued, still ignoring Nell. The white georgette frock shivered with her. At last, it was Nell's turn. Lady Warminster studied her briefly. 'Who are you?'

'The chef at Wychbourne Court.'

A silence, then: 'But you found the body, didn't you?'

'I did.'

112

'What was a cook doing on the ghost hunt?'

Nell decided to take this literally. 'I led the second group. You were in the first.'

'Was I? How strange. I really can't recall.'

'Aunt Clarice says you were,' Lady Sophy chimed in.

'Ah, yes, I do remember now. I had to leave the party early. Like Cinderella.' She gave a tinkly laugh. 'I always leave balls at midnight in case an ugly sister might take her revenge.'

Could she have meant that apparently light-hearted remark deliberately? Nell was appalled, given that Lady Sophy hardly fell into society's standard of beauty. To those who looked no further, she was no Nancy Cunard or Clara Bow. Those who did saw an intelligence and attractiveness that might not pass muster in Mayfair but anywhere else in the world was far preferable. Lady Warminster, Nell decided, was one of those women whose thinking lagged far behind their speech.

'Your chauffeur seems to want you, Cinderella,' Lady Sophy said flatly.

Nell looked up and saw him getting out of the Delage, and Lady Warminster looked over towards him. There was something familiar about him, Nell thought.

'Not my chauffeur, dear child. Merely my under-gardener. A rough sort but he drives well.'

With that, Lady Warminster departed. Nell could see that she had seriously upset Lady Sophy who then hurried away, murmuring that she should join Lady Helen. Nell resumed her place on the ground and reached for the sandwiches. She wasn't alone for long, however.

113

'At last. You're a popular lady, Nell.' To her annoyance, Guy sat down at her side. 'And do stop looking so crossly at the grass. Are you gathering ingredients? You always did love nettle soup, didn't you?'

'Yes, and making daisy chains, but I grew out of that,' she snapped.

'As you did of me?'

'We went in different directions, Guy.'

'And now we've collided again.'

'Nothing has changed, Guy. You're a rover, I'm a chef.'

She thought he would say that chefs could be both, and once – for a brief day or two – she had wanted nothing more. But love is a deceiver and where Guy was concerned she had thought it real when only its pale shadow had been present. Thankfully so far today Guy had not declared that chefs could be both and she was glad.

'I daresay you were right,' he said. 'Still, now I'm back you could at least smile. You always used to say a chef without a smile was like a soup without stock.'

That made her laugh. 'Are you coming back for the inquest?'

'I might stay here. I've had my orders from the police not to go far away.'

'Just you?'

'No. A bunch of us, I believe. Miss Elise is under inspection from the police magnifying glass, as is Rex Beringer, not to mention a lot of folk much nearer home, is my guess. Anyone who was on that ghost hunt.'

114

'But you weren't,' she pointed out.

'I turned up, though. It's the same thing. I thought it would be fun but I didn't know the fun was going to include murder. I didn't even know about this ghost joke as I'm not one of the elite. I didn't join a group. If you recall, when you switched routes at half-time in the great hall I decided just to tag along with yours.'

'Just for fun?' she asked suspiciously.

'No, I wanted to see you, Nell. Later, I said on Saturday. I wasn't going to let you get away without that talk.'

'We didn't have it.'

'Not then. We've just had it and plenty more to follow.'

Her heart sank. 'But nothing's changed, Guy.'

'I'll just hang around until it does then,' he said amiably. 'Lady Warminster is hiring my band for a party, and you never know. Like ice cream, you may grow softer, my frozen lady.'

'I'm told this is the chef's room, Miss Drury,' he said to her politely as he came in – uninvited – through the open door.

There he was: Inspector Alexander Melbray in all his impudent glory and smart grey suit. Nell fumed. This was usually her time for devoting to studying recipes. After today's inquest – or lack of it, however – she was using it to concentrate on the 'why' of Mr Charles's murder. Either way, she was thinking and planning in *her* operations room.

'Are you here to interview me?' she asked coldly.

'I'd have called you to the morning room if I did. That's where we're conducting the formal interviews.'

'What is this then?'

'I don't know – yet. May I sit?'

'Please do.' It would be better than having him looming over her shoulder. He positioned himself, she noted, in a chair where the light would fall on her face. What was he expecting? A confession?

'In that case, may *I* choose what we talk about first?' she asked belligerently when he showed no signs of breaking the silence.

'By all means.' He sat completely at ease, studying her – or so she thought.

She couldn't stand this much longer. 'Why have you delayed the inquest? What are our guests to do?' she asked, trying to sound less aggressive but failing.

'To answer your second question: that's not for me to say. I hope that if guests stay on it does not make too much additional work for you?'

Trust him to make her seem in the wrong. 'And the first question?' she asked.

'That's harder to answer.'

'But does that mean that every guest who stays on and we who live here are suspects? We all expected the jury to deliver a verdict of murder by person or persons unknown. You don't think that Mr Parkyn-Wright's death was an accident, do you, or that he killed himself?'

'No.'

'Well then, to me that verdict would have seemed the right one, instead of inflicting all this waiting on us. Why the wait?'

'Tests, Miss Drury.'

'On what?'

He did not reply for a minute or two. One hand rested on her table and that diverted his attention from her, to her relief. Then his eyes turned straight back to her. 'Does the name Chang mean anything to you? "Brilliant Chang" to be more accurate.'

'No – yes, I think so,' she stumbled, taken by surprise.

'He was an educated gentleman living at the time of his arrest last year in London's East End, in Limehouse. He was a dealer in cocaine, heroin and opium, which he kept at his house, though it defied all our attempts to find it. For the previous few years he had been the leader in the heavy drug traffic we then had. He had owned a London club until our raids forced him to move east and he had been a frequent visitor to other clubs including Mrs Meyrick's Forty-Three Club.'

He paused, perhaps because of her no doubt mystified expression. 'We did finally find cocaine at his home,' he continued. 'Chang was imprisoned but is shortly to be released, after which he will be deported. So far no one has taken his place as a supplier to the same extent and the drug problem has vastly reduced. Every so often, however, someone tries very hard to emulate him and dealers are beginning to reappear. That has happened recently and we were closing in on one of the most successful dealers in illicit drugs. He died here last week, Miss Drury.'

'Mr Parkyn-Wright?' she whispered aghast. '*Dope?*'

'Yes, Miss Drury. Drugs were Charlie's dance.'

Seven

Illegal drugs at Wychbourne Court? For a moment Nell's mind felt like scrambled egg but then it began to focus. Why had the inspector come to her with this? Did he think she was involved in this dope scandal? Her defences began to stiffen in readiness but she tried to calm down.

First, she needed to know more. 'Did Mr Parkyn-Wright use Saturday's party at Wychbourne just for his business – if that's what one calls dealing in drugs? Is that why he came here?'

'I believe so.'

'He was one of the weekend guests.' That could have meant, Nell thought, merely that he wanted a relaxing day or two in the country or that his business hadn't been intended to end with one party. She was aware that the inspector was still watching her closely. Perhaps he *did* think she had killed Mr Charles or that she was an accomplice. No, she told herself. As he had said, he wouldn't be interviewing her here if so. She relaxed a little.

'He almost certainly had clients at the dance on Saturday night,' the inspector continued. 'Chang's method of attracting new and well-off customers was often to approach them at clubs through a carefully composed letter of admiration – his clients were mainly young ladies and he would have the letter delivered to their table.

That was particularly easy at his own club, of course. Chang built up a high-class clientele – as, we believe, did Parkyn-Wright, another frequenter of the Forty-Three Club.'

Nell was still struggling with the fact that the wonderful Wychbourne dance to which she'd looked forward so much had been partly a front for something far different. 'Charlie's dance, you said. Is that what *he* called it?'

'I can't say. It was how his clients referred to it. Think of it. A dance would be a good way of transacting goods and payments without attention being drawn to it. A romantic withdrawal to a balcony or terrace perhaps or just a clasping of hands while a small bottle of powder was exchanged. You may remember the Freda Kempton case a few years ago. She was a dance hostess who killed herself with an overdose of cocaine. At the inquest Chang was heavily implicated.'

Nell shivered. 'Do you know how many clients Mr Parkyn-Wright had here on Saturday night?'

'As yet, we don't.'

'Guests or—' She broke off. How could she ask: is the Ansley family under suspicion? She quickly changed direction: 'Servants?' she finished the question. 'Is that why you're here? You think we're involved?'

'That's *not* the reason, Miss Drury. Lady Ansley—'

Her shock was too instinctive to hide and the inspector allotted her a rare smile. 'Neither Lady Ansley nor you are currently under suspicion.'

Thank you. Nell gritted her teeth at the 'currently'.

'In fact, I've come to explain the situation at Lady Ansley's request,' he continued. 'I should mention, however, that although Lady Ansley trusts you, you'll understand that I'm under no obligation to do so.'

Nell flushed. 'Of course,' she muttered as graciously as she could.

'She felt I should tell you that apart from Lord and Lady Ansley and now yourself no one has been informed by the police about Parkyn-Wright's drug trafficking.'

'Why did you sanction my knowing?' she asked curiously.

'Because, Miss Drury, I'm wary about placing all my eggs in one basket. In this investigation it seemed to me there was a risk in having one basket full of eggs which could be easily cracked. Wychbourne Court has two baskets, however, one of which is relatively empty.'

Nell saw where this was leading. 'The servants' basket,' she said flatly, 'and you have thrown me into it.'

He managed a smile. 'That is one way of looking at it. The other way is that Lady Ansley is placing a great deal of trust in you. And so, therefore, am I. It is a risk.'

'I'm grateful,' she said, wondering whether gratitude was actually called for. 'Should I be?'

'That is a moot point. Only you can decide that, since the risk is also on your side. The more you are involved, the more the danger to you.' He paused. 'May I give you some advice, Miss Drury?'

'By all means *give* it, Inspector.' Whether she would take it was quite another matter. Serious this conversation might be but it sounded as though they were taking part in an Adelphi melodrama, she thought. Nevertheless, the word 'danger' brought what had hitherto only lain at the back of her mind startlingly to the fore.

'I am sure that many people from both Wychbourne Court baskets are talking to you about this case,' he said quietly. 'Put your trust in no one, Miss Drury – or perhaps more accurately *believe* no one without questioning it. Except perhaps myself. You might see me as a useful yardstick. Anyone can mislead, often unintentionally.'

'Or alternatively I might be able to use my own judgement and you might be talking hogwash,' she retorted angrily.

'I might,' he agreed. 'There is, however, a murderer at large. Perhaps my second piece of advice should be to follow my first.'

'The dinner menus, Lady Ansley.'

Still smarting from the previous night's encounter with the inspector, Nell presented her with her choices for Thursday. This used to be a matter of great tension: would Her Ladyship approve of the stuffed cucumber? What were the guests' likes and dislikes? Lord Richard disliked curry but did that extend to curry butter? Lady Sophy had decided she was no longer of the vegetarian persuasion but still could not be reconciled to kidneys. One could not provide a meal to make everyone happy but it was usually an exciting challenge to steer a path through the maze of avenues open to her. Not today.

121

'I'm told we still have ten guests, Lady Ansley,' she continued. 'Is Miss Harlington among them?'

Lady Ansley sighed. 'Unfortunately, yes. Perhaps Elise may be unwelcome at her own home. Her parents live in Hampshire, I believe – not a great distance for her to travel either there or to her London address, but she claims that she needs to be near to where Charlie died.'

Nell trod carefully. 'Perhaps her parents do not approve of her performing Charlie's dance.'

'Ah, I gather that Inspector Melbray has spoken to you, Nell.'

'He has.' She was fully aware that she had been stupid to flare up at him yesterday evening. It wasn't like her and she wondered why she had been so much on edge. After all, both of them wanted to find Mr Charles's killer if for somewhat different reasons, so why had her self-control snapped so suddenly?

'This is a terrible time, Nell, and I'm glad I can talk to you freely,' Lady Ansley said. 'The murder was terrifying, but even though I suspected something was wrong this revelation about Wychbourne Court being used for drugs makes me think that I don't know my own home. I've asked Rex Beringer to stay on and to my relief he has accepted. He will be better company for Helen than—'

'Miss Harlington?'

'Indeed, though I fear Richard does not agree. Oh, Nell,' she burst out. 'How can I tell him about this? The inspector does not want the news to spread further but Elise is probably one of Charlie's clients. I don't know what to do for the

122

best. I can't kick the girl out – Richard would never forgive me. He'd be terribly quixotic and rush after her with a diamond ring. Nor could I tell him the reason just in case it isn't true.'

How to raise the question of Lady Helen? 'I know from my Carlton days,' Nell began tentatively, 'that there's a difference between someone on a high and just normal high spirits. Like soufflés – up one minute, down the next.'

Lady Ansley looked at her sharply. 'As Helen is now. My worst fear, Nell. Perhaps she didn't have her dance with Charlie last Saturday judging by her behaviour since,' she continued steadily.

'Does Lord Richard realize what's wrong with his sister?'

'I don't think so. He's too besotted with Elise to notice. He has no idea what that woman is really like. She's a bully, not a magnet of beauty.'

'He was so friendly with Mr Parkyn-Wright – it's good that he didn't become a client himself,' Nell said tactfully.

'Yes. I cannot believe that of Richard. He pretends to be so worldly-wise but he hasn't the least idea of what's going on around him. Sophy is far more perspicacious, but I don't think even she suspects what's wrong with Helen. The girl needs medical help, Nell. I've spoken to Gerald and it's all arranged. We cannot both leave Wychbourne at such a time, so Arthur Fontenoy is coming with me tomorrow, instead of Gerald, to take Helen to a doctor Arthur has recommended in London. We shall stay at a discreet hotel and be away a day or two. Thank goodness

Rex is staying on. He says he can take a train to London each day if his work requires it.'

'That sounds a splendid arrangement.'

'Yes, but this murder, Nell, brings an even greater fear,' Lady Ansley said hesitantly. 'The inspector means well but Helen, Richard and Sophy were in that first group on the ghost hunt which means . . .'

'And Inspector Melbray,' Nell said levelly when Lady Ansley halted, 'might assume that drugs lie behind Mr Parkyn-Wright's death and that one of his clients killed him.'

In other words, Lady Helen, she thought, trying to see it from the police point of view. Lord Richard too, if he had decided that Mr Charlie was ruining Elise's life. He could fly off the handle so easily and if he *had* found out about the drugs and believed that Miss Harlington and his sister were innocent martyrs to Mr Charles's fiendish plan, he might have seized that dagger and killed his best friend.

No wonder Lady Ansley was worried. After all, who better to know about that dagger on the wall than those who lived in this house? Then there was Arthur. He must know about the drug issue but he had not yet passed this information to Nell. He hadn't yet had time, she thought uneasily. Nevertheless, trust no one, the inspector had said.

A more comforting thought came to her. There must have been other clients here that night and Inspector Melbray would be aware of that. They could have had good reason to kill Mr Charles and could well have discovered his whereabouts

124

on the gallery and crept up there by that far staircase after the first group had passed on its way. No matter what Mr Peters said, the suspect list must surely be based on that possibility – unless, she forced herself to consider, Mr Peters himself had wielded the dagger. But that came back to the same question: why?

'Where do you think they are going, Richard?' Sophy asked anxiously. Richard didn't look as worried as she felt, but he ought to.

'Ma said they were going to see some old friends in London,' he answered offhandedly. He seemed more interested in the *Country Life* magazine he'd picked up in the hall at breakfast time.

'That's what she told me too.' A sudden thought struck her. 'You don't think Helen could have an urge to go on the stage, do you? Follow in Mother's footsteps? It's just the sort of silly idea she would have to get over Charlie's death. That would explain why Pa isn't going too.'

'No. She'd have to work too hard,' Richard said dispassionately. 'My guess is that she's going to see some doctor – woman stuff.'

'Why not our usual one, then? He's not exactly court physician standard but he's pretty good.'

Richard's turn for an idea. 'Do you think Helen could be in the pudding club?'

Sophy gaped. 'Helen? She wouldn't be so daft. Anyway, Rex wouldn't think it proper.'

'Charlie might have. Helen was keen on him, remember,' Richard said darkly.

Sophy shot him a scornful look. 'He was your

chum, Richard. He'd be nuts to seduce your sister, even if Helen was all for it.'

'He *was* my chum,' Richard said bitterly. 'Until he marched in and took over Elise from me.'

Sophy tossed up whether to comment on this or not. Oh, well, he had to be told some time. 'I don't think that Elise gets *taken* by anybody. She does the taking.'

'You don't know a thing about her,' Richard retorted angrily.

'Nor,' said Sophy, 'do you. She just does her impenetrable I'm-a-superior-flapper-of-mystery act and you all fall for it.'

'*I* know her. I've asked her to stay on here, poor little girl. She's suffering from shock after Charlie's death. She needs looking after.'

Sophy decided to say nothing this time. That 'poor little girl' was a tiger disguised as a pussy cat but Richard never saw it. Sophy had her own ideas about Elise and Charlie but her soppy sister couldn't see two inches in front of her dainty Chanel court shoes. Sophy would have put this visit to London down to a dress-fitting appointment at Jays of Regent Street if it hadn't been for the fact that Arthur Fontenoy was going too.

Meanwhile, Elise was going to be a problem. Poor little girl indeed. So far she hadn't made too much of a nuisance of herself, except for yesterday's picnic fiasco. She had stayed in her room sulking while Father went round the village apologising to all and sundry. Sophy was glad that Mother was going away with Helen as even Elise wouldn't play tricks on Father or on the police. She had too much to hide. It wouldn't surprise her if Elise was on dope.

Sophy paused uneasily. Dope? What about Helen? Could that be why she was so up and down, and could that be why she was being swept off to London? The more she thought about it, the more likely it seemed. Poor Helen, though. Sophy was fond of her sister, and the idea that one of those drug dealers had got at her was terrible. Maybe Elise was on drugs too. And Charlie. Was that why he was murdered? If so, that meant Helen might be under suspicion. Sophy was appalled at where this line of thought was taking her. But Helen wouldn't have killed Charlie? Nor would Richard of course, but maybe *Elise* might have done.

Sophy clung to that idea, caressing it in her mind. If Elise came to her with any more hints and questions as to who 'Hugh Beaumont' was just because he had sat next to Sophy at dinner, she would bat them away like ping pong balls. For her 'Hugh' had only been a joke, but as for him, he had been terrified that night. She had changed the seating arrangements so that he would be further away from Lady Warminster – and look how she'd bungled that. She hadn't checked the guest list properly and only saw Lady Warminster's name at the last minute. That had meant changing the seating plan if Lady Warminster wasn't to be close to 'Hugh' and even then she had glowered suspiciously at him once or twice. 'Hugh' hadn't gone on the ghost hunt because he thought Her Ladyship might tackle him. He'd just pretended to go but actually he'd

127

rushed off home. She, the stupid woman, *had* gone on the hunt, and then driven off afterwards to Stalisbrook to check if her under-gardener was at home.

It had begun as a harmless joke on her delightful but stuffy parents to see if they or anyone else would notice if one of their guests, the so-called Hugh Beaumont, was actually a servant of sorts. Provided he was dressed properly and spoke properly, Sophy was convinced he would have no problem. And he didn't, until he saw Lady Warminster there. Her Ladyship would have thought William was at home in his cottage. Sophy had had lots of chats with him when Her Ladyship ordered him to drive her to Wychbourne for discussions with Mr Fairweather over gardens and their design, but that Saturday night wasn't a garden visit and Madam decided to drive herself in the Delage. Perhaps she liked to keep her visits to Wychbourne secret from everyone at Stalisbrook because she had her eye on Charlie, Sophy thought savagely. Or perhaps she was on dope too?

'Do you know where Helen's gone, Elise?'

Rex Beringer was concerned. Lady Ansley had asked him to stay despite the fact that she and Helen would be away for a few days, but he had the impression that there was some mystery about it. He couldn't press them further as he was a guest here, but quite apart from this murder something was afoot. Helen had kept to her room this past day or two save for her appearance at the inquest yesterday. He'd tried to talk to her at the picnic and at one point he had thought she wanted him to do so but then she changed her mind. He had stayed on here so that he could help her after the shock of the murder, and it was strange that she was going away with the police still in the house investigating Charlie's death. As to that, good riddance, Rex thought.

'Should I know?' Elise replied, reclining in one of the conservatory armchairs.

'She's your friend,' Rex said evenly.

'Ah.' Elise smiled and Rex inwardly shrank. He'd put himself in her power. 'I suspect poor darling Helen has had her wrist slapped,' she drawled. 'And perhaps her lovely face too. Hauled off to London for the cure.'

'What cure?' Rex asked sharply. 'Is she ill?'

'Not more than one usually is when one's missed a bindle.'

'A bindle?' he queried blankly.

'Her little package, Rex. Didn't you know? Helen's been missing her sniffs.'

Rex still didn't understand – except that Elise was gloating. But he had to know what this was about. 'Sniff what?'

'Cocaine, Rex. Surely you knew that Helen was a user?'

'No,' Rex said slowly. 'I didn't.' But he began to understand now. Poor, poor Helen. 'I take it it came from Charlie?'

'Don't blame the messenger, Rex. Darling Charlie was just trying to make an honest living.'

'If I'd known I'd have—' He held back. This woman was just as dangerous as Charlie, who must have told her about his past. She *knew* about him, he realized.

129

'Killed him, Rex?' she finished for him. 'How very adventurous of you. Perhaps you did. You remember we had a little chat as we returned from my picnic yesterday. You were so upset, even though I assured you it was Charlie's and my little secret and we never share them. Why would we?'

'Yes,' he said painfully, 'I remember.'

'We must have another little chat shortly. Such a pity Charlie was killed. Everything was spiffing. And I do like everything to be spiffing, don't you, Rex?'

Why did Arthur have to go to London just at this very moment? Clarice Ansley wasn't pleased now the Wychbourne ghosts were entering an active period. Arthur was a pleasant companion and a shield against her mother, but now Mother would be hurrying round to interrupt her Great Project. Clarice was convinced it was time to move forward on her contribution to the Ansley family history. She would have the finished work bound in leather for the library as well as having copies available for the public. There would be a wide public for it with today's interest in the subject. Mr Harry Price himself had expressed an interest in it, as well as the Society for Psychical Research.

After Jasper had been killed in the Boer War, Clarice had put aside all thoughts of marriage and motherhood. Family history had proved much more exciting in the form of *A Guide to the Ghosts of Wychbourne Court*. She was progressing nicely with the tales, many of which she had found so easily in the library that one might almost think the ghosts themselves were eagerly pushing their stories to the front of the shelves. Every so often her brother opened the Wychbourne grounds to the public. May Day was one such occasion but she had pleaded for Halloween to be another. Gerald had meanly put his foot down, however. The house might be opened during the day but not at night.

'When else do you expect the ghosts to appear?' she had demanded.

'My dear Clarice,' he had replied, 'I don't expect them at all.'

Unlike Clarice, Arthur had thought this most amusing and regrettably so had Mother, although Mother had become more understanding after she discovered Arthur did not believe in ghosts. In vain, Clarice had pointed out to Gerald that the very name Wychbourne was derived from the Old English *wicca*, and that there was something mystical about the place which meant it was a suitable home for ghosts. Her brother had pointed out that Wychbourne could equally well derive from the Anglo-Saxon word for farm or farmer, and as Wychbourne was deemed a farm in the Domesday Book that was good enough for him.

The *Guide* had only reached the sixteenth century so far. That nice Nell Drury had been very helpful in small ways and it occurred to Clarice that, in Arthur's absence, she might be persuaded to read some of the sections, particularly the one she had just worked on. She had revised the tragic story of Sir Thomas and would seek Nell out now. She was sure to be around somewhere and would surely help. After all, Nell had had the distinction of finding Charlie Parkyn-Wright's body, whose ghost Clarice was looking forward to meeting – and so his story could be written from first-hand sources.

Why was Lady Clarice hurrying towards her again? Nell wondered. Luckily she didn't think it odd that for the second time Nell was emerging from the old dairy. She'd hoped to see Arthur there but he had obviously already left for London. Perhaps it was as well to have breathing space to mull over what the *nice* inspector had said to her – and unfortunately what she had replied.

'Miss Drury, I wonder if I might ask a small favour of you?'

'Of course,' Nell said guardedly, but Lady Clarice was not waiting for her assent. A huge pile of typescript was being thrust into her arms.

'Just read through this, if you will. It's my guide to the Wychbourne Ghosts. It's so important to convey the right spirit in both senses, both the ghost of the tale together with the way in which my humble pen has narrated it. I must do them justice.'

Nell summoned up her courage. 'I'm reluctant to take it all,' she replied with all the tact she could summon. 'The risk if any pages are lost would be too great.' To her relief, Lady Clarice looked horrified. 'One ghost at a time?' Nell suggested.

'You are right, Miss Drury. Such a pity I cannot yet add Mr Parkyn-Wright as he and Sir Thomas are kindred spirits.'

'But Mr Parkyn-Wright isn't a ghost,' Nell pointed out.

'He soon will be,' Lady Clarice informed her. 'I would not wish to offend any of them so I would be grateful for your critique.'

'Let me do justice to Sir Thomas first,' Nell said firmly, to Lady Clarice's disappointment.

Sir Thomas was a devoted but absentee husband, Nell remembered as she returned to her room ready to do battle with the gentleman after supper in the servants' hall. In Crusading days he had been a gallant and highly regarded military man. Even if the place of the two deaths was the same, Mr Charles had been a far from gallant man; he was a dope dealer. How did the spirits of the two men become kindred? she wondered.

The page was headed 'Sir Thomas Ansley, Earthly life: 1157–1192. Current life: 1192—'

Ah, what a story lies here. He rode forth to war on the Third Crusade with His Majesty King Richard I to fight for his King, his Pope and the Holy Land. His lovely wife, Eleanora, full of tears, remained at their home at Wychbourne. There Eleanora sobbed alone, sorely missing him. For comfort she listened to a minstrel's songs of love written for the simple village maiden he loved. Even as he sang songs of valour in Sir Thomas's honour he was thinking of her and not of Mistress Eleanora. But the call of passion is strong. Who can tell when sin entered their hearts, but as time passed Mistress Eleanora beckoned and he stepped into her chamber.

Sir Thomas, ah, what anguish filled your heart when you returned home victorious to find a mere

133

minstrel had usurped your bed and your wife had falsely given herself to him. What fear entered the minstrel's heart when you strode valiantly into the chamber and he ran for safety, snatching a dagger in his hand but hoping to hide on the gallery where their passion had first been lit by his songs. When you reached him there, he plunged the dagger into your noble heart. The minstrel fled, his songs to be heard no more, and you, Sir Thomas, rail still at your cruel fate as you wait for justice to be done.

Crackling cauliflowers, Nell thought. Sir Walter Scott lives again. Young Lochinvar wasn't a patch on this hero.

Something odd had caught her attention, though. There was something familiar about the story, although certainly Sir Thomas wasn't going to be making any complaints about it. It reminded her of an elderly general in Mesopotamia and Lady Warminster leaving the ghost hunt so promptly. Her Ladyship, she thought, displayed an eagerness for conformity rather than a desire to shock and was unlikely to be taking drugs. She looked all too happy with her current way of life but could there be a minstrel in it? Even if there was, why would that cause her to dash away from the dance so quickly? There were no obvious minstrels around in Wychbourne Court (except for Guy's band), and she couldn't see Lady Warminster developing a fancy for Mr Peters. She did have her own staff, of course. A chauffeur and that under-gardener who drove her around, but she hadn't wanted either of them to

134

drive her that Saturday evening. So there *might* be someone . . .

Nell, she told herself, you're over-sugaring the pudding again.

It was true the world was full of married women laying themselves open to blackmail, just as younger women did the same through taking illegal drugs. A dispute over their supply must be what Inspector Melbray thought was behind Mr Charles's death, but there was another angle, wasn't there? The dope could be a weapon for blackmail. And if Mr Charles was a blackmailer over dope, couldn't he have gone further than that? The whisper in the ear, the threat in casual conversation, all to feed his love of power over people? And where better to gather it than at parties such as the one at Wychbourne Court?

Eight

Mr Charles as blackmailer? Nell tossed this theory around in her mind overnight like a salad, wondering whether the dressing would take to it. Increasingly, it might, as it could have been linked to his dope-dealing activities. Once a client, always a client. Would he have extended his blackmailing beyond his clients, however? Why not, she reasoned, if interesting stories came his way? At the clubs he frequented he could have listened to non-stop gossip and pounced on it if he thought it worthwhile. Perhaps Miss Harlington had provided him with information in exchange for the dope she obtained from him. She would be able to share women's confidences as well as sniff out men's weaknesses, and could have passed the results either innocently or not so innocently to Mr Charles.

That led her to another avenue: Inspector Melbray's two 'baskets' – the main house and the servants' hall. It was highly possible that Mr Charles could have dipped a blackmailing toe into both wherever he was invited, including Wychbourne. Perhaps his attentions to its chambermaids had not been his only excursions into the servants' hall. Servants' gossip could be just as rewarding as that from his own circles.

With Arthur away, Nell had no means of discovering whether her blackmailing theory held water as regards the Ansley family or the guests, but what she could do was tread gently along the path of discovering if there had been other links between Mr Charles and the Wychbourne servants' hall. Miss Checkam and Mr Peters, much as she liked them, had been far from forthcoming.

Nell enjoyed lunching in the servants' hall. It was a comfortable, relaxed room that bore little resemblance to the bleak one in her previous job. At Wychbourne it was officially Mrs Squires's domain but Mrs Fielding took an overclose interest in it. The carpets were old but good, the furniture all made on the estate in years gone by. To Nell it was as much a privilege to enter it as the great hall. Servants, like Ansleys, might come and go, but this room went on for ever.

Today there were about twenty people there when Nell arrived, including Kitty and Michel. There was no sign of Mr Peters or Miss Checkam, but Mrs Fielding, unfortunately, was very much present. No Mr Briggs, but he seldom attended the servants' hall meals because he could not bear too many people around him. Mrs Squires's mutton stew was already occupying most of the diners so Nell held her peace until appetite had been largely satisfied.

'I don't know about all of you but I've had enough of the police breathing down my neck this week,' she observed conversationally when she judged the moment right. 'They keep wanting to know what we thought of Mr Charles.'

Everyone's attention was on her but no one spoke. 'Someone,' she continued, 'must have wanted him out of the way. Obvious, isn't it?

137

And yet the coppers had to postpone the inquest. I ask you, a dagger in the guts and they don't know what killed him.'

Silence, but they were listening.

'What beats me is *why* anyone would want to kill him,' Nell continued. 'We all know he was a rotter but killing him is a different matter. Anyone any ideas?'

No one had, it seemed.

'Anyone see him after the dinner?' she asked in desperation.

Silence, but then: 'He was chuckling when I saw him, Miss Drury.'

Good for Jimmy, Nell thought, relieved. He at least could have nothing to hide – except her arrangement with Arthur. 'When was that?'

'When I was in the hall getting the lamps ready and Mr Peters was in and out helping Lord Richard with the stuff to catch the ghosts. I was doing the lamps by the door to the corridor and there he was by the foot of the gallery stairs. He was laughing and he'd been talking to some woman because I heard a lot of crying and stuff. I had to get on with the lamps and the next time I looked he'd gone.'

That must have been about eleven forty, Nell calculated. 'You could be an important witness, Jimmy. Have you told the police this?'

He looked terrified. 'No, Miss Drury. I didn't kill him.'

'Of course not, but you might provide them with a vital clue. Any of you might,' she added hopefully.

'I saw him in the supper room,' Robert

138

volunteered. 'I was taking coffee over and there he was talking to Miss Harlington. She had a face like she'd lost the Derby, so he went over to the bandleader. Don't know what they were talking about but the band chap didn't like it. Not happy at all. That was about ten because the music started then, but all this was a couple of hours before Charlie boy was done in.'

Guy? Nell thought uneasily. What was that about? 'Anyone else see Mr Charles?'

'I did,' Mrs Fielding's still-room maid Mary piped up. 'I went to the drawing room with the coffeepot just before nine. There was Mr Charles looking very jolly and talking to Mr Peters. Mr Peters wasn't laughing, though.'

'It's not his place to laugh,' Mrs Fielding interjected immediately. 'And how would you know who Mr Charles was anyway?'

The maid looked frightened. 'Polly pointed him out to me, Mrs Fielding.'

The housekeeper turned her ire on Polly. 'And how do you know him, miss?'

Quick intervention needed. 'I expect you see him coming out of his room sometimes, don't you, Polly?' Nell suggested.

'Yes, miss,' Polly said gratefully.

Time enough to sort that one out later and, judging by Mrs Fielding's expression, it would be laid at Nell's door – a battle she would take up with pleasure in due course. It was Mrs Fielding's responsibility to look after the safety of her staff. So Mr Charles had been busy between about nine o'clock and ten. Was that significant or was it just idle chat? Whichever it was, about two or three hours later he was dead.

'Did you see anyone other than Mr Charles going up to the gallery while you were busy with the lamps, Jimmy?' Nell asked.

'No, Miss Drury. Just did the lamps and then I went off.'

'You were there too, Miss Drury,' Mrs Fielding pointed out sweetly.

'From a quarter to twelve because Lady Clarice had asked me to lead the group. Do you think I *wanted* to walk around in the dark when I might meet a ghost wielding an axe?' Nell joked.

'Are there really ghosts at Wychbourne?' Kitty asked nervously.

'Depends whether you see one or not,' Nell said gravely.

That raised a laugh. 'Perhaps one of them killed that gentleman,' Michel said.

'Death by ghost?' Nell managed a laugh. 'I don't think so.'

'No, the rozzers will try and put the blame on us one way or another. That's why they came round here – the inspector and his sergeant,' Robert said heavily and discussions promptly broke out among them.

She was aware she was losing her audience. 'Great babbling barbels,' she cried, 'do you think the coppers are daft enough to believe that one of us here would go prancing into the main house in the dark to bump off a guest? Stand out a bit, wouldn't we? None of us would be dressed up like the Duke of Wellington or Cleopatra, or wearing diamonds and Patou dresses.'

140

The atmosphere grew more friendly. 'The inspector asked a lot about that band,' Mrs Squires said. 'Seven of them there were, all gobbling food like turkeys. It could have been one of them.'

The band . . . Nell groaned to herself. Charlie Chaplin would make a better detective than she was turning out to be. She'd forgotten that not only Guy but his entire band weren't playing during the ghost hunt. But why would any of them want to kill Mr Charles? Were they his dope clients? That was possible in theory. Nell couldn't believe that Guy would be so stupid but one of his bandsmen might be. Was that why Inspector Melbray came to the servants' hall as well as his sergeant? Because he was interested in the band? But surely not Guy, though, even if he had been talking to Mr Charles before the dancing began?

Getting all her fellow upper servants involved in a discussion posed another problem. Nell felt torn between knowing she had to pursue her fear that two of them might be holding information back and feeling like a traitor for even considering that they might have something to do with Mr Charles's death. When she joined them in the butler's room for lunch the next day it seemed to her guilty conscience that they were looking at her with deep suspicion, and so perhaps the inspector's visit to her after the inquest had not gone unnoticed.

At least they were all present, not only Mr Peters, Miss Checkam and Mrs Fielding, but Mr Briggs too. A doubtful asset, she thought, as he looked most unhappy.

141

She braced herself. 'I'm glad we're all here together today,' she said. 'After Wednesday's fiasco at the inquest we're being left simmering like a stew wondering what's happening.'

'I can't see how we can simmer over anything,' Mrs Fielding sniffed. 'It's nothing to do with us.'

'Anything to do with Wychbourne Court is to do with us,' Nell replied. 'We live and work here.' She was treading on quicksand, hampered by the fact that the drugs issue was not yet public. 'This murder must have been because of the kind of person Charlie was, and though it doesn't seem right to think ill of him—'

'Bad man,' Mr Briggs amazingly interrupted, carefully rearranging his knife and fork on his plate.

'That's what some people believe and with reason,' Nell said.

'I hope you're not going to cast aspersions on him merely on the word of a chambermaid,' Mrs Fielding said threateningly.

'He was most pleasant to me,' Miss Checkam said supportively.

Mr Peters added his endorsement too. 'A most sociable gentleman.'

'Then you don't think he could have been blackmailing anyone in the family or any of the guests?' Nell threw at them casually.

An appalled silence. Mrs Fielding recovered first. 'What a thing to say.'

'And I said it,' Nell shot back. 'Somebody killed him. The kind of life he led in London might open a path to his profitably blackmailing others.'

'It's possible,' Mr Peters said suddenly after yet another silence. 'Those giddy young things who came down from London with him. Not family, though.'

'Of course not,' Miss Checkam supported him. 'Blackmail, indeed.'

'We can't be sure but we do hear a lot of what the family and guests talk about as though we weren't present,' Nell persevered.

'That's confidential,' Miss Checkam snapped.

'Of course, but if as a result of our keeping *everything* confidential the murderer isn't found, that would not be right.'

They seemed to be thinking this over. '*We* couldn't have done it anyway,' Mr Peters concluded.

'Certainly not,' Mrs Fielding snorted. 'I was in the still-room all the evening until I heard all the commotion and screaming, Miss Drury. You know that, don't you, Mr Peters?'

'I do, Mrs Fielding.'

That was an odd exchange, Nell thought.

'I do recall,' Mrs Fielding added, 'that I did pop out for a moment to see everyone set off for the ghost hunt and there you were at your post, Mr Peters.'

'Where I remained,' he beamed, 'until I heard Mr Arthur shouting, Miss Drury.'

'And I,' Miss Checkam said quickly, 'went to the dance in the servants' room and then went up to my room until I realized something was going on.'

Her turn. 'I went to the great hall,' Nell contributed, 'at about a quarter to twelve to be ready

143

for my job of leading the group. Before that I'd been at the dance in the servants' hall and then went to the supper room for a quick check before leaving for the ghost hunt. When I reached the hall the lamps were already low and people were beginning to gather to collect their equipment.'

'Did you see Mr Charles there?' Miss Checkam asked abruptly.

'No. He must already have gone up to the gallery to hide.'

'You'd have heard him if he was still in the hall. Mr Charles wasn't the quietest of gentlemen in a crowd,' Mr Peters said drily. 'He liked to be noticed. So there we are, Miss Drury. We all had our duties to perform.'

'And you do yours so splendidly,' Mrs Fielding purred. 'Miss Drury, I do agree that it's nice for us all to be together.'

To Nell all three of them looked as guilty as Kitty or Michel trying to cover up a peccadillo in the kitchen. Only Mr Briggs still looked his normal, somewhat puzzled self. What peccadillos Mrs Fielding might have to hide remained a mystery, however. A nocturnal embrace?

'No!' Mr Briggs suddenly roared. 'G/26420 Corporal Briggs, *sir.*' He was on his feet now and accustomed as they were to this outburst from him at times of stress, it was startling because of his long silence.

'Didn't you see any nightingales that night?' Nell asked gently.

'*No!*' he shouted again.

Tears filled his eyes; he rose to his feet and hurried from the room.

'Well,' Mr Peters said after a moment, 'what upset him? The sooner we get this business of the murder cleared up the better, if you ask me.'

'I do agree, Mr Peters,' Mrs Fielding gushed. 'I'm quite sure the murderer is that bandleader.'

'Why on earth do you think that?' Nell asked crossly.

'Too big for his boots,' Mrs Fielding sniffed. 'Far too superior to eat servants' food. Asked whether there were any leftovers from the house dinner.'

'That doesn't make him a murderer,' Nell said stoutly.

'You would know, of course, as he's an old and close friend of yours.'

Nell froze. 'I've met him before, certainly.'

'Well then,' Mrs Fielding said in triumph.

'Anyone in the band could have done it,' Nell contended.

'Were they *all* old friends?' Mrs Fielding enquired.

Miss Checkam sat primly upright, and even Mr Peters blushed at the innuendo.

'All of them, intimately,' Nell assured her solemnly. '*And* all the king's soldiers *and* all the queen's guards. Every single one of them, every night.'

Mrs Fielding she could cope with, but Nell remained shaken by Mr Briggs's outburst. What had upset him? Did he think that one of them was not telling the truth as he saw it? Whether that truth would have led to murder, however, was as foggy as a London Particular. And then there was Guy and Mrs Fielding's wild allegation. *Trust no one, believe no one.* Easy advice for the inspector to give but so hard to accept. The next step loomed before her. The police had now left their morning-room base at Wychbourne Court and presumably would not be returning until the inquest. Which meant if she wanted to see the mighty inspector she'd have to beard the lion in his den.

Nell felt like a stranger when she stepped off the train at Charing Cross on Monday morning, even though she had been born within the sound of Bow Bells in east London and she had worked only a short walk away from here at the Carlton Hotel on the corner of Haymarket and Pall Mall. She no longer felt a part of London, though, and in some ways she missed it. Covent Garden, a brief walk away in the opposite direction, had been familiar territory. Those early mornings when London was quiet and still. Early workers made little noise and nor did the occasional van or bus, mostly horse-drawn when she was very young. She could still conjure up the smells and colours of the vegetables and flowers in the market, although the walled vegetable garden at Wychbourne was a beguiling substitute. Mr Fairweather mixed flowers with produce, so sunflowers bloomed there side by side with cabbages, nasturtiums and sweet peas climbed the walls, and spring daffodils heralded the first of the spring vegetables.

What lay ahead of her today? It hadn't been an easy decision to come to London. Inspector Melbray might refuse to see her or he might throw her out when he heard what she had to

146

say, if he listened at all. Only the thought that she might help lift a little of the cloud over Wychbourne Court drove her on. That was surely a battle worth fighting.

Who was she to fancy she had anything to offer Scotland Yard, though? Well, she comforted herself, even Scotland Yard had made a few mistakes in its history. Look at Jack the Ripper, who had got clean away, and the terrible mistakes in the Constance Kent case.

Suffering stockfish, Nell, give it your best shot, she ordered herself as she made her way along the Embankment towards Westminster Pier. You can walk in with your head held high even if he does throw you out like a bag of old bones. When she reached the main entrance to New Scotland Yard, however, she almost turned back at the formidable number of people milling around the entrance, many in uniform. She had to remind herself that she had come here on a mission and that she had to see it through.

Her first struggle was to be taken seriously. Not only two uniformed policemen tried to deflect her from seeing the great Inspector Melbray but a woman officer too. 'He's an inspector *first class*,' the latter pointed out in awe. Should she try chaining herself to the railings like the suffragettes, Nell wondered, in order to get taken seriously? She'd have one more shot at it.

'Tell him,' she told the next duty sergeant who came to tower over her, 'that it's Nell Drury, come about the Wychbourne Court murder.' That must have had some effect because a minion was promptly despatched.

147

She waited until eventually she was told that the inspector was with the assistant commissioner but could she wait, please. She wasn't too sure who the assistant commissioner might be but he sounded important, which meant she was going to be waiting a long time. Still, at least she had been asked to wait – like all these other people sitting here so patiently. She passed the time by fantasising as to what their missions were as they awaited their turn for the photographic department, the Flying Squad, Special Branch, the Fingerprint Bureau or any other of the mesmerizing array of departments to which they could be despatched, perhaps never to be seen again.

And then suddenly there he was. That *nice* Inspector Melbray.

'My apologies, Miss Drury.' No smile, just those eyes on her again, obviously appraising why she might be here and whether it was worth his while to see her.

'Do please come with me,' he said flatly, taking her up by the lift to the third floor where a small room holding just a table and chairs awaited them. Not his office, she thought. No such honour for her. This was probably where they interviewed violent criminals and traitors.

She sat down; he sat down opposite her and waited for her to speak but she didn't.

'The murder, Miss Drury,' he said at last. 'Have you come to confess?'

He might have meant this lightly but it riled her.

'No, I've come to help.' Holy herringbones, what made her say something so childish?

'Thank you,' he said gravely, although she detected what might have been a quiver at the edge of his mouth.

'I know you have your own lines of enquiry,' she said crossly, 'and won't be able to talk to me freely. So perhaps I should talk to you.'

'Thank you,' he murmured again. No quiver this time.

'The dope you told me about. Charlie's dance. Could the dance be more than that?'

He frowned. 'In what way?'

'Mr Parkyn-Wright seems to have been the sort of man who liked power. Power over people. I don't mean political power and all that.'

'Go on.' Deadpan voice.

'I mean he could have been gathering information and using it to threaten people. It might have been only his dope clients but it could have been others too. Perhaps Charlie's dance was so named because he was leading them a dance, threatening them.'

'Blackmail?' Then he added, 'Why have you really come here, Miss Drury?'

Nell was taken aback. 'I told you. To help. I want Wychbourne Court to return to normal.'

This sounded feeble and there was no comment on it from the *nice* inspector. 'Do you have anyone in mind who could have been subjected to blackmail?'

'No – yes, I mean yes, but I've no evidence. Just possibilities.'

'About whom?'

'Those who could have killed him but who aren't likely to be on drugs.'

149

'Would one of those be Guy Ellimore?' His voice was very cold.

Nell gasped at the suddenness of the attack. 'He could have been one of them but—'

'And he is a friend of yours.'

It wasn't a question, just a statement. She flushed. 'He was a friend; he isn't now.'

'And yet you are here, Miss Drury. On his behalf?'

Anger rose and she tried to contain it. 'You're hardly likely to stop suspecting him just because I came.'

'It's as likely as your being concerned for the good of Wychbourne Court.'

That did it. She took a deep breath. 'That *is* why I came, for the Ansleys and Wychbourne. I work there, I'm part of it and I love it. I thought you might not have considered the blackmail angle. I came because I know some of the people involved, one of whom was Mr Ellimore. Not him in particular, though. There are others who might have secrets in their lives. Lots of people do have but it doesn't drive them to murder.'

Inspector Melbray rose abruptly to his feet and walked over to the window, beckoning to her. 'Would you come here, Miss Drury?'

Unwillingly, she obeyed. What now?

'Look down there,' he said.

Below she could see the River Thames, people flocking together on Westminster Pier with many others hurrying or strolling along the Embankment, oblivious to what was going on up here.

'Londoners, those who live and those who work here,' he continued. 'It's a sunny day. They'll be

150

eating sandwiches on the grass, or crowding into Lyons teashops, or meeting friends in restaurants. It's lunchtime but I'm not free to do what I choose. If I were, I'd offer the great chef a sandwich for having made you wait so long. But I can't. That's outside my job, just as investigating this case is outside yours.'

'I understand,' she said stiffly.

'Tell me, Miss Drury, what do you put into your vegetable soup?'

She stared at him. What on earth was he talking about now? She was tempted to reply 'arsenic', but she held back. 'Whatever's going. Anything.'

'How do you define "anything"?'

She steeled herself. Presumably this had some subtle point that she had missed. 'Anything I judge that might blend well.'

'That's how a case progresses for me. Cases such as this one.'

She froze. 'And does Guy Ellimore "blend"?'

'Among others. Yes.'

She was trembling but she couldn't tell whether it was through anger, fear or tension. Did she really think Guy could be implicated? She had been stupid to come. Nevertheless, she had to admit that Guy had joined her group on the ghost hunt and she'd assumed that he had only just come from the supper room. If he hadn't he could in theory have killed Mr Charles before that. *Believe no one.* Even Guy. Or even Arthur.

What had she expected to happen this morning? She had had some hazy idea that the inspector would listen to what she had to say and reply,

151

'Thank you, Miss Drury. That was very helpful. I'll look into that.' But no.

She crossed over to the riverside to recover her wits before she set off back to Wychbourne and, looking back at Scotland Yard, she saw him emerge, complete with bowler, and briskly set off perhaps to one of the teashops he talked about or maybe the Savoy. Either way, no sandwich for Nell.

It was mid-afternoon before she arrived back at Tonbridge railway station, by which time she was longing for the comfort of her chef's room. But who did she see appearing out of the blue? Guy.

'I thought you'd like me to drive you home,' he said.

'How did you know which train I'd be on?'

'I didn't. I've been waiting ages.'

She was forced to laugh. 'You're an idiot, Guy. Anyway, my motor car's parked here.'

'Splendid. I'll follow you in stately fashion to Wychbourne and we can have a drink at the Coach and Horses. It's not opening time yet but we can plead for a cup of tea.'

As she parked her Austin Seven at the pub Guy drove right in behind her, but by that time at least she had worked out what to say. 'I have to be back for dinner preparations,' she said as they sat at one of the tables outside. 'I can't stay long.'

''Twas ever thus.'

There was an awkward pause but he slid over it. 'How's it going at Wychbourne?' he continued casually. 'No sign of an arrest yet?'

'No. We'll have to wait until the inquest.'

'Could be adjourned again. I shall be spending the rest of my life in this place, I can see that. Still, I expect they've had time to do the drugs test now.'

'You know?' she asked incredulously.

He laughed. 'I thought it wouldn't be news to you. I made a few enquiries in London about Charlie Parkyn-Wright. Rumour has it he was a dealer.'

'I don't officially know that and nor is it generally known here.' Advance with caution, Nell thought. 'Have you been called as a witness?'

'Not so far. What could I say apart from confirming your story?'

'Why did the police ask you to stay then?'

He shrugged. 'I suppose because I could prove that you opened the cupboard and seemed surprised when a corpse fell out.'

'Why did you come up to the gallery at all?'

'Are you rehearsing me for the inquest or my next grilling by the police?' he asked quietly.

She stood her ground. 'Either or neither.'

'Very well, Madam Inquisitor. Before I followed your group up to the gallery, I had been in the ballroom playing – all the world and his wife will testify to that – and then at about twelve o'clock I went to the supper room.'

'Witnesses for that too?'

He shot a curious look at her. 'Actually, yes. I had a long chat with somebody and when he left I thought of catching you up on the hunt.'

'Who was it?' Drat, she'd gone too far.

'You're really making me wonder, Nell. Do you think I stuck that dagger in Charlie? Why would I?

I've seen him at London clubs time after time. Do I look as though I'm on drugs? I wouldn't be able to hold the band together if I was.'

'I'm sorry, Guy,' she said penitently. 'No, I don't see you as a murderer, but it's because I don't that I have to ask. Does that make sense?'

'Nothing you did ever made sense to me, Nell. Including turning me down.'

'I'm not a rover, Guy.'

'And I am. As you say, things haven't changed. But only because we didn't make them change.'

'It's too late, Guy,' she said gently.

'I lied to you, Nell.'

Instant fear. 'Over the ghost hunt?'

'There you go again. No, this afternoon. I didn't wait for you. I was on the same train and spotted you behind me on the platform. Does that make you feel better?'

It did. He was Guy again. The one who had twisted her heart and hung it out to dry. The Guy she once long ago had mistakenly thought she had loved. Not now. Who to believe? Guy? Or follow the inspector's advice? *Trust no one.*

Nine

The dairy this morning was a refuge and Arthur would add a measure of common sense to her own chaotic thoughts. Nell was relieved that he had returned to Wychbourne Court yesterday evening. She had arrived first at their rendezvous, but shortly afterwards his familiar stocky plus-foured figure appeared.

'My dear Nell, our Baker Street Irregular conveyed your message to meet at our usual trysting place just as I was about to entrust him with a similar task,' he greeted her. 'Well met by moonlight, in the ill-quoted words of Mr Shakespeare, albeit it is daylight and in a derelict dairy unlike the Athenian woodland of his *Dream*.'

The usual flower was in his buttonhole and he duly presented a rose to her, for which she gravely curtsied her thanks. His line of nonsense was a great cheerer.

'Myself alone, I fear,' Arthur continued. 'Helen and Gertrude are staying with old friends for a few more days. I'm sure you can interpret that correctly.'

Nell could. A nursing home for Lady Helen, perhaps? 'Will their old friends permit them to return for the inquest next Tuesday?'

'Gertrude, at least. The police have been making the same enquiry, somewhat to my alarm.'

'They're only wanted as witnesses, I hope?' she asked uneasily.

'Fortunately I believe that to be the case. However, we have no idea what lines the police are following and we must defy augury. *The readiness is all. Hamlet*, I believe. Not a fortunate choice of play for me to quote, considering that most of the main characters end up dead.'

Nell shivered and he must have noticed, for he quickly added, 'I jest, Nell. I do indeed. Have the police descended on Wychbourne Court in my absence?'

She hesitated, wondering whether to tell him about her visit to Scotland Yard. No, she still felt raw about that. After all, Sherlock Holmes hid plenty of information from Watson.

'No, but they'll be here for the inquest.'

'It appears that as yet they have not troubled Gerald. They are keeping us in the dark like mushrooms but we shall spring up and make the most delicious soup. Tell me what you have been up to in my absence, Nell.'

She laughed, glad of his company. 'I have a whole new theory.'

'Do tell. I'm agog.'

He listened attentively as she relayed her theory that Charlie's dance went further than distributing drugs. 'He was blackmailing people, either about the drugs or other secrets.'

Arthur looked taken aback. 'You have excelled yourself, Nell,' he murmured. 'It could explain so much. It fits the facts like a Lus and Befue suit. We must ask ourselves who such victims might be and into whose sphere of interest they

156

fall. In mine, poor Helen is a former client who surely can be excused. No blood sullied Helen of Troy's beauty, and she was too upset to have planned such details as daggers or the blood-stained cloth the inspector told me had been found. He still asked to see my garb for the evening, however, and no doubt inspected that of the other participants. Which brings me to hidden secrets. How does your garden grow in that respect, my pretty maid?'

Nell laughed. 'As we arranged, I tackled the servants' hall.'

'Ah, the fount of all knowledge. Ignore it at one's peril. More can be gleaned among the pots and pans than from the elegant Meissen marmites and centrepieces of the diners for whom they labour.'

'The pots and pans department was persuaded to chatter,' and Nell told him the results. 'And then there are the upper servants – Mrs Fielding, Miss Checkam, Mr Peters, Mr Briggs – and me.'

'Do not look so doubtful, Nell. I exclude you from suspicion. Mr Briggs too.'

'No,' Nell said slowly, remembering his outburst. 'He has something on his mind about the murder.'

Arthur looked grave. 'Can you pursue that with him?'

'I'll try. Perhaps he is just picking up the general tension – he doesn't like that and Mr Peters and Miss Checkam seem to me to be more tense than just concern on the family's behalf would cause.'

'I'm not a medical man despite my mask of Doctor Watson,' he commented, 'but I don't see

157

Peters and Miss Checkam indulging in cocaine. However, do be aware that we might open a can of dangerous worms instead of tasty anchovies if we delve too deep into the secrets of others. A murderer has nothing to lose by killing twice. We should tread carefully, Nell.'

Trust no one, she remembered. No one.

'Let me give you an example,' he continued. 'Miss Checkam, who thought Charlie such a pleasant gentleman and was, she claimed, on friendly terms with him. It seems, alas, that those friendly terms were only on one side. Hers. As for Charlie, I'm told it was the subject of a bet that he could not or would not seduce the unfortunate woman.'

Nell reeled in horror. 'How far did that go?'

'The whole way, Nell. To be blunt, he bedded her. She apparently believed that this romance would be kept secret to avoid his parents' disapproval but would end in marriage.'

'They hardly ever met,' she cried in astonishment. If true, this was a terrible story.

'They met here and also in London when she accompanied Lady Helen or Lady Ansley there. I believe, however, that according to the agreed terms, one bedding was enough to win the bet.'

'Who was the bet with?' Nell was beginning to feel sick on poor Miss Checkam's behalf.

'I was not told. It might have been with the Honourable Elise Harlington.'

'Did Miss Checkam discover the truth?'

'I believe so, but only shortly before Charlie's death and probably therefore at Wychbourne Court. You see what this means, Nell?'

'That Miss Checkam could have had reason to kill him.' Nell's stomach was lurching with the shock. Well, she had set out to seek reasons why Mr Charles might have been murdered and she couldn't escape the consequences.

'I'm sorry, Nell. This is the tarnished side of the Bright Young Things. My source for this was Helen and it might therefore not be accurate, but I do believe it is. And there is something else.'

Nell made an effort. 'You've discovered that Mr Peters was Jack the Ripper?'

He laughed. 'Little to fear on that score. Lady Ansley asked me to give you a message and it is not about Peters. She believes there might be some mystery hovering over Rex Beringer, Helen's forlorn admirer.'

'And still a guest here,' Nell said. 'Lady Ansley asked him to remain as she feels he is a calming influence on Lady Helen. Is that still the case?'

'Why not? I have no idea – yet – what this mystery might be. Who else still remains a guest here?'

'Miss Harlington of course, and Guy Ellimore, although he's at the inn. But I really can't see any reason for his wanting to kill Charles Parkyn-Wright.'

'Then he has little need to worry. Many people have secrets that they prefer to keep from examination from themselves, let alone others, but murder is not normally the path to salvation on such matters. The danger lies in deciding which, if any, is the exception.'

Usually Nell would have thought little of a summons to Lord Ansley's office while Lady

Ansley was away. In the current circumstances, however, it did not bode well. 'I've been honoured – if that's the correct word,' he explained, 'with a request from Lady Warminster. She is holding a party on Saturday the eighteenth of July and has asked for your assistance with a buffet. I'm sure it's the last thing you want to do, and frankly she's a most annoying woman, but I feel an obligation to General Warminster. That's only two weeks from this coming Saturday. Could you cope with that? I expect she will want you to visit her to discuss her requirements.'

'My guess is that her requirements would simply be that she should not be bothered,' Nell replied forthrightly.

He laughed. 'His first wife was so different to his second. So you'll do it, Nell?'

Of course she would do it. For one thing, she could find out more about Lady Warminster, who had so abruptly left the party that Saturday night.

Two days later she was driving into the forecourt of Stalisbrook Place. It was a stone-built residence looking bleakly ornate compared with Wychbourne Court. *I'm here for you to witness how grand I am*, it seemed to be saying to her. The large reception room where she was asked to wait did nothing to contradict this assessment. Gentlemen in military uniform glared down from every wall and their long-suffering wives smiled weakly at their painters. Nell wondered whether they ever got together with the Wychbourne Court ghosts.

It took some time for Lady Warminster to arrive, sweeping in with diamonds already

160

glittering around her throat. *Never* wear diamonds before the evening, Nell remembered the dowager decreeing. With her short blonde hair, blue eyes and laden with jewels, Lady Warminster must fancy she looked like an innocent from Hollywood – though how innocent was that? In fact, Nell could see the beautifully rouged mouth was already drooping and looked more like Lady Macbeth's than a Cupid's bow.

'So good of you to agree to cook for our little party, Miss Drury,' Lady Warminster purred without enthusiasm. 'A mere sixty or so.'

'Will your husband be among them?'

'But of course.' Lady Warminster looked hurt at the mere suggestion he should be omitted. 'It is a welcome home party for him, the darling.'

It occurred to Nell that if she had been an ageing husband coming home from Mesopotamia or Persia after many months or years away, a cosy dinner *à deux* might be preferable to a party for sixty.

'My butler will escort you to the kitchens shortly. As for the menu—' Lady Warminster continued but then broke off. 'Haven't we met before?'

'After the inquest and at Wychbourne Court, just before the ghost hunt,' Nell explained patiently. 'I was leading the second group.'

'A cook leading it? How quaint.'

'Cooks,' Nell explained with a straight face, 'are said to be very good at divining the presence of ghosts because ghosts sense the food they're missing in the other world.'

'Oh.' Lady Warminster looked blank. 'I didn't

161

know that. How super. I didn't see any ghosts, though. We marched round and I heard a groan and so on, but nothing creepy. I was so bored but I couldn't leave because it was dark and I didn't know where we were until we were back in the hall. My new shoes were hurting too. By the time I returned to the ballroom the dancing had stopped, so I left.'

'That would be when Mr Parkyn-Wright's body was discovered?

'Probably. I heard some screaming and everyone rushed back to the hall. So I went home.'

'It must have been horrible for you,' Nell sympathized, tongue in cheek. 'Even worse if the police interviewed you because you were in the first group.'

'Oh, yes, that duckie Inspector Melbray. He can't keep away from me. My husband wouldn't like his behaviour at all but the inspector does seem bemused by me.' One hand clutched the diamonds to underline their presence.

Bemused by her? Was he indeed? Nell thought savagely. So the great inspector was a 'duckie' kind of man attracted by babylike far-from-innocents like Her Ladyship.

The menu took little time to discuss as Lady Warminster merely glanced at the ones that Nell had brought with her, pointed to the most expensive and rang the bell for the butler. He seemed as bored with life in Stalisbrook Place as Her Ladyship was, but probably he was merely giving his own interpretation of a superior being worthy of this great mansion.

The servants' hall to which he ushered her was

162

in the midst of serving lunch. Faces stared back at her blankly. It didn't – admittedly at first glance – seem a happy gathering. She did recognize one face, however. From his general build he could have been Lady Warminster's driver on the day of the inquest but it couldn't have been there that Nell had seen him at quite close quarters. Strange. He looked like someone one might see at the pictures – a Hollywood Douglas Fairbanks.

She tried to imagine this man sitting stolidly at the table doing anything as dashing as that tasty dish. No fear of that. On the contrary, the only dish this man seemed interested in was his lunch. He was studying his plate with great devotion, which was strange since only one carrot remained on it – and even that looked overcooked.

'We've met, haven't we?' Nell said politely, stopping for a moment. 'At Wychbourne?'

His face instantly paled in a way that Douglas Fairbanks would never have permitted. 'No,' he managed to stutter. Then seeing his neighbours staring at him, he added in desperation, 'The gardens there. Not the house.'

'That must be where I've seen you,' Nell agreed. But it hadn't been there. She was sure of that. Curiouser and curiouser, as Alice in Wonderland had remarked.

In the absence of Lady Ansley and Lady Helen, the task of approving menus at Wychbourne had devolved on Lady Sophy, whose interest in the food she consumed was slight. When Nell returned from Stalisbrook Place she was nowhere to be found, until Mr Peters told her she was

163

somewhere in the gardens. Nell could find no sign of her at first, until she eventually tracked her down to a remote bank by the lake, where she was sitting under a tree reading.

'Menus,' Nell said cheerfully.

Lady Sophy sighed and put the book aside and glanced at the menus. 'All smashing,' she immediately pronounced.

'Excellent. That's just what Kitty's been preparing, Lady Sophy.'

'I suppose I must still be Lady Sophy to you or Helen will nag me when she gets back,' she sighed. 'I hope she's cured, Nell. I hate it when she's ill.'

'It may take some time,' Nell warned her. 'It depends how long she's been taking the drug.' Too late, she remembered Lady Sophy might not yet know the cause of her sister's illness, but it became obvious that she did.

'I don't think that's very long. She's only begun getting keen on Charlie for the last few months. He was just one of the crowd before he turned into Mr Wonderful.' She picked up the book again. 'Have you ever read this? I found it in the library. Recipes from a Roman cook.'

'Yes. Apicius. He poisoned himself because he ran out of cash to spend on good meals.'

'I'll never be poor then. But I do want to learn to cook,' Lady Sophy said vehemently. 'I think I should, don't you? I've already been learning from Mr Fairweather about how to grow vegetables and fruit.'

How strange that Lady Sophy had little appreciation of the finished products of the recipes, but plenty of their history and in knowing how they worked. 'I'd be happy to teach you,' Nell told her.

'Would you? Oh, Nell, none of those stuffy other chefs would. None of them liked me being in the servants' wing. You'd think they owned it. But that's all tommy rot nowadays. I mean, there's you and there's me. Why should there be a wall between us just because my parents pay your wages?'

'No reason except established tradition.'

'Not that established. I think those socialist people in Russia are on the right lines. Look at history: we know all about the sirs and madams but when did you last read a gallant tale of a medieval kitchenmaid – not one who married a lord but one who married the village woodturner? There's that tame ghost of Aunt Clarice's, though. She was a cook. She dates from the eighteenth century when women could go into their own kitchens without their chefs throwing them out.'

'I promise never to do that,' Nell said gravely.

'Good. It's only the stuffy Victorians who set all these rules about housemaids not being seen in the main house after midday. Ridiculous. You can dress anyone up in a dinner suit and tails and he looks no different from a duke.'

'Got it!' Nell cried. She remembered where she had seen that familiar face at Stalisbrook Place before. 'It was him, wasn't it?' she exclaimed. 'He was your guest at the dinner that night. He works for Lady Warminster.'

Lady Sophy went very pink. 'That was Hugh Beaumont, not William Foster.'

165

Nell laughed. 'You'll never win a game of poker. How did you know which of her servants I was referring to?'

Lady Sophy giggled. 'Don't tell anyone, will you, Nell? It was all a joke to see if anyone would notice, but then it went wrong.'

'Because Mr Parkyn-Wright died?'

'No, worse than that. Worse for William, anyway. Lady Warminster arrived and we didn't know she was coming until the last minute. I didn't check the guest list until too late. William's her under-gardener and his father's the head gardener. William was off duty that evening and didn't know she was coming to Wychbourne. She drove herself here and William took his father's van. I'd met William when I was with Mr Fairweather one day. William comes here to talk to him about garden design because he wants to do more than just mow lawns and boring things. So in May I drove him up to the Chelsea Flower Show in London. He was worried about it at first, my being a lady and so on, but I told him that was rubbish. This is a new age and we're all on the same level now, like Russia. It's only clothes and jobs that make us seem different.'

'And how did he come to be at the Wychbourne dinner, Lady Sophy?' Nell enquired grimly.

'My idea,' she confessed. 'My parents are so stuffy about my ideas, and I thought it would be a great joke if they didn't notice any difference if he was all dressed up and chatty. And it *would* have been funny, if it hadn't been for everything else. He was so worried about Lady Warminster being suspicious that it was him. We began dancing together so that she couldn't get near him. Then we crept off into the gardens. I thought he might kiss me and I'd wanted to know what that's like, but he didn't even bother. He was terrified of Her Ladyship finding us and decided he would leave as soon as he could. I knew she'd follow him or go looking for his van, so I went over to Aunt Clarice and told her loudly in that woman's presence that my guest would be coming with me on the ghost hunt. As soon as the lights went out in the hall and we knew Her Ladyship was safely on the hunt herself, I told William and he had gone by the time of the changeover in the hall.'

'Why was he so scared she would catch him?'

'If he got clean away he could say that she'd made a mistake and he'd been home all the evening. She couldn't have proved he wasn't, so she wouldn't be able to give him the boot. That would mean his having to leave his tied cottage and perhaps his father too.'

Nell was still puzzled. 'Why would she want to *sack* him, though? A dressing-down, perhaps, or a complaint to Lord Ansley would do.'

'General Warminster wouldn't like it,' Lady Sophy explained simply. 'He's a stickler for protocol.'

And yet, Nell mused, he had married Lady Warminster who, according to his standards, was hardly out of the top drawer. She was still mulling this over when Lord Richard strolled up looking disgruntled, which undermined the nonchalant effect of the Oxford bags he wore.

'There you are, Sophy. I've been hunting

everywhere. Good afternoon, Miss Drury,' he added stiffly.

'Don't glare at Nell, Richard,' Lady Sophy reproved him. 'She's on our side, aren't you, Nell?'

'Of course,' Nell replied. 'Provided I know what the side's all about.'

'Getting this awful murder solved, isn't it, Richard?'

'I don't see how Nell can help,' he muttered. 'Not unless one of the servants is involved.'

'That's possible,' said Nell quickly before Lady Sophy could restart her campaign for communism. 'We in the servants' hall want to get it solved just as much as you do. We see ourselves as a humble part of the greater house community.' She thought she had gone too far in smoothing feathers but Lord Richard didn't seem to think so, though Lady Sophy was trying not to giggle.

'It must have been one of the guests,' he compromised graciously. 'Of course I don't see our servants committing murder.'

'Plenty of murders here in the past, according to Lady Clarice,' Nell pointed out.

'Not nowadays, though. Poor old Charlie,' Lord Richard added. 'He invited all those people from London and his killer must have been among them.'

'Is that the police's line?' Nell asked.

'It should be. They must have the evidence. Must have been fingerprints on that dagger unless they were wiped off by his murderer.'

'Unlikely,' Nell pointed out. 'There wouldn't be time in such a public place. The killer would want to get away.'

168

'Poor old Charlie,' Lord Richard repeated. 'He didn't deserve that.'

To Nell's ear that struck a distant tone; it wasn't best chums' talk.

'All this stuff about drugs is hogwash,' Lord Richard continued. 'He told me that himself. I'd heard these rumours months ago and so I talked to him man to man.'

'And you believed him?' Lady Sophy enquired.

'My dear girl, I went to school with him. It's a matter of honour.'

OK, Lord Richard had asked for it, Nell decided. 'He didn't seem to consider his honour when he carried on dancing with Miss Harlington who had promised to dance with you.'

'She's right, Richard,' Lady Sophy crowed.

'What would you know about it, Sophy?' he asked crossly.

'I have eyes,' she snapped. 'I could see Helen was just as furious as you were. She was keen on Charlie.'

'Yes, and not because he was a dealer,' he threw back at her. 'Wherever Helen got that dope it wasn't from him.'

'It *was* from him. Charlie's dance, Richard. Not Another Person's dance. And where's your beloved Elise this sunny afternoon? At a low, is she? No supplies?'

Taken by surprise, Lord Richard looked suddenly very young. 'Elise?' he said. 'Are you telling me she's on dope too? That's all my eye. Come off it, Sophy. Do you really think that someone as elegant, as talented, as beautiful as Elise needs drugs to buck her up?'

169

'Why not? You only have to look at the way she behaves. And anyway, Helen's beautiful and she's on drugs.'

'She only took it the once, she told me,' Lord Richard retorted. 'And anyway, Sophy, we shouldn't be discussing this in front of *her.*' He jerked his head towards Nell.

'Nell knows more about life than you ever will, Richard,' Lady Sophy replied scornfully.

'I'm sorry, Nell.' He looked abashed. 'It's this awful business. I can't think who would want to kill Charlie. There are people who fell out with him, but kill him? Never. Old Peters had an exchange of words with him after dinner that night but he wouldn't go and stab him to death, would he? That bandleader had a dust-up with him too round about the same time.'

Just as Robert had told her, but now it was evident that what happened was more than just an exchange over the music or coffee. 'Did you hear what it was about?' Nell asked, trying to sound offhand.

'No. I asked Charlie about it later and he said the band was proposing to play all ragtime or this new Charleston or something, but he wanted to canoodle with—' Lord Richard came to a sudden stop.

'With Elise,' Lady Sophy finished sweetly. 'That's when he was passing the dope. You're the dope, Richard, for not believing it.'

'I still don't,' he shouted, almost crying.

'That's very loyal of you,' Nell said gently. 'But don't be too surprised if it all comes out at the inquest.'

'Are you giving evidence?' he asked, calming down with some effort. 'Must have been rotten for you, finding him like that. I miss him, old Charlie.'

'I don't,' Lady Sophy chimed in. 'He was nasty all round. To you and Helen and that nice Rex, and even Mr Fontenoy.'

'Why him?' Nell asked sharply. 'What had he done to stir Mr Parkyn-Wright up?'

'How should I know?' Lord Richard said. 'Some old scandal, I imagine. Mother mentioned one once.'

Nell gulped. Is that why Arthur had talked of a house full of secrets? Once Mr Charles's murderer had been found secrets could lie undisturbed again – and perhaps it was better that way.

'Anyway, Fontenoy wasn't on the ghost hunt until later,' Lord Richard continued. 'And Sophy and I were in that first group, Nell. It was dark, but if someone had tried to slip away or stay behind we would have noticed.'

'Not if they were at the back of the group,' Lady Sophy said. 'Tell her who was, Richard.'

There was a silence, then he replied sulkily: 'Helen and I were. We wanted to be at the rear so that we could slip away to carry out the Pepper's Ghost joke in the library. At one point we nearly did. We argued about it but Helen said it was too early, so we stayed on until the change-over. But none of us three killed him, Nell,' Lord Richard concluded anxiously.

'We could have done,' Lady Sophy amplified. 'But we didn't. Anyway, Helen would never have killed Charlie. She was cuckoo about him, no matter what he'd done.'

Lord Richard looked relieved. 'So it seems, Nell, as though the guests *and* the servants' wing are back in the picture. I told you old Peters was having a dust-up with him as well as that bandleader. Peters has a thing or two to hide, if you ask me.'

'I am asking,' Nell said lightly.

'Lips sealed,' he said mysteriously.

'Oh, come on, Richard,' Lady Sophy said crossly. 'In a murder case you can't seal your lips.'

'Nell isn't Scotland Yard,' he pointed out.

'No, she's better than them. She'll know if it's important or not. She can *help*.'

He surrendered. 'I don't know the full story but there was something during the war that happened. Noel knew about it. You were only a child, Sophy, and he told Kenelm and me when he was on his last leave.'

'Did your father know?' Nell asked.

'I spoke to Pa when he hired Peters and he said he knew the story perfectly well. So you see, there's nothing to it.'

'There is,' Lady Sophy said immediately, 'because Peters might not have known they knew. And somehow Charlie did. How, Richard?'

He blushed. 'I might have mentioned it to Charlie – just for fun. He liked teasing the old boy.'

Ten

Here, on Tuesday, 7 July were the same people in the same place, the upper room at the Coach and Horses, but to Nell there was a sense of urgency that had been lacking during the brief earlier inquest hearing nearly two weeks ago. The jury was being sworn in, including Mrs Brown, who ran the sweet shop and tobacconist in the village and was visibly proud of her new status. The witnesses were present, save for one empty seat, and they inevitably included Inspector Melbray. In the main part of the hall there were now two rows full of newspaper reporters and behind them in the public seats sat the Ansleys, save for Lady Helen, not apparently a witness now. Nell could see Lady Warminster too, no doubt being ogled from afar by Inspector Melbray (or 'duckie' as Her Ladyship termed him). What a blister he was. Her Ladyship was doing her best to look like a *femme fatale* and Guy was at her side. Could it be he *was* an admirer of Her Ladyship's charms? she wondered. No, he was far too sensible.

The missing witness must be the Honourable Elise Harlington. She had been a far-from-ideal guest over the last few days, unpredictable in mood, punctuality and demands. True, that was from the servants' hall perspective, but Nell suspected she was no more popular with Lord and

Lady Ansley. At times she had been sweetness itself, at others the reverse. Mr Beringer, on the other hand, had proved a model guest throughout.

Once the coroner was seated and he had explained that evidence of identity was not necessary as it had been given at the earlier hearing, Nell felt her tension level rise. It was the witnesses' turn now. The first witness this time was the local inspector, who was summoned to take the oath. Would she be next? Nell fidgeted as he went through the time of his arrival and subsequent actions. No, the duckie Inspector Melbray came next.

'I first saw the body of Charles Parkyn-Wright at four twelve a.m.,' he informed the coroner, 'at which time it was still on the gallery floor on to which I was told it had fallen earlier.'

For the first time she could see the inspector in profile: the stiff way he held his head, the aquiline nose, the chin and the mouth that spouted such oh-so-correct, confident words. 'It appeared,' he continued, 'he had died by the wound from which the weapon still protruded. There was another wound to the abdomen which had bled profusely.'

'Could the wounds in your experience, Mr Melbray, have been self-inflicted or by accident?' the coroner asked him.

'Not in my opinion.' He went on to be more specific while Nell tried to distance herself from the memories his words evoked. It was hard, however, and even the technical medical evidence that followed from the doctor was more bearable. It did, as Nell had expected, include references to cocaine and opium.

When the court clerk finally called for Miss Eleanor Drury, she rose to her feet with such speed that her gloves and bag fell to the floor and had to be rescued. Flustered, she took the oath in a blur but the first question was simple enough.

'You are the chef at Wychbourne Court?' the coroner asked.

'Yes, sir.' She steadied herself for the next question. Yes, she had opened the door in the middle of the gallery screen.

'Why did you do that?' he asked.

'It was dark and I thought I saw something liquid coming from under the door. So I put my lantern into the other hand so that the right one was free to open the door. I only pulled it gently but the weight of the body resting against the door on the other side made it fly open.' So far so good. She was over the worst.

Then she was aware of a disturbance. There were people coming in or out at the back of the room and there were gasps from the public benches. Someone must have fainted or made a flamboyant entrance.

To her dismay, she saw a slender woman dressed entirely in black from her shoes and stockings to the chic hat and full black veil over her face. Only when she tremulously drew back the veil and dabbed her eyes with a lace handkerchief was Nell sure who it was. Miss Elise Harlington. Nell's first ignoble thought was that she couldn't have brought that outfit with her. She must have dashed up to London to acquire it.

'I am late. I do apologise, My Lord.'

The coroner would love his elevation to the peerage, Nell thought meanly.

'I was too upset earlier. Where should I sit?' she asked plaintively, looking around as though this were the dress circle at His Majesty's Theatre.

The coroner's clerk rushed to assist her, leading her the entire remaining two yards to the witness seats where, with a pathetic smile to her neighbour, Inspector Melbray, she continued to dab her eyes with the handkerchief.

'Shall I continue, Coroner?' Nell asked loudly.

'By all means.' His voice was frosty, as though she had little right to be so composed in the face of the woe and tragic emotion displayed by the lady in black.

Nell managed to get through the rest of her evidence, even though it was clear that the jury was far more fascinated by Miss Harlington than by the details of whether or not Nell had known the deceased or moved his body. Even the story of the ghost hunt and the intended joke to follow it went down like a damp squib.

The jury was even more fascinated when Miss Harlington took the stand and repeated the oath in a tremulous tone to indicate the ordeal through which she was bravely struggling.

'Are you the widow of the late Mr Parkyn-Wright?' the coroner asked her gently.

'Oh, no, Your Lordship. We were pledged, however. But . . .' Another handkerchief came into play as the court was left to ponder on the happily married life and innocent children of which this unfortunate woman had been deprived.

'Water, please, sir,' she begged the clerk, who rushed to obey.

'Tell the court – when you're ready, of course – what happened that day. Was anything weighing on Mr Parkyn-Wright's mind? Did he seem troubled in any way?' the coroner persevered.

'Oh, no. That afternoon we had driven down to Wychbourne together in his motor car. Such a perfect day. We were so *happy*. So full of our plans for our life together. It was going to be *so* wonderful.'

'Were you aware of this so-called joke in which Mr Parkyn-Wright was to play a part and which resulted in his hiding behind the gallery screen?' There was disdain in the coroner's voice.

'Of course not. He must have reluctantly agreed to do that after we arrived.'

'You had no knowledge at the time of how he came to be in the gallery?'

'No,' she sobbed. 'If I had I might have prevented this awful murder.'

'In what way?' the coroner pressed her gently, ignoring the fact that as yet it hadn't been established as a murder.

'I would have warned him of the dangers.'

Nell stirred uneasily. This sounded ominous.

'Charlie was so wonderful,' Miss Harlington continued, 'that there were some who resented him. He was so much in demand that people would confide in him and then regret that they had done so. He was so honest that when he heard those confessions he felt he should warn his informants that he might have to report them. I could tell you who those people are—'

'No, Miss Harlington,' the coroner interrupted, almost regretfully, Nell thought, and he was obviously fascinated by the husky voice that his witness had suddenly acquired. 'This court has to determine how the deceased met his death and not who might have meted it out to him.'

'But is there to be no justice?' she wailed heartrendingly. 'Is the murderer of my beloved Charlie to walk free?' She burst into tears and indicated that she would like to be escorted back to her seat – perhaps, Nell thought, intending to seek the comforting shoulder of the duckie inspector.

Before she got there, however, the inspector stood up. 'One moment, Coroner. As the representative of the Metropolitan Police, I have a question for Miss Harlington. And if it reassures you, Miss Harlington, no murderer will walk free from this crime.'

She looked at him with fluttering eyelids. 'Thank you, sir.'

'Before you arrived here,' he continued, 'sworn evidence was given that medical tests revealed the presence of cocaine in the deceased. The Metropolitan Police also has evidence that Mr Parkyn-Wright dealt in drugs. Were you aware of that, in view of the fact that you were going to marry him?'

Miss Harlington's eyes had narrowed. 'I can't believe that, sir,' she managed to gasp. 'Not of darling Charlie.'

And then she swooned. But not before, Nell noted, she had tottered conveniently near to the coroner's clerk. Perhaps she had unhappy memories of the inspector's handling of her delicate frame at the last hearing.

Nell emerged into the sunlight with relief. The inquest was not yet over but at least during this adjournment for lunch she could feel normal again – even if Guy Ellimore was at her side with Inspector Melbray watching them from a distance. As Lady Warminster suddenly appeared from nowhere, that was doubtless the reason for his attention.

'Mr Ellimore,' Her Ladyship cooed. 'At last, we can talk. So difficult in that courtroom. You still have evidence to give?'

'I'm not to be called,' he told her, smiling down at the too perfect doll-like face. 'The police have already taken details of the period my band was playing in the ballroom.'

'And playing so splendidly,' she murmured. 'We have to discuss – when this unfortunate business is over – the music for my little party.'

'My pleasure,' he replied.

Lady Warminster was as expert a vamp as the Honourable Elise Harlington. Nell was highly amused. Guy was good looking, of course, and running into ladies with too much time, money and energy must be a familiar hazard in his line of business.

'Why don't you walk with me to my motor car?' Lady Warminster asked him, dismissing Nell's presence with, 'I'm too fatigued to talk to you now, Miss Drury. All this emotion. To think I was present when he was killed.'

Nell blinked. 'You saw it happen?'

179

'Not in front of me, of course,' Lady Warminster replied hastily. 'But, as you know, I took part in that ghost hunt, and was so close to where it happened that I can imagine it all terribly vividly. Shall we go, Mr Ellimore?'

Nell watched them for a few moments and then gave some thought to her lunch. It had been arranged for those who wished for food to be available at the Coach and Horses but Nell had little appetite. She gave a last look at Guy and Lady Warminster, who had reached the far side of the green where William Foster was presumably waiting, as he'd been in court. Did the inspector know about Lady Sophy's joke? she wondered. She couldn't see how it could affect the murder case as Foster hadn't been on the ghost hunt, but who was she to judge that? Nevertheless, remembering the possibility that there was a time gap during which in theory anyone could have gone up on the gallery, she felt uneasy. That applied to Guy too. Mr Peters was there all the time, of course, and he was sure he would have seen or heard anyone moving up there, but he could be wrong about that.

Nell could not bear the idea of being cooped up inside so she bought herself a sandwich and a glass of lemonade and then selected a spot on the far side of the oak tree where the afternoon sun, dappled by the shade of the branches overhead, looked far more attractive than sitting inside in the Coach and Horses. Revelling in the solitude, she closed her eyes.

Not for long.

'May I join you, Miss Drury?' Standing there

180

was Inspector Melbray, also with a sandwich in his hand.

This was the last thing she wanted, but how could she refuse? The investigation into Mr Charles's death lay in his hands.

'Please do,' she managed to say graciously. He sat down by her side but he didn't begin interrogating her, which was something for which to be thankful.

'We have achieved our sandwich lunch after all,' he said presently, 'although I apologise for your having to buy your own.'

'You couldn't buy me one anyway,' she joked. 'You'd be bribing a witness.'

'That is true. You were talking to Lady Warminster just now.'

She stiffened at this pointed sign that she was second best for his choice of companion. 'She's over there.' She pointed. 'If you hurry you might catch her. I'm sorry I deprived you of sharing your sandwich lunch with her.'

He looked at her puzzled. 'Why would I do that?'

'Well' – she was disconcerted – 'I thought you might after your visits and personal attentions to her.'

'Visits and attentions?' He actually laughed, which wiped the grim look of dedication from his face. 'Miss Drury, I told you to believe no one.'

She longed to ask him more about Her Ladyship but that might make it seem too important when really it was nothing.

'In fact,' he continued, 'I can't spot Lady Warminster but I do see your friend Mr Ellimore bearing down on us. He seems upset.'

He did indeed, and Nell scrambled to her feet in alarm as he approached. The inspector, however, remained seated on the ground.

'I saw him, Nell,' Guy began without preamble. 'And Inspector Melbray . . . that fellow I said I was talking to in the supper room. My alibi, you'd call it. It turns out it was Lady Warminster's gardener.'

'William Foster?' Nell exclaimed. Too late, she realized she had put her foot in it.

It didn't escape unnoticed. The inspector immediately stood up. Grim dedication was back. 'Details, please, Miss Drury.'

'It *was* him,' Guy continued, 'but he's refusing to admit it. He says he was nowhere near Wychbourne Court that night. He was at home at Stalisbrook Place, but I swear it was him I was talking to until just before twelve thirty when he dashed off somewhere and I came along to the great hall.'

'You know William Foster?' the inspector asked Nell non-committally.

Nell inwardly groaned. 'I don't *know* him. I saw him that evening at Wychbourne Court, just as Guy did. And again at Stalisbrook Place. I'm catering for a buffet dinner there on Saturday week.'

'But you definitely saw him on the night of the murder?'

'Yes, I saw him at the dinner that night but I didn't know who he was.'

'At dinner?' He frowned. 'In the servants' hall?'

'No, the Ansleys' dinner.'

'That seems unusual for Wychbourne Court.'

How could she tell the inspector to speak to Lady Sophy? The inspector was staring at her. Never had she wanted to be safe in her kitchen so much. She knew what Foster had been doing at Wychbourne and here she was making a first-class disaster of a stew.

'I'll speak to Foster,' Inspector Melbray finally said. Nell's face felt redder than a radish. 'I'll also speak to Lady Warminster – again. And who else should I speak to, Miss Drury?'

There was no way out. 'Lady Sophy.'

The jury dutifully returned its verdict of murder due to a sharp instrument by person or persons unknown two hours later. By then the verdict was almost an anti-climax after the Honourable Elise Harlington's performance and nothing, as far as Nell could see, had emerged to indicate who had killed Mr Charles. The funeral had, she'd gathered, taken place near Derby, where he had been born and his parents still lived, but it had been a family funeral only. Miss Harlington had been the only person at Wychbourne who had attended, and she was now wooing his bereaved parents.

'Was there any truth in their being engaged?' Nell had asked Lord Richard, perhaps tactlessly as he was clearly mortified by his beloved's public desertion.

'Not from what Charlie told me and he would have done,' he told her miserably. 'Helen won't believe a word of it. I'm sure Elise is sacrificing herself for the sake of his parents.'

The only significant moment in the inquest after

the verdict was that Inspector Melbray, after discussion with Lord Ansley, had requested all those present who had been at Wychbourne Court on the night of the murder to return there immediately.

Nell was flummoxed. Why not announce that earlier? Because of Miss Harlington's evidence? she wondered – if it could rightly be called that. She had referred obliquely to knowing who Mr Charles's victims were, save that she didn't refer to them by that name. That, for Nell, at least, confirmed the blackmail theory. Mr Charles could have ruined careers, relationships or marriages, either for money or for power. Had the inspector dismissed her theory outright or would he be following it up now that Miss Harlington had implied she was Mr Charles's confidante? Why did the inspector need everyone to return to the house, though? That would include her – which meant a speedy visit to the kitchens for catering arrangements. Mrs Fielding's still-room would bear the brunt of a sudden tea for everyone but Nell still needed to be on hand.

When she arrived in the east wing both the kitchen and the still-room were in a flurry of dainty biscuits, scones and cakes which were miraculously appearing in many pairs of flying hands.

'Lady Ansley wants to see you in the parlour right away, Miss Drury,' Kitty panted as she hurried by with a tray of rock cakes. 'What's going on?'

'I wish I knew,' Nell said ruefully, automatically whisking one imperfect specimen from it. Tottering turbots, what next? With an agonised look at the kitchen, she hurried up the east wing staircase to the parlour. There in the familiar room was not only Lady Ansley but Lady Helen, who managed a wan smile.

'The prodigal daughter returns, Nell.'

'Lucky we've several fatted calves roasting in the range,' she laughed.

'I have to stay here with Helen,' Lady Ansley said, 'and you'll be needed in the drawing room. Will you be my eyes and ears as to what on earth is going on?'

'Of course. If I can work it out myself,' Nell added. At the moment she was more at sea than the Flying Dutchman.

'The inspector wants Mrs Fielding there too, and Miss Checkam. And Peters,' Lady Ansley said despairingly. 'Tonight's dinner will have to be at eight thirty and not seven o'clock to allow for whatever it is the inspector has in mind.'

That meant she would have to cancel her nine o'clock meeting with Arthur, Nell realized. She'd given Jimmy a note to arrange it, but with any luck she could catch Arthur in the drawing room to cancel it.

When she arrived there, it seemed that egalitarianism had come to Wychbourne Court in a big way. Lord Ansley was present with Lady Enid, Mr Charles's parents and the inspector, and so were Lady Sophy, Lord Richard and Mr Beringer. Arthur was sitting next to Lady Clarice, on whose other side were Mrs Fielding and Mr Peters. Robert the footman and Jimmy the lampboy, both looking very uncomfortable, were perched side by side on a sofa. Lady Warminster was also there and Nell could see William Foster too, although not next to Her Ladyship or to Lady

Sophy. The Honourable Elise Harlington was lounging on another sofa and surprisingly Guy was with her as her chosen comforter, although he didn't look happy at this arrangement. Longing to get back to Lady Warminster, perhaps?

It was evident to Nell that Inspector Melbray, whose eye had fallen on her the moment she entered the room, was about to 'address the meeting' even though tea was still in progress. He did so with little pomp, merely standing up and thanking everyone for coming. A sure sign that trouble was on its way, Nell thought.

'As you probably all know by now,' he continued, 'the coroner refused speculation on those who might have had reason to kill Mr Parkyn-Wright but the jury's verdict was that somebody most certainly did. It's my job to find out who and I need your help for this.'

She had been right, Nell thought. What was this going to involve?

'Distressing though it might be to relive that night,' the inspector continued, 'I'd like you all to walk through your movements again, whether or not you were in the first ghost hunt group. Take it from twelve o'clock and at the same pace as you did before, even though it won't be as dark. It may be that something might occur to you that you have previously forgotten. Any detail, any noise or movement I want to know about. I'll be here waiting in the great hall.'

Those who weren't on the hunt were asked to stand near where they were that night, or at the nearest door to the hall if they were further away in the supper or drawing rooms.

'I do have a question,' Lady Clarice asked anxiously. 'How can we re-enact that night? There will be no ghosts and they are the essential factor.'

'Only for the ghosts themselves,' the inspector replied seriously, 'and none of them is likely to be around at teatime. But I do need to know about any sightings or sounds that took place in connection with the ghosts.'

She'd be touring the house on her own, Nell realized with dismay as they began to assemble in the great hall. No one else from the second group was still at Wychbourne, save for Guy and Arthur, who had both appeared later. She was glad that Mr Charles's parents had remained in the drawing room with Lord Ansley. At least they would not be put through more agony.

'What do I do when I reach the screen door?' she blurted out.

'As you did then, please,' the inspector replied calmly.

Nell could see that no one seemed happy about the task ahead of them as they waited for the inspector to begin the proceedings, and it was a relief when he looked at his watch and gave them the signal. Guy had already walked off to the door nearest to the supper room, unwillingly followed by a stony-faced William Foster. Miss Checkam and Mrs Fielding had disappeared to the entrance nearest the servants' wing and Mr Peters remained in the hall by the doorway closest to the gallery stairs.

'I'll go round the west wing on my own then.' Nell tried not to make it sound like a plaintive cry for help.

187

'I'll go with you, Nell.' Arthur stepped up.

The inspector glanced from one to the other. 'I'd prefer not. My sergeant will come with you, Miss Drury.'

'Why?' she all but snapped back. She had already managed to tell Arthur that this evening's meeting would have to be postponed so there was no logical reason she should object, but she did.

The inspector did not answer that. 'Would you leave now, Miss Drury,' he said instead. 'Mr Fontenoy, you can join her at the point you did before.'

Off Nell set to march up the grand staircase to the west wing, feeling somewhat ridiculous with a lantern in her hand and the sergeant behind her. She forced herself to stop where she had done so on the Saturday night but the sergeant decided to do without her explanation of the ghosts that she should, according to Lady Clarice, have encountered on the way, each snugly confined to its own cold area. Coming back through the library, however, she hesitated. The curtain, glass and mirrors in place that night had of course vanished, but the sergeant watched without comment as she flicked her hand mid-air, having judged roughly where the curtain had been concealing the mirrors.

When that ordeal and the changeover period had been surmounted, she took a deep breath. It would be time to face that gallery again. At least Arthur and Guy would be joining her here. She was beginning to see what the inspector might be looking for: the gaps in timing when the murder could have taken place, exactly where

188

Mr Peters was standing and how much he would have been able to see of the gallery.

Conscious that she was being closely watched from below by the inspector, she climbed the stairs furthest from Mr Peters' position and made her way along the gallery. She was alone now because the sergeant's presence, the inspector had decreed, was no longer necessary. She hadn't even been conscious of Arthur and then Guy joining her until she felt their presence. She was concentrating once again on that screen door and her heart was pounding. Suppose the inspector had put a dummy behind that door just to make this reconstruction more real? Her hand hovered, but telling herself not to be such a fool she pulled it. Nothing fell out to her relief, but even so it took courage for her to kneel down once more. Arthur and Guy were pressing her from behind now. Then mercifully the whistle blew – the signal for everyone to return just as the screams had brought them back that Saturday night.

'Thank you, Miss Drury,' the inspector called to her. 'You can all come down now.'

With relief she joined the group gathering again in the great hall, just as Lady Clarice was telling the inspector imperiously: 'There was something wrong. I had one person fewer that night when Lady Dorcas was about to greet us. Someone had disappeared.'

'Must have been a ghost,' Lord Richard said lightly.

'Lady Dorcas *is* a ghost. It was not a ghost who disappeared,' Lady Clarice said reprovingly.

Lord Richard glanced at Lady Sophy. 'Helen,

Sophy and I left, Aunt Clarice, when we reached the great hall for the changeover. We had something to do,' he added airily.

Lady Clarice fortunately dismissed this impatiently. She might have taken Mr Charles's rendition of Sir Thomas reasonably well but Pepper's Ghost floating across the library balcony would have been quite a different matter, Nell feared.

'It was earlier,' Lady Clarice insisted.

'That could,' Lady Warminster said airily, 'have been myself, Inspector. I have a sensitive nature and the ghostly tales of murder were beginning to upset me. I did leave as we reached the change point or perhaps just before.'

'You told him, Nell,' Lady Sophy said reproachfully as the last of the party departed from Wychbourne Court, even, thankfully, the police – or so Nell hoped.

'I had to do so.'

Lady Sophy sighed. 'I'm sorry. I should have told the inspector myself, I suppose, but it would have caused trouble for William and he had nothing to do with this at all. I wouldn't put it past Lady Warminster to be involved, though.'

'Because she has an eye for the men?'

'Both eyes, if you ask me.' Lady Sophy laughed. 'She does have the reputation of being a maneater, and if Charlie found that out she would be terrified out of her Chanel boots with her husband due to come home shortly. I bet Charlie did know.'

Nell almost pitied Inspector Melbray if he had been lured by Lady Warminster's charms, whatever they were. But what about William Foster? Supposed he'd been lured and succumbed? That could be why he was so scared when he saw her at the dinner. It wasn't just his being there that would have annoyed Lady Warminster, it would have been seeing her fancy-man cavorting around with Lady Sophy. He was two-timing her, as the Americans phrased it at the pictures. And that would definitely have led to his getting the sack, especially with her husband returning shortly.

The inspector was next to delay her return to the east wing. 'I'm sorry to have put you through that ordeal, Miss Drury.'

'It's your job.' Surprised at what seemed a sincere apology, her reply was more stilted than she had intended.

'Also, I want to thank you.'

Thank her? This was indeed a new approach. 'What for?' she asked cautiously.

'For your theory about this case. It has been most helpful. I can't tell you any more than that, and this charade – as you no doubt consider it – has been of use. It was necessary given the evidence this morning.' He hesitated. 'One point about—'

'Yes?' she asked encouragingly when he broke off.

'No matter.'

Dinner was not over until ten o'clock, with the result that the kitchen was so disrupted that Nell was helping out in the scullery, to Mrs Fielding's delight. Lady Helen had twice refused anything to eat in her room and then changed her mind at ten thirty. Mr Peters was in an unusually snappy mood, and for once Nell fell into bed not caring what she would put on the menu for tomorrow. She awoke at dawn, as so often, not through choice but because the cocks were crowing. They never took any notice of how late you went to bed, she thought crossly. She managed to doze off again before she reluctantly had to leave her bed and begin dressing.

Still in her brassiere and panties, she became aware of an unusual amount of noise outside and peered down through the window to see people shouting and running through the kitchen yard, some into the stable yard, some towards the gardens and some heading through the other exit towards the forecourt of the main house. What the flipping flounders was going on?

She threw on the rest of her clothes, fingers fumbling on hooks and eyes, quickly brushed her hair and hurried down to the yard. There she found Mr Peters with Mrs Fielding in his arms – still with her curlers in – obviously consoling her over something. And, of all things, Lord Ansley with them.

'What's happened?' she cried.

White-faced, Lord Ansley turned to her. 'Elise Harlington is dead, Nell.'

Drugs was Nell's first thought once she had pulled herself together from the shock, but that could not have caused all this commotion.

'It appears she was strangled,' Lord Ansley told her bluntly.

'Where?' she blurted out. Murder? *Again?*

'Not in the house. Outside in the grounds. In the old dairy.'

Eleven

Nell clutched at routine as a lifeline as she wrestled with this new disaster for Wychbourne Court. The elegant, supercilious Miss Harlington murdered? This was more like something out of Fu Manchu or Sherlock Holmes. The kitchen was understandably already buzzing with talk when she arrived. A house such as Wychbourne came to life in stages each day and many of the servants would already have been at work when the alarm was raised. At present work had ceased, and she was quickly under siege from anxious and curious staff. She told them what little she had heard from Lord Ansley, but it was clear that routine had to be abandoned.

The facts she had to face were these: until she and Arthur had decided to meet in the old dairy, it had been unused; yesterday she had cancelled their appointment and that very night Miss Harlington had been murdered there. That was too much of a coincidence for there to be no link. Had Miss Harlington known of their plans to meet or had it indeed been chance that took her there? If the former, the probability was that Miss Harlington – and her murderer – were expecting Nell and Arthur to be there, not knowing of the cancellation.

One fact was obvious. She would have to tell the police, which would probably be in the form of Inspector Melbray. The nearer she drew to the dairy, however, the more formidable the task seemed. The moment she walked through the gate from the kitchen yard to the stables, she could see police vans, motor cars and, sure enough, there was the inspector talking to the local police, intent on his job. Worse, a covered stretcher was being loaded into a police mortuary van. Nell shuddered. If she had gone to the dairy last night, as originally planned, would she have been the victim? No, she wouldn't dwell on that. If Miss Harlington had heard about the rendezvous, though, it must have been either through Arthur or Jimmy, and the latter was much the more probable.

Her next step was clear. Find Jimmy, who would have been up and about long since with the lamps to look after, but it took a surprisingly long time to track him down. She eventually found him skulking in the library and his face went bright red when he saw her. He looked round for an escape route but she managed to block the door.

'Morning, Miss Drury,' he began tentatively.

'Fine Baker Street Irregular you are,' she said severely.

He did his best to look innocent. 'Why's that, Miss Drury?'

'You did deliver my message to Mr Fontenoy yesterday, didn't you?' she asked.

He looked relieved. 'Yes, miss.'

He wasn't getting away with that. 'You delivered it yourself, Jimmy? *You* put it through the letterbox at Wychbourne Cottage?'

His feet suddenly seemed of great interest to him.

'*Did* you, Jimmy?'

Guilt was written all over his face. 'The lady told me she was going there and she'd hand it over to Mr Fontenoy,' he mumbled. 'And she did, miss. I saw Mr Fontenoy later and he said he'd got it. Was that the lady they're saying got murdered last night?' A quiver in his voice now.

Nell thought back. Had she sealed that letter? No, she hadn't bothered as the contents were innocent enough. 'I believe it was, but what happened last night wasn't your fault,' she consoled him. She could see real distress on his face.

She'd have to tell the police this, but next, she managed to convince herself, she simply must organize her daily work. Anyway, the inspector seemed to have disappeared now. With Kitty's help she succeeded in concocting suitable menus, but then of course she had to discuss the vegetables with the gardener and telephone the butcher – who proved only too eager to deliver to Wychbourne Court. Clearly the news had travelled and newspaper reporters would be hot on his heels. Nevertheless, the household still had to eat, despite the circumstances. The menus were basic but would do.

Lady Ansley didn't notice whether they were basic or not. She stared at them as though she wasn't sure what they were.

'There's a guest fewer now, Nell.' She burst into tears and, alarmed, Nell knelt beside her, taking her hand. 'What's happening here?' Lady Ansley continued. 'What was she doing in the

195

dairy so late at night? Elise only made a very short appearance at dinner and then she said she was going to retire for the night. I suppose there must have been a tramp sleeping in the dairy.' She must have picked up Nell's silence. 'It *was* a tramp, wasn't it?'

'Probably,' Nell said soothingly. She had to pave the way for the obvious. 'Although it's possible the police might think she was killed because she knew who killed Mr Parkyn-Wright.' Or, she thought, Miss Harlington might have known too much about Mr Charles and his clients.

'The silly girl. Helen's distraught, Nell. Could you look after her for a while? I don't know what's happened to Miss Checkam. There's no sign of her. Most unusual. Richard is playing the bereaved lover and won't budge from his room, and Sophy has gone very quiet and shut herself into *her* room, so poor Helen is on her own because I have to be at Gerald's side and the police – oh, Nell!'

'Don't worry about Lady Helen. I'll stay with her.' Lunch might be delayed, Nell calculated, but with luck Mrs Squires might have begun preparations in her absence.

Nell didn't flatter herself that her company would do Lady Helen much good, though. She was still mourning Mr Charles's death – in her own way. She was right, for her welcome was not warm.

'What do *you* want?' Lady Helen threw at her.

'Your mother didn't want to leave you alone. Any company's better than none at present, even mine.'

Lady Helen looked very pale, obviously ill, Nell thought, but at last there seemed to be a glimpse of the real person underlying the Bright Young Thing.

She didn't answer for a few moments, but then: 'The police will want to see me, won't they?'

'It will only be a formality. Where you were at the time she was killed and so on.'

'But when was that?' Lady Helen asked plaintively.

'Probably sometime last night. She was found this morning by one of the gardeners.'

'I hated her, Nell,' Lady Helen said abruptly. 'But the thought of her dead is just awful. And here at our home too. I can't bear it. It almost looks as though one of us must have killed her. But then there's that bandleader – he's still around. Or Rex—' She broke off. 'No, not Rex.'

'Why on earth would he want to kill her?' Nell asked practically.

'He wouldn't, of course,' Lady Helen said after a moment. 'It must have been a tramp or a poacher.'

Another vote for the convenient tramp. And Lady Helen was remarkably reticent about Mr Beringer. 'That's possible,' Nell agreed. Then she had an idea. She'd persuade Lady Helen that she was needed elsewhere. It would both flatter her and be true. Lord Richard *did* need help.

Lady Helen agreed immediately. 'Of course I'll go. Richard was crazy about Elise. Oh, Nell, suppose he . . . He couldn't have, could he? If she'd really been horrible to him?'

'No, he couldn't,' Nell said firmly, hoping she was right. True, Lord Richard was given to impulsive reactions, but strangling someone he loved? No, not he. But if Lady Helen was right about ruling out Mr Beringer, that brought Nell back to considering the servants' hall for suspects – and by extension to Guy. Ridiculous, because he had no reason for killing Miss Harlington – unless of course it was he who had killed Charles. Her mind began to spin, remembering that William Foster had not confirmed Guy's alibi. How could she even be thinking of Guy as a killer, though? She just couldn't believe it, just as Lady Helen couldn't believe it of Mr Beringer.

What Nell *could* believe, however, was that luncheon and dinner had to be served. She was relieved to find on returning to the kitchen that Mrs Squires had indeed begun the preparations. That was a good omen, otherwise how was she going to manage with her head full of police and murder and wondering where Miss Checkam was? It was so unlike Miss Checkam to desert her post.

Meanwhile, her own post was here, and its most immediate demand was for a raspberry fool to which she had to give full attention. Cooking was an art, not just a craft. It responded to moods and emotions. Why else, Nell had always argued, would a recipe work perfectly well one day and fail miserably the next? The rational explanation was that one was too confident, too blasé about it to give attention to detail or that the ingredients had varied in quality or quantity. In her view there was much more to it. On a happy day, inspiration cooked at your side. On a bad day, inspiration sent his companion Mr Plod in his place. Variations between good and excellent might not be noticed by most diners but she could tell which of the two was in charge, just as an actor repeating the same words each night could tell the difference between one performance and another. One night the audience rose to applaud him and the next it stalked out in disappointment.

Today she was Miss Plod, Nell quickly realized, and took a brief pause from the raspberry fool to see what was happening at the old dairy. She *must* tell the inspector about her appointment with Arthur. Mr Peters had reported that the police were moving back into the morning room. That put an end to Nell's forlorn hope that Lady Ansley's tramp had already been arrested, and when she reached the vegetable garden gate she could see that investigations were still in progress at the dairy. People were swarming everywhere, on the road leading to the rear exit from the estate, on the narrow path leading to the dairy and in the bushes surrounding it.

The dairy had been built in the coldest corner of the garden in the eighteenth century, and was so tucked away that it was hard to see it from where she stood. No one would go there by chance, which made it all the more probable that Miss Harlington had known of her planned rendezvous with Arthur but not of its cancellation. But why would Miss Harlington want to eavesdrop on them? Was she hoping for blackmail material? Had she a companion with her who then murdered her or had someone followed her?

Stop speculating, she told herself, and get moving. Tell him now. She could see the inspector by the roadside talking to a group of officers. At least he wasn't going to think that she and Arthur were lovers. But she remained frozen to the spot. Go, she ordered herself, but then she saw Arthur walking towards her.

'My dear Nell,' he said, 'what splendid good fortune. I wanted to talk to you and to see what was going on here, being a nosy fellow, and here you are already. This is bad news, Nell. Very grave. I have left a message for the police that I can be found here. Have you spoken to them yet?'

'No, I needed to talk to you first. Jimmy tells me Elise delivered my message to you yesterday.'

'Did she? It came through the door as usual.'

'Could it have been opened and read?'

'I recall it was unsealed. How unfortunate. I presume she did not know that our meeting was later cancelled. What could have interested her in our arrangement, Nell? I saw the police just now gathering clues in their little test tubes and glass bottles. They seemed also to be taking plaster casts which I presume are of footprints. Ours, do you think?'

'Perhaps, but unlikely. It was dry when we met here last week. There'd be fingerprints, though.'

'Ah. They will still no doubt have ours on record adorned with that nasty black powder. I see that Inspector Poker-Face Melbray is still here.'

He was rather poker-faced, now she came to think of it. 'Yes, so he must believe the two murders are connected.'

'It looks that way, Nell. Was the body found inside the dairy?'

'I don't know. They seem to be working inside, though.'

'Perhaps Miss Harlington sought the diary out as a convenient if uncomfortable place for love and therefore it has nothing to do with our visits? I assume her killer was a man, but of course it could be a woman. I don't see Lady Enid strolling down here in the middle of the night, however.'

Nell managed a laugh. 'That's better, Nell,' Arthur continued approvingly. 'Incidentally, I believe the Dowager Dragon might awake again and roar at any moment. Miss Checkam is currently with her – I cannot help observing such matters from my cottage – and I do wonder why she is there.'

So did Nell, but there were more urgent issues. Such as Inspector Melbray walking purposefully towards them.

'I'm told, Mr Fontenoy, that you wished to see me. Shall we adjourn?' he said after nodding briefly to Nell.

It was an invitation for her to leave, Nell realized, inexplicably annoyed.

'Miss Drury is involved in this matter too,' Arthur told him mildly. 'Her footprints and fingerprints might well be found as well as mine by your indefatigable gentlemen over there. Left, I should make clear, from our earlier meetings, not last night.'

The inspector looked from one to the other, his face, as usual, impassive, but a steeliness had entered it.

'They were not meetings of mutual passion, Inspector,' Nell told him curtly.

'I note that.'

She was already mishandling this, she realized, but it was too late to draw back. 'We were

201

hoping to help.' She stumbled onwards, but it sounded to her more childish with every word.

'In short,' he commented when she had finished her explanation, 'you saw yourselves as Mrs Christie's Hercule Poirot and Lady Molly of Scotland Yard respectively.'

Her cheeks burned, part in embarrassment and part in anger. 'We might hear details that you would not that might give some clue as to *why* Charles Parkyn-Wright was killed.'

'That's true,' he conceded. 'On the other hand, you could be hindering every step the police make. I need the times and dates that you met in the dairy and to be told of anything that might be relevant for the case. And I need you to stop these activities immediately.'

Anger was winning over embarrassment. 'Relevant to Miss Harlington's death or to Charles Parkyn-Wright's?' she asked.

'Both,' he replied briskly.

'There's more to tell you, Inspector,' Arthur put in. 'We had arranged a meeting here for nine o'clock last night, which we cancelled.'

This time it was the inspector's turn for anger. 'And you tell me only *now*?'

Hold on to your hat, Nell, she told herself, but failed. 'You weren't here earlier and Miss Harlington would not have known it was cancelled.'

He listened grimly and without comment as she told him about the message and Arthur confirmed it. By the time they had finished he looked almost weary of them. 'Miss Drury, would you come with me, please. Mr Fontenoy, I'll call on you later, if I may. I need a statement from you.'

It was only a short walk back to the house but it felt like a mile as she marched like a naughty child beside the inspector through the kitchen garden towards the forecourt. There were roses in bloom on the walls of the kitchen garden and in front of the house. They seemed incongruous in the light of today's news, yet on the Western Front birds had still sung and what trees remained had still struggled to blossom.

'Miss Drury,' he said as they reached the entrance to the house, 'have you ever seen the body of someone who has been strangled?'

Was this some kind of test? 'No. Dead bodies, yes.'

'In a hospital?'

'No,' she said curtly. 'During the Zeppelin raids during the war. There was a terrible bomb dropped in the Strand, you may remember. I was working not far away and went to help – many people were killed there.' She swallowed. 'Do we have to talk about this?'

'No. We could talk about flowers and the beauties of this countryside and how it doesn't seem right that a murdered body should be lying amid all this luxury. Especially hers.'

Much as she had been thinking herself. 'Why especially?' Nell asked, sounding more aggressive than she had intended.

'Wouldn't you agree that Elise Harlington was an exotic hothouse bloom at home in London but out of her depth among these roses and green lawns and fields full of wild flowers or sheep? And Charles Parkyn-Wright too?'

Nell considered this as he led her into the

203

morning room, now once more a place of work, not the comfortable room she was used to. 'Yes, I would agree,' she answered him, 'but nevertheless, Miss Harlington seemed content to stay on here as a guest. She wasn't really his fiancée, you know.'

'I do. We searched her room this morning. She had a supply of cocaine with her. A very large supply. Does that suggest anything to you?'

Nell put her mind to it, although she was puzzled. She had thought she was here for a severe lecture on her activities by the inspector, if not an official arrest. Instead he was talking to her as though she was a human being.

'Only that Mr Parkyn-Wright had just sold her some,' she replied. 'No, that doesn't work, does it? He would want to keep his clients coming back for more so he would sell only a limited amount at a time.'

'I agree. What does work then?' He was watching her keenly, she thought uneasily. Perhaps he was about to arrest her after all.

'That she did some of his work for him?' she suggested, warming to the idea. 'She could have been distributing the drugs for him, maybe to the men, while he looked after the women.'

'Good, but you don't go far enough.'

'Thank you, sir. I'll try harder,' she murmured humbly.

A glimmer of a smile. 'Don't mock me, however tempted you might be, Miss Drury. I might not deserve it. And today I don't need it. I don't enjoy seeing murdered bodies, particularly of young women.'

'I'm sorry,' she said genuinely. She hesitated. 'How far should I have gone to answer your question?'

'I'm sure you'll work it out for yourself. *Yourself* only, please. About the dairy business, though – I'll have to interview Jimmy again. He's already been hauled in front of me once. He's a bright lad.'

'He didn't know what was in the message he delivered for us and I'm sure he wouldn't have bothered to read it. And in giving it to Miss Harlington, he meant no harm.'

'Very few of us do. However, as a result of his not delivering it in person, it's probable that Miss Harlington read it and went there hoping to find – well, who knows what? Yourself and Mr Fontenoy, perhaps, in a clandestine embrace.'

'Just a tottering turnip,' she retorted indignantly. 'Why would we go to a damp dairy when Arthur has a cottage not far away?'

He actually laughed. 'You forget that you thought I might automatically assume that a lovers' tryst was taking place. However, I'm sure that both Miss Harlington and you would have been aware that his tastes do not include ladies, not even you, Miss Drury.'

She calmed down, although she was not sure whether this was a slur or a compliment. 'Miss Harlington must have gone there out of curiosity to see what we were up to.'

'And someone followed her. I'm told she made only a brief appearance at dinner. She died, we think, between nine and eleven o'clock, and your appointment had been for nine. Perhaps she thought you or Mr Fontenoy knew who had killed Parkyn-Wright. At the very best she knew she could embarrass you and tell the Dowager Lady Ansley of your rendezvous with her neighbour, whom I gather she dislikes.'

'An understatement.'

'Or she might have hoped to get you into ill repute with your employers.'

'That's possible,' she frowned. 'But even if someone followed her who would want to kill her? It wasn't me or Arthur.'

He remained silent.

'You can't think that?' she asked in alarm.

'I have to for my job. Facts will emerge from the evidence we've collected from the dairy and will reveal the truth in the end, but meanwhile we have to consider every possibility. My opinion is that the answer lies deeper than with you or Mr Fontenoy, though.' He paused, then began again: 'Miss Drury, I've gone further in speaking to you than I should have done in view of my job and your being a witness in the case. I intend to go even further, however, back to the murder of Charlie Parkyn-Wright and then to your friend, Mr Ellimore.'

She stiffened. 'He couldn't have killed him. I've been thinking about it. Mr Peters would have seen him, heard Mr Charles cry out, seen Guy up there on the gallery.'

He ignored this. 'I thought you might wish to hear this. Despite his earlier denial, William Foster has now admitted that he was talking with Mr Ellimore in the supper room until twelve twenty-five. He then left for the reasons you gave

206

me, and Mr Ellimore's story of joining your group about five minutes later is therefore confirmed. And before you ask whether I think either of them is lying, I do not. Lord Ansley's chauffeur saw Foster leave in a van and we have a witness who remembers seeing Ellimore leave the supper room at the same time as Foster. However, I'd be grateful if you would keep this to yourself.'

'Guy can know, surely,' she said impulsively. 'That's wonderful news. You can't leave him in suspense.'

'*I'll* tell him that his alibi stands up when *I* choose.'

A silence and, knowing she was in the wrong, she made an effort to break it. 'You told me how Miss Harlington had died. Could a woman have killed her? Arthur says it's possible.'

'And he is correct.'

At that moment the door was flung open, Inspector Melbray half rose to his feet and Nell turned abruptly round. It was Lady Clarice but not as Nell was used to seeing her. Today she was flushed and angry, her whole body trembling.

'This,' she announced, ignoring Nell and addressing Inspector Melbray, 'is not good enough.'

'What's disturbing you, Lady Clarice?' he asked.

'It's not something disturbing me that you should worry about. It's my ghosts. When are you going to stop these murders and see justice done? First one, and now I understand there's been another murder and the police are doing nothing, but nothing!'

'We could discuss this later, perhaps—'

'No, we could not. I came here to tell you that

as you appear to be incapable of solving these murders, my ghosts will advise you. I will inform you of where and when.'

Time to step in, Nell thought. 'Lady Clarice,' she said firmly, 'that's very good of you and of your ghosts, but Inspector Melbray needs to get on with his job. He can't wait for the ghosts.'

'You mean well,' Lady Clarice replied, 'but the ghosts won't be long in coming.'

'For what?' the inspector asked, remarkably politely, Nell thought, in view of the provocation.

'Young man,' Lady Clarice explained coldly, 'one murder in the house might be tolerated by my ghosts, but two is too much. Do you realize that there is *silence*? Nothing comes from them at all. It is most peculiar. I believe it means they are planning something quite terrible. They accepted Mr Parkyn-Wright's murder and welcomed him into their number, but this new death is something quite different.'

Nell tried again. 'Miss Harlington died very recently. Perhaps after the funeral she will settle down.'

'It is not as simple as that. I repeat, there is something ominous. They are gathering. We shall see what we shall see, Inspector. The ghosts will settle this matter for themselves.'

'How shall we know the results?' Inspector Melbray enquired, as though this was a routine procedure for a murder case.

'You will know because I shall inform you. But I think it is a matter of days. And please do not say I have not warned you.'

Twelve

'My fate cries out, it seems,' Inspector Melbray remarked wryly as the door closed behind Lady Clarice. 'But Hamlet only had one ghost to cope with and I appear to be facing a whole army. Unfortunately the psychic world doesn't fall within the Scotland Yard criminal procedure training. We are taught to provide more tangible evidence. Do you believe in ghosts, Miss Drury?'

Nell gave her standard reply. 'No one does until they see one.'

'Or sense them, perhaps?'

'There can be an odd atmosphere where a murder has occurred.'

'As here in Wychbourne Court,' he commented. 'Is Lady Clarice a medium or a spiritualist as well?'

'She feels deeply over the people who have lived in this house,' Nell said defensively. 'And that's good, isn't it? It's not the bricks and ragstone but the people she cares about. She doesn't use Ouija boards to commune with the dead, though.' Nell remembered being told that Lord Ansley, in the first wave of grief over the loss of his son Noel, had hoped to contact him by such means, just as Sir Arthur Conan Doyle had tried to reach his own son that way, but there had been no suggestion that Lady Clarice had done so. 'Perhaps Lady Clarice is suffering from the anxiety that everyone here is feeling but it's conveying itself to her as the ghosts becoming upset.'

He looked at her keenly. 'Do you really believe that?'

'I'm sitting on the fence,' she admitted, 'and it isn't very comfortable.'

'I'll join you there. Lady Clarice believes ghosts are gathering because they want to see justice done. Can they tell, do you think, whether the right person is being condemned?'

Could the inspector be serious? Nell tried to see it from his point of view. Making the wrong decision, despite all the legal proceedings that would have to be gone through, could lead to the death of an innocent person. That could well be what was troubling him. 'We can do our best,' she replied, 'but how can we know if it *is* the best? Who judges that, save God?'

'There's only ourselves to do so, Nell.' He reddened. 'My apologies. I should say Miss Drury. We await our ghosts then. They might indicate their displeasure.' He paused. 'Tread carefully, Miss Drury.'

'I will.' Nell felt unexpectedly lighthearted. 'And I'll trust no one.'

'Except me,' he reminded her.

The encounter with Lady Clarice left Nell in a quandary. Should she talk about this threat with Lady Ansley? No, she decided on her way back to the east wing. Ten to one, Lady Clarice would already have forgotten about it and, even if she hadn't, it would probably amount to nothing more than her periodic cry of 'Sir Thomas is abroad'

210

or 'Violet is awake' or whomever she picked on. Nevertheless, she would keep an eye on Lady Clarice to see if the subject arose again. She wondered if she should warn Arthur, however, as he was closest to Lady Clarice. Nell then remembered that she had promised the inspector – she wondered what his Christian name was as he had made free with hers and remembered it was Alexander – not to actively investigate the case with other people. Did the ghosts count as part of the case or not?

'Visitor for you by the yard entrance, Miss Drury,' Mrs Fielding announced disapprovingly on Thursday morning, as though Nell was in the habit of entertaining guests for coffee during working hours.

Who was this? Nell wondered crossly. Mr Fairweather's queries had been settled and the butcher's order had been placed. What else?

It was Guy. Now what was she to do? Her lips had to remain sealed over the matter of his alibi. He didn't look in need of comfort, however. In fact, he looked remarkably cheerful.

'Time for a chat, Nell?'

'Of course. I can chat all day. Lunch and dinner will wait while I do it,' she said, irritated.

'Ah, well, it won't take long. I thought I'd let you know that I'm off the hook. Whoever killed Parkyn-Wright, the police are satisfied it wasn't me.'

The inspector had relented after all. Good. 'Come into Pug's Parlour,' she said, 'and I'll make you coffee after all.'

'*Where?*'

'The butler's pantry. It's an old name for it.'

'That gardener chap, Foster,' he explained, ensconcing himself in the best chair, 'has finally come clean and admitted he was talking to me at the time in the supper room, just as I said. He told the police the reason he hadn't confirmed it earlier too. Not sure what that was, but it's clear I'm not a murderer. Thought you'd like to know.'

'That's good news,' she said. 'Does Lady Warminster know what's happened? Has she sacked him?'

'No idea. He's told the police and that's all I needed.'

That was Guy all over, she thought. Odd how one could after a time still feel an affection for someone but also see the failings one missed the first time. Guy had always put himself not only first, which might be natural enough, but second and third too. And here he was, the same old Guy.

'Are you free to leave Wychbourne? Where are you heading next?'

'Stalisbrook Place. That party's coming up so soon that I won't bother to shift. After that I'll take off, though. Any chance of your coming with me?'

'Chained to my job, Guy,' she told him quickly.

'Doesn't the idea of Paris attract you? Pruniers, the Eiffel Tower, the Folies Bergère . . .'

'One day.'

'You're a stay-at-home by nature.'

'You think Wychbourne Court is my home?' she rejoined. 'Smashing. I'll have some calling cards printed.'

He laughed and clasped her hand in his.

'Seriously, Nell, the offer's open. What a team we would make. You could still be a chef. Why not? We'd hire out our services for every grand ball in London and Paris. Music by Guy Ellimore, cuisine by Nell Drury. And at night we'd be two married turtle doves. Doesn't that appeal?'

He was more persistent than usual. He really meant this, she realized. How to deal with it, though? Keep it light, she thought. 'Guy, there's a time for everything and ours was either in the past or hasn't yet come.'

He was silent for a moment but then he shrugged. 'You always did know the best recipes, Nell. Are you giving evidence at the inquest?'

Inquest? Hopping haddocks, she'd been so preoccupied with ghosts that she had forgotten there would have to be an inquest on Miss Harlington. She had heard no word about it yet. Would her parents come here? There'd been no talk of it so far.

By the time she had persuaded Guy to leave and returned to the kitchen it was once again in turmoil. Instead of everyone quietly getting on with their jobs, they were talking in twos and threes with someone making the occasional quick dash to the scullery or ovens. Rumours were buzzing around like bluebottles and she tackled Kitty to find out what on earth was happening. It turned out that Mr Peters had been interviewed again, as had Mrs Fielding and Miss Checkam too. Even Jimmy had been grilled once more. Where was Miss Checkam, though? She had not appeared in the servants' hall for the whole of yesterday, nor this morning. Lady Ansley had murmured that Miss Checkam was spending a lot of time with Lady Enid but even so she seemed to be keeping out of their way. Typical of the dowager, Nell thought. Power depended on control and the dowager achieved it by maintaining her grip the old-fashioned way – at a distance. So far Nell had had little to do with Lady Enid but she had no doubt that her friendly terms with Arthur had been duly noted.

Once lunch was over and Nell had restored the normal working pattern to the kitchen, her plans were again disrupted when she was summoned by Lady Ansley. What now? she wondered. She had discussed the menus with her this morning, so this must be something new. At least she wasn't being hauled up in front of the inspector again. It was true he was friendlier now, which must surely mean she was off the suspect list – or did it? Perhaps that was one of his techniques – to put people at their ease and then pounce. Nonsense, Nell, she told herself briskly, but she remained uneasy.

When she reached Lady Ansley's room she saw she was not the only visitor. Surprisingly, Mr Beringer was present. No sign of Lady Helen, though. She took the seat Lady Ansley indicated, noting that their eyes were fixed on her in the same way as Guy's had been: as if in her lay some kind of answer. Nonsense, she told herself once more. You're getting above yourself, Nell Drury, thinking you're so important. She was a chef not a magician. As a child she had once seen Maskelyne and Cooke's automaton Psycho, and marvelled at the way it answered the

214

questions thrown at it by the audience. She, alas, was no Psycho.

'We were hoping,' Lady Ansley began, 'that you could tell us what's happening over Elise's death. Gerald is as much in the dark as we are, and you seem to get on so well with the inspector.'

'Me?' Nell squawked in surprise.

'That's what we've heard,' Rex said apologetically.

'I don't get on with him *well*. I've had several grillings from him but he doesn't talk about the investigations. Either of them. He couldn't do so.' She had had to bend the facts a little in view of the Guy episode but it was essentially the truth.

'Even your impressions would be valuable,' Lady Ansley said pleadingly. 'I know you've been doing your best to help.'

Nell thought hard. What could she say? 'He seems to be interviewing everybody again,' she tried, 'which might mean that he believes the two murders are connected, just as I imagine we all do.'

It wasn't much of an offering on her part but at least it gave Mr Beringer something to seize upon. 'I told you, Lady Ansley,' he said, 'this is all about drugs. I'm sure of that. Charlie supplied them and Elise was a client.'

'That's possible,' Nell said diplomatically. Mr Beringer's contribution merely took them right back to the beginning but perhaps, it occurred to her, that's just what he meant to do. Was he clinging to this explanation for reasons of his own? Arthur had passed on the suspicion that he might have secrets in his past.

'Look what he did to Helen,' Rex continued.

215

'Helen thought the world of that rotter but all he wanted to do was to sell her dope. Thank heavens he was caught before it was too late for her. Elise was a victim too, of course,' he added, rather too hastily in Nell's view. Rex was very definitely eager to push the drugs angle but how would guarding Miss Harlington's reputation help that? He wasn't suggesting that she was a confidante of Mr Charles's – far from it.

'The evidence they gathered after her death has to go to scientists to be examined, just as they did with Mr Charles's,' Nell pointed out. 'That takes time.'

'What evidence?' he shot back at her sharply.

'The usual,' Nell said firmly, crossing her fingers that she wasn't talking rubbish. 'Footprints and collecting items. Scientists can detect all sorts of things from hairs and bits of fluff and so on.'

'Did they do that for Charlie's death?' Rex demanded.

'They must have done.' Nell was feeling more and more like little Jack Horner, trapped into a corner, but in her case there would be no plums to pull out of the Christmas pie.

'How much longer do you think this will go on?' Lady Ansley asked. 'My husband tells me the inquest on Elise was adjourned for two weeks and that Elise's family is holding the funeral at their Hampshire home. Although that's natural, I feel we are pariahs here in Wychbourne.' She made an obvious attempt at humour. 'We are a house of ill repute, it seems.'

'That will pass,' Nell said stoutly. She hesitated but decided she should warn Lady Ansley about

216

the ghosts in case this was the first she had heard of it. 'Lady Clarice,' she began, 'feels that the ghosts are gathering in discontent.'

Lady Ansley sighed. 'That's only to be expected of her.'

'She has told Inspector Melbray that the ghosts will appear together shortly to indicate their displeasure at the police's progress.'

'They didn't appear when Charlie died,' Rex pointed out.

'This is bad news, Nell,' Lady Ansley said seriously. 'Clarice is of course eccentric in her views about our so-called ghosts, yet there's something about this house that gives some weight to her beliefs. It's warm and welcoming most of the time, a house of love, but occasion-ally it feels like it's giving itself a shake, as if all those people in the portraits looking down on us have come together and decided something was amiss.' She glanced at them and smiled. 'You must think I'm dotty too, Rex,' she continued. 'Even you, Nell.'

'You're not,' Nell assured her. 'I felt it when I first came here. I put it down to the way Monsieur Antoine behaved as chef and, indeed, that might have had something to do with it. It seemed a house at war with itself, as if the old house resented the two newer wings. Perhaps it's for a different reason now but perhaps something is wrong and we're all fastening on to the police investigation as the cause.'

'No, houses take their cue from people,' Rex replied. 'You said so yourself, Miss Drury. They don't have a separate life of their own. If there's an odd feeling about the house, it's picking it up from us and, when we're at peace again, so will it.'

'And that can't happen until the person who committed these murders is found,' Lady Ansley said despairingly.

What on earth was wrong now? Nell thought. Yesterday had been bad enough with unexpected visitors and Lady Ansley's distress but Friday was boding no better. Nell had returned from the daily menu discussion to find that there seemed to have been a strike in the kitchen for no one was working. No one was attending the ovens and the entire kitchen staff was clustered at the kitchen table, regardless of the clock ticking by towards the time for lunch. The reason quickly became clear. Mrs Fielding was crying bitterly with Mrs Squires's arm round her. The faces of the rest of the servants looked stricken.

'What's wrong?' Nell asked in alarm.

For once, Mrs Fielding forgot Nell was the enemy.

'It's Freddie,' she sobbed. 'They've gone and taken him off. Dragged him out. Arrested him for murder.'

Mr Peters? Nell couldn't believe it. There must be a mistake. Mr Peters couldn't have anything to do with high society drugs. Then she remembered her blackmail theory and that it seemed to her that he might have a secret, perhaps dating back to his wartime years. Moreover, he had been talking to Mr Charles in the supper room and he had had the opportunity to have killed him. For about twenty or more minutes, she thought in growing dismay, Mr Peters had been the sole person on guard in the great hall while Mr Charles was upstairs, with the dagger and the dark photographer's cloth within his reach to shield him from blood. But that was theory and she couldn't believe it had actually happened that way.

There had been no hint while she had been with the inspector to suggest he was on the point of arresting someone. It was true he had talked generally of the responsibility of possibly arresting the wrong person, so did that mean Mr Peters was already in his sights, now that Guy was in the clear?

She couldn't plead with the inspector for more information or discuss it with Arthur because she had been forbidden to carry out any more detective work. It occurred to her, however, that the inspector had specified not conferring with other people. Even Inspector Melbray couldn't stop her conferring with herself.

She gathered from Kitty that Mr Peters had been taken to Sevenoaks police station, and when she went into the great hall there was no sign of the police in the morning room. The east wing butler's room would be empty today, she thought, with Mr Peters gone and Mrs Fielding indisposed. Right, she decided, I'll confer with myself there instead of lunching in the servants' hall. She gathered a tray of food for herself and took it to this chosen refuge, but it wasn't empty after all. Miss Checkam was there, and it looked to Nell's practised eye as though she wanted to talk.

219

'Have you heard?' Miss Checkam asked anxiously the moment Nell put the tray down.

'I've heard a lot of things.' She tried to look encouraging. After all, she had wanted to talk to Miss Checkam. 'Do you mean the news about Mr Peters?'

'Yes. I just can't believe he would murder two people. He went through the war and that should be enough, although I suppose they got used to seeing death.'

Nell decided not to take her up on this argument. It was the other way round in her view. Men who had been through the war had, like Guy, indeed seen enough of death, too much for them to want to see any more. Instead, she murmured something sympathetically.

'Madam would like to see you,' Miss Checkam said diffidently. 'Lady Enid.'

'What about?' Alarm bells went off like rockets. Arthur had mentioned that the dragon was waking and it seemed she had. 'Mr Peters?'

'I think about the murders in general.'

Not again. 'I know no more about what the police are doing than anyone else,' Nell replied carefully.

'Everyone seems to think you do and that you see it from all sides.'

Useless to fight this, Nell thought, and Miss Checkam had been through so much with Charlie that she couldn't turn her back on her. Miss Checkam wanted help and there must be a reason for that. She braced herself to tackle the problem. 'If you're afraid the police might suspect you because of your friendship with Mr Charles, you're wrong. They can't do that because Mr Peters was there all the time that Mr Charles was probably murdered. He would have seen you or anyone else on the gallery.'

'Someone did it,' Miss Checkam muttered. 'If Mr Peters was there it must have been him that killed Mr Charles – and that's why they've arrested him.'

'They would have to have other evidence too.'

Miss Checkam grasped at this eagerly. 'You're right. The police must be certain he did it.'

Were they, though? Nell wondered, recalling Inspector Melbray's strange question. *Was* he convinced that Mr Peters was guilty? Meanwhile, the dowager was demanding her presence. 'When does Lady Enid want to see me?' she asked in resignation.

'Three o'clock.'

Super. Just when she should be beginning dinner preparations.

'I have,' the dowager informed Nell an hour later when she arrived promptly at the Dower House, 'maintained silence over these terrible events at Wychbourne. However, the time has now come for me to intervene.'

With her old-fashioned long skirts and hairstyle she looked as formidable as Queen Mary, Nell thought. She had great presence and an implacable air of being right about everything. Nell liked this house with its Jacobean grandeur, and Lady Enid was a splendid chatelaine for its stateliness.

'I'm told,' the dowager continued, 'that you know a great deal about what is going on here.'

221

For the umpteenth time, Nell denied it. 'Far less than Lord and Lady Ansley.'

'Of that I cannot say, but you have the advantage of having an ear to the ground in the servants' hall as well as among my family.'

'I *am* a servant,' Nell pointed out uneasily, hoping she wasn't expected to relay gossip.

'Some might regard you in that way. I do not. I have a high opinion of your intelligence.'

Buttered bananas, what was this all about? 'Thank you,' Nell murmured.

'My views of this outrageous situation are these,' Lady Enid swept on, 'and I should be glad to know if you are of the same opinion. Firstly, I wish you to understand that these rumours of drugs are ridiculous. My granddaughter was merely indisposed for a few days. If Charles Parkyn-Wright took pain relief for some ailment, that is or was his own affair.'

Nell knew she would be falling at the first fence, but she had no choice. 'I can't share that view, but I can respect it.' She mentally crossed her fingers.

'Very well.' The dowager's shrewd eyes fastened on her. 'We differ. Next, Elise Harlington, poor, unfortunate girl. She knew who had killed Charles and was brave enough to confront the murderer. Do you agree?'

'That is a possibility,' Nell said, relieved to be able to agree with her up to a point.

'Next, Miss Drury. If we accept that there were no illicit drugs in use, there must be other reasons for either or both these deaths. Melodramatic as it sounds, I suggest blackmail.'

222

Nell's opinion of Lady Enid shot up. 'I agree.'

'Blackmail of whom is the question. May we assume that Charles was the blackmailer himself and not a victim threatening to spill the beans, as I believe the American phrase goes?'

'Yes, I agree,' Nell said weakly. The dowager was in full Boadicea mood now.

'Then we must ask ourselves whom he black-mailed. I have to tell you that Miss Checkam was one victim, although in a modest way. It appears from what she tells me that Charles made advances to her, to which she was foolish enough to respond. She tells me he threatened to inform Lady Ansley of their liaison which would, in a household of such good reputation as Wychbourne Court, have brought about her dismissal. Murder, however, would be an inappropriate method of dealing with that problem.'

'Yes,' Nell agreed again, but fear of dismissal must surely be outdated in this day and age. 'Although it could be that—'

She was mightily relieved that she had no time to finish the sentence: that Mr Charles had been killed by Miss Checkam in the passion of her rejection by him.

'Then there is Peters,' the dowager interrupted, 'now arrested, I gather. There was some story about his war career. You are young but you will discover that unfortunate episodes are apt to reappear in one's life – the wheel turns remark-ably accurately at times. The same is true of a gentleman I do not care to discuss – my neigh-bour, Mr Fontenoy. My late husband was prepared to overlook his foibles. I am not. It has not

223

escaped my notice that you, too, tolerate such modes of life.'

'There may be other victims too,' Nell said quickly. 'Others who have past lives they prefer to forget.'

'You have courage, Miss Drury. To you the possibility of murder caused by a long-buried past might seem remote. When you are older you will realize that the past is but yesterday. There remains, unless I include my own family, Mr Rex Beringer.'

'And Lady Warminster,' Nell put in.

'Ah, yes. I have heard tales and no doubt Charles also heard them. Lounge lizards – I believe that is the current word for such paramours – are all the thing, but spooning with one's gardener is quite another. I am acquainted with General Warminster and have little doubt of his reaction should I wish to cause trouble. Mr Beringer, however, is a different matter. I do not doubt that he is extremely fond of Helen but I have, like that odious playwright's Lady Bracknell, been unable to discover anything of his heritage. I do not consider Mr Beringer was placed in a handbag and left at Victoria Station, but nevertheless were something similar the case it would undoubtedly impinge on his career and his suitability as a husband for my granddaughter.'

'Surely Lady Helen would not—'

The dowager raised her hand. 'Quite. But Mr Beringer would not wish to place himself in the position of someone, shall we say, moving up in life, a factor on which Charles might have swooped.'

224

Nell gulped. 'Why are you telling me this, Lady Enid?'

'My daughter-in-law, Lady Ansley, tells me you are on good terms with the inspector and that you are discreet. You may wish to make use of my thoughts to him. If Peters is guilty of murder they will be of no use and you may forget them. If not, they might be invaluable. And, Miss Drury, if you have any jars of that delightful rose petal preserve, I should be delighted to receive some.'

Typical, Nell thought. The preserves came from Mrs Fielding's still-room.

Thirteen

Today would be Armageddon, Nell vowed as she wrenched her dress over her head and prepared to face the day before her. It seemed to her that Wychbourne Court grew daily more divided. Every house had its secrets, as did every family and every person, but there came a point at which they had to shake them off and heal the wounds. That point, she decided, was now. It was Monday morning, 13 July, over three weeks since this nightmare had begun. The police would be concentrating solely on proving Mr Peters was guilty and she had to do what she could to find out if they were right.

Brave words, but could she do it? Well, you never knew whether a new recipe would work until you tried it. Now that Lady Enid also seemed to think Nell had some magic powers enabling her to whisk all the ingredients into an acceptable dish, she couldn't bury her head in the sand. Inspector Melbray might regard her as a squashed tomato where detective work was concerned but even squashed tomatoes have their uses.

Nell made a face at her reflection in the mirror. Her face cream hadn't managed to turn her into the bewitching beauty the advertisement had promised, nor did her curly brown hair lend itself to the obligatory sleekness demanded by the fashion magazines. She just had to work within

226

her own limitations, squashed tomato or not. After all, Dumas, the great French novelist and cook, had not been deterred by limitations. He had bragged about the day his wife had sacked all three of their cooks within hours of a host of friends arriving at his home for a grand dinner. The larder proved to be bare, except for a large stock of rice and tomatoes. With these two ingredients Dumas had concocted a marvellous dish which had his friends rapt in admiration (admittedly with the help of good wine to accompany it). That's what you should do when you were driven into a corner, although she doubted whether the diners at Wychbourne Court would be enraptured by rice and tomatoes. She could, however, see where working within her limitations on the murder investigations would take her.

With Mr Peters absent, it seemed wrong to be asking people to gather in the butler's room that lunchtime, but there was no alternative as it was the only place that Mr Briggs would feel comfortable. He was now sitting there with a pleased smile on his face.

'I can't think what you want to talk about, Miss Drury,' Mrs Fielding complained.

'It is inconvenient,' Miss Checkam chimed in. 'I was about to begin Lady Ansley's ironing.'

'It's about Mr Peters. Do you want him to stay in prison if there's any chance we can help free him?' Nell asked mildly.

'No.' Mr Briggs shook his head vigorously.

Nell was startled by his rapid response. It was

227

so firm that it might be he knew something he hadn't yet told them.

'What can you do about it, Mr Briggs?' Mrs Fielding snarled.

'What *we* can do is more the point,' Nell replied. She had been ready for this attitude. 'We don't know what evidence the police have against him, but part of it must be that it looks as if he was the only person who could have killed Mr Charles. He was alone in the great hall for about twenty-five minutes between twelve and twelve thirty, which means he must have seen who killed him or committed the crime himself. He would have spoken out if he'd seen anyone else.'

Mr Briggs looked alarmed. 'No,' he cried. 'Not there.'

'What do you mean?' Mrs Fielding snapped. 'Of course he was there.'

'Kissing you in the cellar room.'

A red flush slowly spread over Mrs Fielding's face. 'Load of nonsense,' she said. 'Really, Mr Briggs, you should be careful what you're saying.'

Mr Briggs looked puzzled. 'Going to see the barn owls. Saw you through the window.'

Nell held her breath. 'Can you be sure of the time, Mr Briggs, and that it was that evening?' He could indeed have taken a route along the pebbled gap between the main building and the east wing. The cellar room, on the ground floor but close to the basement cellar entrance, was at the end of a row of china and other storage cupboards lining the corridor that ran alongside the wall of the great hall – and only a few yards from where Mr Peters had been on duty that evening. The small room was used as a staging post for small quantities of the required wine as it came up from the basement. That Saturday evening it seemed to have had a more interesting purpose.

There was a dead silence in the room. Nell could hear Mrs Fielding's heavy breathing as she watched Mr Briggs's bewilderment. Then he fumbled in his jacket pocket and took out a battered leather-covered notebook.

'Diary,' he said proudly, turning the pages, found the one he wanted and thrust it under Nell's nose.

There it was in Mr Briggs's all but indecipherable handwriting under *Saturday, 20th June.* 'Quarter past midnight. Went to castle. Saw Mrs Fielding and Mr Peters and Albert.'

'Is Albert one of your owls, Mr Briggs?' she asked quietly.

'Yes. Mr Ball, VC.'

The flying hero during the war who'd won the Victoria Cross. An appropriate name for a swift-flying hunting bird. Nell had no doubt that Mr Briggs had indeed seen Mr Peters and Mrs Fielding together in that room, but it might need more than this diary to convince Inspector Melbray.

She took a deep breath. 'Mrs Fielding?'

Silence. Where to go now? Nell thought despairingly. Then it was broken so suddenly that she jumped.

'He's right,' Mrs Fielding blurted out. 'Mr Peters was with me. We were having a quiet word together, just as Mr Briggs said. He went back

229

into the hall just before you all returned at half past twelve.'

'Didn't you tell the police about that?' Nell asked incredulously.

'I never thought,' Mrs Fielding moaned. 'They never asked me about Mr Peters, just about what I was doing and seeing as how most of the time I was in the still-room, that's what I told them.'

'Why did Mr Peters keep quiet about it?' Miss Checkam asked. 'It's his alibi.'

'He's a gentleman,' Mrs Fielding sniffed. 'I suppose he didn't like to say. It was that dance in the servants' hall,' she added with obvious reluctance. 'He couldn't get away for it, and he liked a bit of a dance, so when I popped into the hall to see how he was getting on with all that ghost stuff, he said to me, "Let's have our own dance in the cellar room. They won't be back for twenty minutes or more".'

There wouldn't be space in the cellar room for much of a dance, save perhaps a bunny hug, Nell thought, repressing an image of Mr Peters and Mrs Fielding employed in a spirited Black Bottom together. It seemed more likely to have been a kiss and a cuddle.

Mrs Fielding began to weep. 'Is that why my Freddie's in prison? I thought it was earlier that gentleman was killed. Before you all came trooping in.'

'I don't know,' Nell said gently, 'but it's certainly going to help if you tell the police where you were. If he was with you, not only could he not have murdered Mr Charles but anyone who knew he was in that cupboard could have got up there unseen.'

Mrs Fielding began to reclaim her usual self. 'What about you, Miss Checkam?' she asked. 'Where were you?'

'You said you were at the servants' hall dance,' Nell said, as Miss Checkam seemed reluctant to reply, 'and then went to bed.'

'To my bedroom,' she amended, 'not to bed.'

Mr Briggs looked eager to help again. 'I saw you too,' he said, and Miss Checkam went very pink. 'With that bad gentleman who attacked Polly.'

Miss Checkam stiffened. 'That was *before* Mr Charles went up to the gallery. We just passed a few words.'

'That's what *you* say,' Mrs Fielding snorted.

'Tell us, Miss Checkam, please,' Nell pleaded. 'We need to get this straight for Mr Peters' sake.'

Miss Checkam looked mutinous. 'I was upset,' she said unwillingly. 'I was in my bedroom but I had to lay out Lady Ansley's night attire. When I was on my way to the grand staircase I saw Mr Charles about to go up the stairs to the gallery. I wanted to talk to him but he wasn't very pleased to be stopped. He was very rude, so I went away. I'd forgotten all about meeting him since nothing happened. Mr Peters was still in the great hall so he would have seen me if I had come in to take the dagger. But I told you – all this was *before* he was killed.'

'It's still relevant,' Nell said firmly, 'and you should both tell the police.'

Mrs Fielding swung in again. 'Miss Drury's

right. I can't have my Freddie hanged for something he never did, the darling man.'

It was a start, Nell thought, no matter if she had broken her word to Inspector Melbray that she wouldn't go foraging for information. After all, this had been a mere chat between workmates and they hadn't even mentioned Miss Harlington's death. Could Mr Peters have been involved in that? Suppose he had killed Mr Charles and Miss Harlington knew that? The key must lie in Mr Charles's death. Nell had a moment's doubt – but if she listened to all the doubts in her mind she would never get anywhere.

Forward then: Lord Richard, she reasoned, had no strong motive for killing Mr Charles, despite his jealousy of him. Anyway, he couldn't have killed him without his sisters seeing him leave the group. With Mr Peters spooning in the cellar room, however, any of the group might well have slipped away and killed Mr Charles. Poor Lady Helen was in no state to kill anyone, though, and Lady Sophy had no reason to do so, which left Mr Beringer and Lady Warminster. And Arthur? Nell forced herself to consider. Would his sangfroid stretch to killing Charlie? He had chosen to join her group *after* the change-over. Where had he been before that? Guy now had an alibi, otherwise he would have been in the same position.

Nell sighed. It was all very well for the likes of Sherlock Holmes to tread on the toes of Scotland Yard but she knew the dangers of *her* stepping on the inspector's investigative feet.

It occurred to her that every morning Arthur

232

set off for his morning stroll to the village at about midday, and if she bumped into him by chance she could hardly be blamed for their having a casual conversation, no matter what the subject.

'My dear Nell, what a pleasure.' Arthur swept off his Panama hat. 'Do pray join me if your time permits on this delightful morning. We might take a glass of cider at the Coach and Horses.'

'That would be delightful,' she agreed solemnly.

'I'm most perturbed to hear that Peters has been arrested,' he said as they strolled down the drive to the inn.

'Wrongly, I'm sure,' Nell said stoutly. 'He has an alibi but seems not to have taken advantage of it.'

'Unfortunate, but gentlemen will be gentlemen if a lady is involved. I take it that is the case?'

She laughed. 'It is.'

'Or indeed if another gentleman is involved,' he continued. 'We have our own code, but I doubt if Lady Enid would approve. I'm surprised that she has not tried to fix the blame on me for killing Charlie or the beautiful Elise. She does have a nose for old scandals. I'm sure if you have spoken to her, she has remembered mine.'

'She didn't mention it, even if she knew, and of course—'

'You don't want to know?' His turn to laugh. 'You do, Nell, and I've no objection to telling you or anyone else, come to that, save our police, of course. It is a sad story. It preceded my friendship with Lady Enid's husband, Hugo, the present

233

Lord Ansley's father. A young man, the son of a well-known family, who was very dear to me. He killed himself when our liaison became as public as the law permits, and his parents discovered his preferences. He was my first love, and first love runs deep. It is never forgotten but lies in a guarded portion of one's heart. It does *not* emerge nearly sixty years later and result in murder. It is true, however, that dear Elise murmured in my ear that I might not like the Ansley family or anyone else to know of my inclinations.'

'What did you tell her?' First love, Nell reflected. Was Guy hers or was her first love the boy on the oyster stall at Spitalfields who had seemed so Godlike to a humble girl of twelve?

'That everyone I care about already knows and that those I don't wouldn't be interested. She suggested the police would be. I suggested that she find proof. As both of my loves are, alas, dead and I have not, as did Mr Oscar Wilde, lived an indiscreet life, there is no proof available, merely gossip and rumour and tittle-tattle. Elise was most disappointed, I fear, especially when I informed her that Charlie had made similar threats to no effect.'

'Thank you, Arthur,' Nell said. Putting aside having to consider whether he could have played a part in Mr Charles's death, her liking for him grew. It must have taken courage to tell her that sad story of love. True, he might have calculated that the story would become public knowledge at any moment, but she overruled that angle. That was her privilege and one Inspector Melbray was unable to claim.

'Lady Enid also mentioned Mr Beringer,' Nell continued as they seated themselves outside the Coach and Horses with their cider. What a contrast between this peaceful scene before them and the subject that had brought them here.

'Dear Rex, ah, yes.'

'She told me his heritage was hard to trace. I presume that implied he was either an imposter or' – she intoned solemnly – 'presuming to a station in life to which he was not born. But that can't be a matter for blackmail, surely?'

'He wishes to marry Helen, my dear.'

'Even if the Ansleys did not approve, they would never stand in the way of her happiness. Lady Enid, however, thought that Mr Beringer might not wish it to seem as though he was courting money. Is that reason for blackmail?'

'Charlie Parkyn-Wright would doubtless have said that it was. Elise, also. Nell, I happen to know Rex's heritage thanks to a conversation I had with Charlie's parents at the inquest. They know Rex – or did once. He is the son of a local gamekeeper in Derbyshire and is extremely intelligent. Thanks to his father's wealthy employer he was able to study at Oxford and he has since done well in the Colonial Service. He is far from poor but has hardly enough to support Lady Helen in the style to which she has become accustomed.'

'That's a good story, though,' Nell said stoutly.

'For you, yes. Some see it differently.'

'Does he deliberately conceal it?'

'No. It is merely that it never emerges. I don't doubt that Charlie tried to blackmail him, however.

What else troubles you, Nell? I can see that something is on your mind.'

Nell smiled. 'Apart from Mr Peters, ghosts are. Has Lady Clarice told you that she believes her ghosts are gathering for a united battlefront against the police?'

'She has, although not in those words. She has told me at great length. If Peters is charged with murder, however, they will have no cause to gather. Justice will have been served.'

'But if he isn't?'

'Then I fear she is serious.'

'What does she think will actually happen?'

'Of that, not yet being a ghost, I have no prior knowledge.'

She might find out all too soon, Nell discovered on her return to Wychbourne Court. There had been a special request from Lady Clarice that she would like tea served in the Blue Drawing Room that afternoon and that Nell might care to take tea with her.

When she arrived, Lady Clarice was sitting by the window overlooking the drive and forecourt and scribbling furiously in a notebook. She looked so thin that Nell wondered where all the cream went. Lady Clarice had a weakness for chocolate cake and French *crème anglaise*.

'I have been making plans for the ghosts,' she explained, waving a hand for Nell to sit opposite her.

'Do they permit you to do that?' Nell asked seriously.

'In certain circumstances, yes, such as the

236

events that have overtaken this household. I do not believe that Peters could have committed these murders, and therefore I have decided to make plans now. I would be glad of your coop-eration. The suitable places for the gathering are only two in number: one is the great hall and the other is the chapel.'

'The chapel is in the newest part of the house,' Nell pointed out. 'Would the older ghosts travel there?'

'That is the new chapel,' Lady Clarice said. 'I talk of the old one. Although that is no longer holy ground its former use might prejudice the results. At least one murderer will be present, albeit penitent.'

Nell was confused. 'The murderer of Mr Charles and Miss Harlington?'

Lady Clarice looked irritated. 'The murderers among the *ghosts*, Nell. I believe they will choose the great hall, however, which means that Charlie, at least, will join them.'

'Who will be coming? I mean,' Nell added hastily, 'among their audience.'

'Everyone involved in this terrible affair. The police, of course. I'm also informing my brother, since it's his house, and you, Nell, should inform anyone you feel should be present. I've no objec-tion to the presence of servants, even gardeners, if they are relevant to the purpose.'

'When do you expect it to happen?' Nell had been peering out of the window at some new arrivals in the forecourt.

'The ghosts will tell me in due course. We need to know about Peters first.'

'Then we will know soon.' Unexpectedly, Nell was full of hope. 'He's walking across the forecourt.'

But so, she saw, were the police. Inspector Melbray and his sergeant had just stepped out of the van.

'Released without charge.' Mr Peters sat down in the servants' hall looking very tired to Nell's concerned eyes, and all the kitchen staff were crowded around him, together with Miss Checkam. Mrs Fielding stood proudly at his side. 'Thanks to Mrs Fielding, here,' he added, 'and to Miss Checkam.'

'We told them, didn't we, Miss Checkam?' Mrs Fielding boasted, pressing a cup of tea on him. 'Why ever did they think it was you in the first place?'

'All a mistake,' Mr Peters said delicately.

'Why would you want to kill him, though?' Mrs Fielding was getting into her stride now. 'They're daft. All them coppers. And to think we pay their wages. Arresting good people like you and letting murderers go free. I don't know what the world's coming to.'

'It won't be coming to much harm with people like you around,' Mr Peters said valiantly.

A mistake? Nell pondered that. There must have been more evidence against him than his lack of an alibi. Was Mr Charles blackmailing him? Very possibly. But there must be more to it.

Nell skipped back to the theory that Miss Harlington knew who had killed Mr Charles. *How* could she have known? Answer: she was in the

238

first group on the ghost hunt and noticed someone had slipped away or did she merely deduce who had killed him? She had been dancing with Mr Charles non-stop that evening. If blackmail was the root cause of his murder and she, as well as he, had been gathering gossip, then that could have provided the reason for her murder. She knew Mr Charles's clients, she moved in the right circles, and she was a determined and beautiful woman.

Hold on, Nell, she warned herself. Where are you going with this?

Evidence. The police had been looking for evidence in Elise's room. Of what, though? Of who had killed her? Of drugs? Yes, but what about the blackmail angle? Assuming that Mr Charles and Miss Harlington were in that racket together, how did that affect the drugs issue? Why did Miss Harlington have a *large* supply in her room and Mr Charles did not? She recalled that the inspector had asked her whether that suggested anything to her and when she answered he had told her she hadn't gone far enough. Very well, she'd go further. Could it be that she and perhaps the police too had been seeing it the wrong way round? That Miss Harlington was the blackmailer-in-chief and the dealer too?

Excitement began to well up inside her. Suppose Mr Charles was as much a victim as they had thought Miss Harlington to be, and that he was under her control? Wouldn't that work? Inspector Melbray had said that in the drugs scandal of 1922, Chan's clients were mainly high-class women, not men. Why shouldn't they be dealers too?

'Miss Drury, what brings you here?' Inspector Melbray looked trapped when she invaded his sanctum in the morning room on Wednesday morning. 'Is this about Frederick Peters?'

'No. Well, yes. I'm glad he's not guilty.'

'Not quite accurate. We haven't enough evidence to charge him now that Mrs Fielding's evidence, true or false, has to be taken into the equation.'

He must have taken note of her surprise. 'I'm being remarkably frank but I believe it's time to be so. I understood that you were behind the two ladies coming forward with their stories. Thank you, but what are you here for now?' His stern expression almost persuaded her it might be wiser to flee the room. He clearly was not in the mood for discussion.

'I have a theory—' She broke off, seeing his face change, but then braced herself. 'I shall tell you what it is and you can judge whether it's true or false. It might be a line that you're working on anyway.'

'Go ahead,' he said stonily.

'Miss Harlington might have been the drug dealer and the blackmailer, not Mr Parkyn-Wright. You told me that Chan's clients were women.'

His expression was unreadable. 'Brilliant Chan, he was called,' he said absently. 'He smuggled the stuff out of Germany through Holland. It wasn't illegal in Germany. I believe Chan did

240

have some women dealers.' He didn't seem over-whelmed by her contribution.

'And the blackmail?' she persevered.

'She could well have been Parkyn-Wright's partner in that,' he agreed – grudgingly, it seemed to her.

'What about her being the driving force in that too?' she said obstinately.

He looked at her steadily. 'I'll consider that. She could have taken over after his death.'

Silence. 'I had to tell you, anyway,' she said inanely.

Still silence. Then at last: 'Diaries,' he said after a while. 'We keep them, you know. Every day. It's the Scotland Yard rule. We write down everything that has happened to us that day, and on the same day, not later. We write down our expenses too. They're checked every week. It's a good system. That's why I can give precise evidence in court. Elise Harlington kept a diary too. She died roughly between nine and ten o'clock and we found the diary when we searched her room in the morning. It was well hidden. It looked like a leather-bound Bible until we opened it and found it was a wooden box with a diary inside. Charlie Parkyn-Wright didn't keep a diary, or at least didn't have one among his possessions. Her diary had all the details of the clients, all the gossip which could have come in handy. We thought that meant she was his secretary, Miss Drury, but the world is changing. Perhaps you're right. I'll consider what you've said.

'And now,' he continued, 'I'll tell you why we

241

arrested Peters. In confidence, of course. We suspected, and now we know, that his evidence about his whereabouts that night was false. We also checked his past record, particularly during the war. Checking records is all part of our job. Dull work, mostly, unless you come across something interesting. This case has proved far from dull in one or two instances. War records are seldom checked in later life. A private can call himself a colonel and no one will doubt it if he behaves like a colonel. In Peters' case, he had been in a military court on charges of theft. It was noted that there had been too many queries over missing items among the possessions of the fallen for it to go uninvestigated. It was traced to Frederick Peters. Major Noel Ansley saved his bacon and Peters has never put a foot wrong since. When Noel Ansley was killed, the service warned Lord Ansley, and it could be that his sons know the truth as well. Nevertheless, Peters is a reformed man now. A powerful motive for killing Charles Parkyn-Wright if he, working – as you would have it – with Elise Harlington, discovered Peters' background.'

'Not if Lord Ansley already knew the story,' Nell pointed out.

'Peters wasn't aware that Lord Ansley knew, so his motive remains. Motive, opportunity, means. That's why we arrested him.'

'Did Miss Harlington's diary have more victims in it, other than Mr Peters?'

He remained silent. Capering carrots, she'd gone too far. 'I know about Mr Beringer,' she blurted out, 'and probably Miss Checkam and Lady Warminster.'

'Ah.' He managed a smile. 'Lady Warminster. You told me you were to be the chef at the party on Saturday.'

'Will you be there?'

'She has been kind enough to invite me, so yes. As to whether she was in Miss Harlington's diary, you probably already know the story and there is no need for me to tell you.'

Checkmated. She longed to ask if the Ansleys were in the clear but managed to refrain. Instead, she asked mildly, 'Where do your investigations go now?'

'Officially, we carry on interviewing, digging away like archaeologists. Some day we'll find our Troy.'

'And unofficially?'

'I'll consult the ghosts on what we do then.'

Fourteen

Nothing so simple, nothing so glorious as the menus she had suggested to Lady Warminster, Nell thought wistfully. French cuisine was mandatory for Her Ladyship. Nell's own ideas had been for the most exquisite dishes yet devised by man – or woman – but haute cuisine to Lady Warminster went no further than price and name, alas. Faced with the dilemma of whether the garnish should be the true black truffle of the Périgord or the more expensive artificially produced one, the taste came second, as it had with Nell's Kentish cherry wine jelly, which had been replaced with a more showy *pêches à l'Aurore*. Nevertheless, Monsieur Escoffier would have been proud of her, Nell thought. He too believed in simplicity, and by dint of her assuring Lady Warminster that this or that dish was a favourite of his she had ended up with a compromise, which remained as French in appearance as Monsieur le President Deschanel or the Comte d'Orleans themselves could desire. Pity they wouldn't be coming.

'What about the ices, Miss Drury?' Kitty asked anxiously. The buffet was to be served at nine p.m. and it was already eight. The party was in full flow and, even from the Stalisbrook kitchen, Nell could hear Guy's band.

'Not yet, Kitty,' she called back. Thank goodness she had been able to bring Kitty and Michel with her, she thought. Mrs Squires would be looking after Lord and Lady Ansley who had deemed it improper for them to be attending a ball after the two recent deaths in their home. Lord Richard, Lady Helen and Lady Sophy were here, however, as was Mr Beringer. Nell was beginning to warm to him. He almost seemed part of the family as he had been a guest for so long. Luckily he was a force for good. He kept Lady Helen calm, he was good company for Lord Richard and even Lady Sophy approved of him. 'He discussed the *Iliad* with me,' she had told Nell in awe. 'He was up at *Oxford*.'

The dowager had declined her invitation but Arthur had murmured that he could not resist. 'Lady Warminster,' he had declared, 'is such a character. I do wonder what her poor husband will make of this merry-go-round. I fear the Charleston, which I understand Her Ladyship has demanded, is not yet known in the wilds of Mesopotamia.'

While sharing Arthur's views on Lady Warminster, Nell had unexpectedly enjoyed working with the kitchen staff at Stalisbrook Place. She had over-come their natural resentment of her intrusion by the simple method of asking their advice from time to time, even pleading for their help. Their interest had increased when Lady Sophy bounced into the kitchen and, to their astonish-ment, instead of demands and complaints they heard her say: 'Can I help, Nell? Oh, please let me.'

Nell had to stifle a laugh. 'Thank you, Lady Sophy,' she replied grandly, 'but I have such excellent assistance from everyone here' – she swept an all-encompassing arm around the kitchen – 'that everything is in hand.'

Lady Sophy understood. 'I can see you have,' she enthused. She looked at the array of dishes on the kitchen table awaiting the footmen who would carry them in. 'It all looks *wonderful*. Do show me the supper room, Nell,' she pleaded. 'I can't wait.'

Nell took the hint, and as soon as they were out of earshot of the kitchen, Lady Sophy announced: 'This place gives me the creeps. It's got the curse of Tutankhamun hanging over it.'

'Just because it's done up like an Aladdin's cave?' Nell asked curiously.

'It's all so artificial. Not like Wychbourne Court. I know that's home but I'm sure guests find it welcoming. Look at those mock lilies and lotuses. Why not give the general a bunch of roses?'

Nell laughed. 'You can take him for a walk in the garden for his roses. Anyway, Mr Escoffier rather liked artificial flowers.'

'It's more than that, Nell. This place is full of money with no heart. It's that woman, of course.'

'Could you possibly mean your hostess?' Nell solemnly enquired.

Lady Sophy giggled. 'Yes. Oh, Nell, if you see William, do tell him I want a dance with him – he'll be too embarrassed to ask me.'

Nell grimaced. Lady Warminster would pass out with shock if she saw the servants joining her precious ball, particularly her beloved gardener. 'Is that fair on William?'

Lady Sophy pouted. 'I suppose not.' Then she brightened up. 'Suppose I clear it with the general? Everyone now knows the story about William coming to the Wychbourne dinner and if the general hasn't heard it, I'll tell him. It would be a scream.'

'On your head be it,' Nell warned her.

'I'm a let's-see-what-happens person. Just like you.'

Nell grinned. 'Bully for you, Lady Sophy. Go ahead if you think you can stand Lady Warminster bearing down on you in full force.'

'The general's word goes, so madame would find it hard to give William the boot now. Anyway, the general's a real sport. She wouldn't moan too much because he might think her majesty had been carrying on with the gardener in his absence.' She glanced at Nell who, caught by surprise, was too late to react innocently. 'Oh ho,' Lady Sophy continued with glee, 'I do believe you've been holding out on me, Nell. *Has* she been getting off with William?'

'Go and ask a policeman,' Nell retorted crossly.

Phew. Thankfully Lady Sophy didn't seem upset at the notion that there might be more to Lady Warminster's relationship with William than had previously occurred to her. That put an end to Nell's fears that Lady Sophy might have a romantic interest in William as well as her seeing him as a guinea pig for her social equality programme.

'It looks grand, Nell.' Guy strolled up to her, clarinet in hand and in evening dress; with his

247

medals prominent, he looked as dashing as the Prince of Wales. She'd just finished her inspection of the buffet table and there was only fifteen minutes to go now. 'All set?' he asked, looking quizzically at the loaded table. 'Does the band get a share of this?'

'Ask the hostess.'

'She's nowhere to be seen. Last spotted dancing decorously with an ancient mariner otherwise known as vice-admiral something or other. Leftovers in the kitchen?' he added hopefully. 'Better than their usual rations, I'd guess.'

'You'll have to wait, Guy,' she said in exasperation. 'Leftovers won't be back in the kitchen for hours.'

'Feed the troops and keep them happy, that's what we reckoned in the officers' mess during the war.' With that Guy seemed prepared to go, but then they were joined by an elderly man of medium height, grey hair and, Nell noted, sharp eyes. His uniform and medals immediately made it clear who he was.

Guy's demeanour changed instantly. 'We met earlier, General. Miss Drury, may I introduce General Warminster, our host. Miss Drury is your chef for the evening, General.'

'An honour, Miss Drury, but one glance at this table would immediately have informed me you were present. I dined frequently at the Carlton during the war and remember you as Mr Escoffier's favourite apprentice there, although I don't believe we ever met. He told me you have a fine line in expressing your feelings.'

Nell laughed. 'Tipsy turtles, fancy your remembering that.'

248

'You're at Wychbourne Court, of course,' General Warminster continued. 'Two murders, I understand. I have sent my condolences to Lord and Lady Ansley. My wife tells me she was there on the night of the first murder. A great pity she was there alone. It was the chauffeur's night off but our under-gardener could have driven her there. It seems he too was otherwise engaged. A gentleman with ambitions in his field, I gather. I'm told that he and Lady Sophy met through their mutual interest in horticulture. Unusual, but we must keep up with the times. Miss Drury, busy though you are, I trust you will keep a dance free for me?'

It was clear, Nell realized, that whether from his wife or from Lady Sophy, General Warminster did know about William's escapade at Wychbourne, if not the full story. Before she could answer his question, though, Lady Warminster appeared out of the blue. She was a vision in bright yellow Arabian trousers and a sleek tunic, glittering in diamonds and looking for all the world as though she were to do a belly dance, save that her dress was decorously covered in the relevant portions of her body. Nell had to admit that she looked spectacular.

'You can't dance with the hired help, darling Tiddles.' Lady Warminster issued a tinkling laugh. 'Really, you can't. That will be all, Miss Drury.'

'Until later, Miss Drury,' the general remarked, apparently oblivious that his wife had spoken.

'That will be *all*,' Lady Warminster snapped.

Not, Nell thought with amusement, if the

general had anything to do with it. Nevertheless, this whole evening had a jarring element. The décor looked like something out of *The Arabian Nights* and, extreme though it was, it was well done. Rich hangings made a tented roof, palm trees stood by the walls and above them photographs from *The Sheik* showed Rudolph Valentino's smouldering eyes surveying the dancing beneath. If only she had been able to provide a buffet drawing on the exotic fruits and spices of the East, with rose water and apricots and aubergines. Back to reality, Nell. It had to be French. And that perhaps was why it jarred. There was no heart in this ball, no warmth. It was merely a statement, a show without substance.

The buffet over, Nell stood in the doorway to the ballroom watching General Warminster. He was wandering affably – and looking rather lost – among his guests as the dancing began again. She could see Lady Helen with Mr Beringer, his arm protectively around her. Arthur was walking over to chat to the general, though what they had in common was hard to imagine. Guy was performing his best with his band and Lady Sophy was cavorting – yes, with William. The person Nell could not see was Inspector Melbray. He must be here, unless he had been joking when he said he was coming. Of course, she had been busy with the buffet and might have missed him.

Then she spotted him. He was hardly recognizable in his dress suit and he was dancing a tango with – what a surprise! – Lady Warminster. It looked to her at first as though he was enjoying it immensely, but as she watched more closely, it dawned on her that every time a turn of direction might suggest a closer embrace with the lady he promptly turned her in a different direction. Was that purposely to annoy Her Ladyship? Nell wondered. Perhaps that was sheer imagination on her part, although why would her imagination be dwelling on such an unimportant point? More interesting, she instructed herself, was that Lady Sophy was still dancing with William Foster. Was that something to applaud? Had Lady Warminster noticed? Nell's attention was diverted when General Warminster came over to her.

'I claim my dance, Miss Drury,' he said. 'A foxtrot, I believe.'

Nell speedily whipped off her apron, glad that she had worn her chiffon dancing frock and not her working clothes.

'Are you interested in motor cars, Miss Drury?' he asked as they danced.

'I have one and very grateful I am for my Austin Seven. Travelling to and fro by horse with banquet food would be most inconvenient.'

'My wife has bought yet another new motor car in my absence,' he reflected. 'It is fortunate we have not merely a chauffeur but a splendid additional driver in our gardener. In fact, I thought I saw Foster dancing with Lady Sophy but he seems to have left the floor. No doubt they will dance again. It seems the episode in which he was involved at Wychbourne Court is quite a talking point. My wife regards it as a splendid joke.'

'It was,' Nell replied on cue. 'And such fun to see them dancing together now.'

251

'It is indeed. I wonder, Miss Drury, if I might talk to you about that night. You might care to see the new motor car.'

'I would indeed.' What else could she say? Where would this lead? Nell wondered, dismayed. Was General Warminster yet another person who thought she had the answer to everything? She tentatively tried a diversionary tactic.

'Inspector Melbray is here, I believe, General. He would be able to tell you more than I can.'

'I've met him. Good fellow. Not an army man but good all the same. He was in the police force during the war. London had it bad at times. But Melbray wasn't at Wychbourne before the murder, nor was he there when the body was found. That's why I wanted to talk to you. It's always my strategy to listen to hear how the campaign went at the time and then I'm ready to judge the results.'

Without more ado he escorted her into the gardens and round to the yard which now boasted motor car garages as well as the horse stables. The guests' cars were parked in front of the house for the evening, and so the Delage together with a Bentley were its sole occupants apart from the incurious horses. The presence of other garages was another testament to Lady Warminster's passion for motor cars.

The general waved a hand at those before him. 'They're the future,' he said. 'The horse's day is done, more's the pity. I was a cavalry man so horses have been good friends of mine, which is more than one can say for lumps of metal like these. Nice looking, though, I grant you. There's Foster now. Here for a cigarette, no doubt.'

Nell looked over and saw William standing with Guy Ellimore in the porch of what must be a rear service entrance.

'My wife has a rule, Miss Drury. No smoking in the house,' General Warminster remarked.

'The guests were smoking in the supper room.'

'Guests,' he said, 'appear to be different. It's servants' smoking that my wife objects to. She doesn't want them dropping ash into anything she might be eating. I beg your pardon,' he added instantly. 'I'm not implying you—'

'I only smoke salmon,' she reassured him.

By the time they reached William and Guy, however, the cigarettes had disappeared.

'Good playing, Ellimore,' the general congratulated him. 'More used to the trumpet myself. Reveille. Play during the war, did you?'

'I was in the air force, sir. Squadron leader.'

'That's the future too,' General Warminster said reflectively. 'Aircraft. The Navy's day is over. Were you playing at Wychbourne Court when the murder took place at the ghost hunt?'

'Yes, sir.'

'And you were there too, Foster, Lady Sophy tells me.'

'Yes, General.' Foster looked more like Douglas Fairbanks than ever, Nell thought, but in his case a very unhappy one, judging by his expression. 'It's not her fault, sir. I agreed to it.'

'Subject's over, Foster. These murders are not, though. Tell me about them, Miss Drury, if you please. You can speak out as both Ellimore and Foster were there.'

Nell took a deep breath and related the story

once again. She noted that General Warminster was concentrating on the first murder, although his wife had been in Wychbourne on the day of Miss Harlington's murder too. It was true she hadn't been at the dinner, though, having left after the reconstruction. She could see the general listening intently to what she had to say, and then he turned to Guy and William.

'You two were talking in the supper room at Wychbourne, so my wife tells me. Poor little woman felt queasy – nothing to do with your food, Miss Drury – and she decided to leave early.'

'I left just before twelve thirty, General,' William said miserably.

'Then I went to join Miss Drury's group,' Guy added.

'And you found the body not long after that.' General Warminster's keen eyes fell on her. 'Why was Parkyn-Wright killed? Wasn't married, was he? Not one of those *crimes passionnels*? I don't hold with that sort of thing. Once you're married, you're married whether you like it nor not. Then there was this other murder two weeks or so later. Was the girl a wife, girlfriend, rejected lover, that sort of thing? We had enough of that going on in the war.'

'They were bad days then, sir,' Guy said. 'Bad for wives and bad for men away at the front.'

'Worse for them,' General Warminster grunted. 'And look at the mess it's left behind. Persia heading for trouble too, despite the Teheran agreement. I commanded in the South Persian Rifles, thought we had it all under control, then along comes that Reza Khan chap and makes himself dictator, throwing the Russians out and us. I've spent the last four years advising the air force in Mesopotamia. Your field, Ellimore. Sorry, Foster, I know Lady Sophy's a fan of the Russians and perhaps you are too, but they're looking for expansion, believe me.'

'They're doing wonderful things there,' Foster said miserably – and in the circumstances foolishly, Nell thought.

'They'll be doing wonderful things wherever they walk into next,' General Warminster said drily. 'Well, goodnight to you. Good car, that Delage,' he added. 'My wife's got an eye for' – Nell thought she detected a pause here – 'motor cars.' He watched as Foster and Guy returned to the house. 'Rum fellow that,' he said to Nell. 'Something odd about him.'

So General Warminster's eye was still on William, whose Douglas Fairbanks looks wouldn't help one little bit if he put a foot wrong again. Nell wondered why the general had been so eager to hear her account of the day of the murder. Was it mere curiosity or did he fear his wife had been involved?

As she entered the supper room again, Mr Beringer greeted her, bowing politely. 'Another triumph, Miss Drury.'

'Is Lady Helen coping with the dance?' she asked him. 'She seems better now.'

'She is. I love Wychbourne but it's time for me to return to London now.'

'After the ghost gathering, I hope,' Nell said.
'The what?'

'You haven't heard? She explained and Mr Beringer looked dismayed.

'I should certainly stay for that then. Helen may need me. Are the police attending?'

'I fear I am.' Inspector Melbray had materialized seemingly from nowhere to answer his question. 'I have been convinced by Lady Clarice that it will speed up the case investigation. The ghosts will assist me, she assures me.' He turned to Nell. 'Miss Drury, may I claim a dance with you?'

Her initial surprise vanished. Why not? 'Later, perhaps?' she suggested. 'I have to finish here first.'

Dancing with the *nice* inspector, Nell Drury – whatever next? she thought.

What came next was the kitchen where Kitty and Michel would be hard at work. The buffet might be over but all too soon it would be time to serve the late supper. As she was passing the servants' hall, however, she saw a very unhappy William Foster sitting at a table, alone, with his head in his hands.

'What's wrong?' she asked tentatively. She couldn't just walk by.

'Everything,' he growled. 'I owned up and told the inspector and General Warminster about how I came to be at Wychbourne Court that Saturday, but now the cops are trying to pin the murder on me.'

'How can they?' Nell asked practically, sitting at his side. 'You left the building at about twelve thirty, to which there is a witness, and before that you were talking to Guy Ellimore. He confirms that.'

'But the blighter was dead by then. From what he said, I reckon that inspector's trying to prove I did him in before you all went up on the gallery.'

'The butler would have seen you.' Nell knew she was plunging into deep water. 'He was in the great hall preparing for the ghost hunt and before that, but in any case we know Charlie was alive until after the hunt began because he groaned – as a joke,' she added hastily.

'He might reckon I could have slipped up there while the groups were changing over. You wouldn't have noticed then if anyone who shouldn't have was nipping up those stairs. Anyway, they think I did it because of all the Hugh Beaumont stuff.'

Nell stared at him, aghast. 'But why would you want to kill Mr Parkyn-Wright? You didn't even know him.'

He flushed. 'He knew about me. Picked up gossip last time he visited about me and Lady Warminster.' He broke off, embarrassed.

'That you are or were friends,' Nell said helpfully.

'Yes, nothing bad,' he said hastily, avoiding her eye, 'but General Warminster wouldn't like it.'

'More importantly, does the inspector know about your friendship?'

'Yes,' he said unhappily.

Nell sighed. 'You're probably worrying for nothing. After all, he can't blame you for murdering Miss Harlington, can he? This house is miles away from Wychbourne Court.'

He looked puzzled. 'But we were there that night she died.'

Nell blinked. 'You couldn't have been. You came to the inquest and reconstruction earlier in the day but Lady Warminster left before dinner.'

From a Douglas Fairbanks about to sweep her off her feet, Foster now looked more like a frightened rabbit. 'We went down to the inn for supper,' he said miserably. 'Her Ladyship took a private room. Didn't want to be seen, she said.'

This was beginning to look grim. 'Do the police know this?'

'Don't know. Then she said after we'd eaten there was somebody she had to talk to at Wychbourne Court. That suited me. She said she'd come back to the inn later on.'

'And did she?' Nell asked blankly. 'What time?'

'Not sure. I fell asleep and she found me there. Must have been about half nine. The police might know all this, though,' he said hopefully. 'They've talked to her.'

'But you didn't tell them yourself?'

'Can't remember. Might have.' His voice lacked conviction. Then he added, 'You tell them, Miss Drury. Ten to one there'll be nothing to it.'

'They'll want to talk to you, not me.' This was the last thing she wanted.

'You could maybe pave the way,' he said pleadingly.

'I'll think it over,' Nell said. 'Meanwhile, I've supper to think of.'

That was something much more pleasant on which to concentrate. It should all be laid out there now, the *tartlettes à la Tosca*, the *croquettes de Camembert*, the *delices de foie gras*, the ices, the soufflés and the *anges à cheval* as Lady

Warminster had insisted – no simple angels on horseback for her. And then she saw Inspector Melbray approaching her.

'Later has arrived, Miss Drury,' he said amiably. 'Our dance. Shall it be the Charleston or the waltz?'

It was a trap, she could see that immediately. Choose the Charleston and they would be flying legs and arms, partnering but not together. Choose the waltz and he would be holding her close, his arms round her. He would be in control. Or was she merely imagining this trap? It was just a dance, after all, and she would enjoy it. Nevertheless, in case it *was* a trap, she would take up the challenge. 'The waltz, please.' She smiled at him.

'Excellent. I'll tell Mr Ellimore.'

'Are you sure Lady Warminster won't object to our dancing together?' she asked sweetly.

'She will not.'

And here she was a few minutes later, dancing with the *nice* inspector. Of all things the band was playing Jack Caddigan's 'The Sweetheart Waltz'. Still, no matter. He was a good dancer, she realized, and being close to him was no problem at all. She began to relax – then tensed again as she remembered Foster. She did her best to forget it but she couldn't.

'I've something I must tell you,' she said awkwardly.

His grip tightened. 'And what is that?'

'Some evidence you might not have.'

'And you think I should know it this very moment?'

259

How could she say no? 'I do.'

He stopped. 'Then we must leave the floor, Miss Drury,' he said formally. 'It would be inappropriate to concentrate on work here. This is not Charlie's dance. It is the Inspector's dance and that is far different.' His voice was very cold and formal now and she bitterly regretted her stupidity. She had wanted to get this unpleasant job out of the way and all she had done was infuriate the inspector when she had had no intention of doing so.

'Come, Miss Drury. Let us go outside and find somewhere where work might seem more attractive.'

She was disconcerted, yet again feeling like a naughty child. Outside on the terrace lights twinkled and, below the steps to the garden, lights stretched into the dusky distance. Wherever he intended to take her she couldn't retreat now.

'There was a quiet spot I found the other day,' he said as they walked in silence through the rows of lights hidden in the trees. 'We might as well be somewhere pleasant if we are doomed to work.'

The somewhere pleasant was by a pond tucked away beyond the main lake but close enough to the lights for the path to be lit and for it still to be secluded by trees and shrubbery.

'Tell me,' he said at last when they were seated on a bench. Nell had to force herself to speak with the ordeal seeming more and more insurmountable.

'Lady Warminster—'

'It is as well we left the dance floor,' he

260

interrupted. 'She is our hostess and it is hardly polite to impart detrimental information while accepting her hospitality.'

'I'm serious,' Nell protested, angry at being checkmated again.

'And so am I. Tell me, if you please. I will not interrupt again.' She could see muscles working hard in his face. He was furious – but now so was she.

He kept his word and was silent as she told him what William Foster had to say. When she had finished he remained silent, however. 'You know it already?' she asked.

'No,' he said. 'Not this much. Is Foster telling the truth, do you think?'

She considered this. She was aware of his breathing close to her in the silence. She could smell the late scents of the evening, hear the occasional late night cry of birds. 'I do believe him.'

'Why?'

She had to consider this too. 'Because he had already told you about the joke that led to his presence at Wychbourne Court and when he was talking to me the words just came tumbling out. He could just have said that he had told you the story. Also, he was so worried that you would suspect him for Mr Charles's death that he had given no thought to Miss Harlington's. If he had been lying he would have covered both.'

'Well argued, but there's no evidence. I must speak to Lady Warminster – tomorrow,' he added. 'The etiquette books fail to specify what to do if one wishes to interrogate one's hostess about

261

a murder, especially a strangling, but I am sure they would recommend postponement.'

'And William?' Nell asked uncertainly, wondering if she was stepping on toes again. 'His job . . .'

He surprised her again. 'He's unlikely to suffer through your telling me this unless he is a murderer. If his peccadillos catch up with him, however, he would always have a future in Hollywood, and if by any foolish chance he was overlooked, his training as a gardener would not make it hard for him to find another job.'

'Thank you,' she said. It was heartfelt.

'Our dance, Miss Drury,' he said matter-of-factly. 'I believe I can hear the waltz. Shall we return to the floor or continue our earlier dance here? The waltz still plays and we can hear the music.'

'Why go inside?' she asked, now at ease. Why shouldn't she dance under the stars for once, among these green and silent trees? 'Don't waltz us into the lily pond, though. It's very close.'

'I am excellent at avoiding obstacles.' He was and they said little as they danced until the music stopped.

'The supper must be cleared,' she said, unexpectedly embarrassed and stepping back from him. 'I should go now.'

'And I too.' He took her hand and kissed it. 'Goodnight, Nell.'

Fifteen

'Nell,' Lady Clarice said with barely concealed excitement, 'I sense it is upon us.'

'The Gathering of the Ghosts?' Nell asked. Lady Clarice had summoned her to her dressing room at breakfast time to make this pronouncement, and Nell's hopes that Inspector Melbray would resolve the murder investigations before it happened seemed doomed. Instead he appeared to be in favour of the ghosts' intervention. The inspector, Nell decided crossly, was an enigma that would puzzle Einstein himself.

'I am certain of it,' Lady Clarice replied earnestly. 'There is a most exceptional cold area by one of the staircases to the gallery. I have been monitoring the temperature daily and it has already dropped significantly. I am now convinced that the gathering will be tomorrow evening and I have informed Inspector Melbray. Having failed to find the culprit himself, he is bowing to the superior power of the Wychbourne ghosts. He asked the most intelligent questions, however, and I was most impressed. Could ghosts leave their own particular locations in the house in order to commune with each other? he asked.'

'And can they?' Nell dared to venture.

Lady Clarice was only too eager to tell her. 'There are many instances of ghosts moving either individually or in groups. Take the monks

263

at Bilsington Priory, for example, and the group of Dickensian ladies and gentlemen at Cooling churchyard.'

Nell had another question. 'The Wychbourne ghosts are from different ages. Would they mix?'

'They will. It's Monday, the twentieth of July, Nell, and there will be a full moon. The ghosts will be at their greatest strength. Tonight is too soon for the gathering but the energy they absorb must not be wasted. It will be tomorrow. I fully expect Elise to be reunited with Charles. He and his comrades have been strangely silent since her death. Charlie is waiting for her to join him.'

Nell decided not to comment. 'Is Inspector Melbray definitely attending?'

'Everyone concerned with this wretched affair must attend, he told me, including himself. He will inform Lady Warminster, her husband and for some reason her chauffeur, and Mr Ellimore too before he departs. Also, he wishes Miss Checkam, Mr Peters and Mrs Fielding to attend, and of course yourself. Even Mr Briggs. Lady Ansley will be informing them all. I do have to admit that it is a very strange world when chauffeurs, bandleaders and butlers are among the guests, but the ghosts, as well as Inspector Melbray, wish it to be so. Now, Nell, more importantly, we must discuss the menu.'

'*Menu?*' Jumping jellies, what was this?

'One cannot merely provide a late-night supper of ham sandwiches for such a distinguished gathering,' Lady Clarice explained.

'Of course. For the family, General and Lady Warminster—'

'I speak of the ghosts, not their audience,' Lady Clarice said reprovingly.

The *ghosts*? 'But ghosts can't eat,' Nell said cautiously.

'Not physically. I am aware of that. But it is a well-known fact that ghosts display a great deal of interest in the food around them, particularly of food which they themselves were accustomed to enjoying in their earlier lives. They eat emotionally, Nell. The very best must be provided. It does them honour. It takes note of their feelings. They feel part of the life and soul of the house again. It draws them to us and us to them. No, Miss Drury, never overlook the power of food on such occasions.'

A ghost menu. Nell despaired. What in the name of pickled pollocks would that consist of? The nightmare of the Ghosts' Gathering was bad enough without having to entertain them to supper. She must have a discreet word with Lady Ansley about it. Nell had only just managed to pull herself together when another disruption occurred.

A scream made her leap up from the kitchen table and with her staff again at a standstill she rushed into the scullery where Muriel, one of its two maids, was weeping with a broken plate at her feet.

'It flew at me,' she sobbed as Nell reached her.

Mrs Fielding had already appeared from nowhere and swept into action. 'You'll be dismissed for this, my girl. Sheer carelessness. That plate's from the Wychbourne Service.'

'I'll look after her, Mrs Fielding,' Nell said quietly. Kitchen servants fell within her domain, although Mrs Fielding stoutly refused to accept that.

'China's my responsibility,' she snapped back.

'I didn't drop it. The plate just flew over me. It's that ghost,' Muriel sobbed.

Ghosts again. Nell sighed. 'Tell me exactly what happened.'

'It happened yesterday too, only it was a saucepan then,' Muriel said tearfully. 'Flew right through the air from behind. It's one of those poltergeists. They don't like what's going on in this house, Miss Drury, and that's a fact.'

'There must be some other explanation for it.' Nell's eye fell on Jimmy standing by the door into the kitchen yard. He was looking far too innocent but she had no time to sort it out now.

'Jimmy,' she said warningly, 'you can take all this china back to Mr Peters' room *now*.'

'Jimmy's Mr Peters' responsibility,' Mrs Fielding weighed in again.

'Today he's mine, *aren't* you, Jimmy?' Nell said meaningfully. 'Sweep up the shards, get the china back to its proper place and then give Muriel a hand.'

When she at last reached Lady Ansley with the day's menus, Lord Ansley was also present, which was unusual. Ghosts' Gathering discussions, she presumed, or perhaps Inspector Melbray's progress or otherwise with the case.

It proved to be the ghosts. Lord Ansley was as courteous as ever although clearly worried.

'There seems to be something going on, Miss Drury, in this household but neither Her Ladyship nor I can determine what it is. We know about my sister's plans for tomorrow night in the great hall and that ghosts are involved, but what exactly is it for? We aren't hunting them again, I trust?'

Usually Lord Ansley would either avoid an obstacle or deal with it in his own way, so this was an extraordinary departure from normal times. Nell did her best. 'Not quite. Lady Clarice is sure that the Wychbourne ghosts want to add their weight to the investigation. She senses they are dissatisfied with the police's lack of progress.' Putting this into words made the gathering seem even more ludicrous than it was, Nell feared.

Lord Ansley glanced at his wife. 'We must attend then.'

'Lady Clarice would like everyone who was here when Mr Parkyn-Wright was killed to attend tomorrow,' Nell explained, feeling more wretched every moment. 'Inspector Melbray is coming.' At least that seemed to add a note of credibility to the situation.

'He'll think we're all potty,' Lord Ansley declared.

'It's his choice to come,' Nell pointed out.

'Knowing my sister is in charge?'

'Yes.' She saw another glance exchanged between the Ansleys.

Lord Ansley sighed. 'Is Lady Warminster coming?'

'I believe so. And her chauffeur. Also Lady Clarice,' she added bravely, 'would like you to invite Mr Peters, Miss Checkam and Mrs Fielding,' Nell said. 'And Mr Briggs too.'

'Briggs?' Lord Ansley looked horrified. 'We'll have to look after him, Gertrude.'

Now for the worst. Make this sound as normal as possible, Nell told herself. 'Lady Clarice has also requested a special supper to be served there, one that would appeal emotionally to the ghosts. Would ten o'clock be suitable?'

'Ask the ghosts.' Lord Ansley managed a smile. 'There seems to be no harm in granting her request, Miss Drury. By ten o'clock night should be falling fast, if not already with us, but let us hope that light is not far afield. Serve what my sister wishes provided it is manageable for you.' He paused. 'Could you by any chance tell us what the police are doing over these murders? My wife and I have very little idea save that investigations are proceeding and the inquest on Miss Harlington has also been adjourned. It seems unfair to ask you but we felt the servants' hall might, as so often, know more than we ourselves. We do know about Peters and that the poor man was being blackmailed, but nothing further.'

'We're in the dark too,' Nell said apologetically. 'As the inspector's cooperating with the Gathering of the Ghosts though, perhaps he expects something to come of it.'

'That's completely batty,' Lady Ansley declared. 'Harry Price's investigations are well known but never have I heard of Scotland Yard making use of ghosts. What does Inspector Melbray hope will happen? That one of them will step forth and give him the answers?'

'The ghosts would have to provide some tangible evidence too, if the inspector's to be satisfied,' Nell said gloomily. And that wasn't going to happen.

'Two murders at Wychbourne Court, Nell,' Lady Ansley said despondently. 'I would not have believed it possible. Clarice tried to reassure us by pointing out that we'll be gaining two new ghosts in the family home. Set beside such tragedy and loss of life that seems out of place, to say the least. I take it, incidentally, that the inspector will want Lady Enid to be present as she was here that evening?'

'And Mr Fontenoy,' Nell murmured.

Lady Ansley groaned. 'Another seating plan will be called for. I fear one of our children had a part to play in rearranging the last one. It won't happen again.'

'I'll arrange a buffet supper,' Nell said. 'Seating could then be at small tables and guests may choose their own seats.'

'Will the ghosts know where they are supposed to be sitting?' Lord Ansley enquired.

Nell laughed but then wondered whether this was out of order. It might have been because he continued soberly, 'What's going to happen if nothing spectral occurs tomorrow night? Do we repeat this performance?'

Nell had no idea but decided to add a note of cheer. 'I'll plan my menu so that at least that pleases everyone, even if it adds nothing to the investigation.'

Her confidence stayed with her through the rest of the morning but mysteriously vanished when she was at last able to contemplate a menu for the ghosts. Inspiration failed to come and she walked through to the great hall, hoping its grandeur and silence would do the trick. Mr Peters was crossing the hall, but like an eerie ghost in black himself he did not even glance at her. She looked around her at the portraits, the closed doors, the heavy furniture smelling of lavender polish, and thought of all the people over the centuries who had passed through this hall and those who had attended great feasts by the roaring fires. Tomorrow all that would happen again, save that the feast would be supper and there would be no spit roasts, no ornate roast swans, no prime cutlets. After all, bones thrown casually over shoulders as of old might injure the ghosts.

Nell, she reproved herself, don't mock them. Whether there were 'real' ghosts or not, those past Ansleys infiltrated the mind. Perhaps that's what ghosts were. Memories of past people or events imprinted so vividly on the atmosphere or on one's own mind that they attained a reality of their own. Tomorrow, however, Lady Clarice was convinced that ghosts of some sort would be gathering here, wherever their usual haunting locations.

At last, the idea for the ghost menu began to emerge and she—

'Ah, Nell.' Lady Clarice was almost running across the hall towards her. 'Another word with you, please.'

'The menu?' Capering carrots, she had to hold fast to the idea in her mind before it vanished.

'No, no, no. The *poltergeist.* How exciting. I'm told that one of the scullery maids has had an experience. How old is she?'

'About fifteen, but—' Nell didn't have time to relay her suspicions.

'That is splendid. Just the age for a girl to attract such manifestations. But it does mean that *they* are gathering. Do tell the young lady to take extra care tonight. Do not let her be alone in the scullery. She must be present tomorrow night, of course.'

Nell could see trouble ahead. Muriel would be terrified, even if she sat with Mrs Fielding. 'Don't—'

'Let's discuss the table arrangement, Nell. The girl must sit with my brother and mother.'

Ghosts or not, this would not work. It was an even bet as to whether the dowager or Muriel would faint with shock first. She had to speak out. 'Lady Ansley has agreed to arrange separate tables where everyone can sit where they wish, and the supper itself will be a buffet. Some people may not wish to be close to the colder areas where the ghosts may congregate. Others might want to be next to them; others to move around to investigate phenomena.'

'Oh, but I thought—'

'It will work very well,' Nell soothed her. 'I'll see to that. Now allow me to tell you about the menus I have planned.' That idea of hers would have to be aired before it was fully fledged.

'It must be the best food,' Lady Clarice pleaded anxiously.

'Certainly. Each ghost shall have his or her very own dish,' Nell informed her, 'so that each one recognizes the food they once enjoyed so much.' She mentally crossed her fingers as she waited for the reaction.

Lady Clarice looked spellbound, fortunately.

'How splendid,' she breathed. Then a slight frown appeared on her brow. 'How will they know which *is* their own dish? They might not recognize it if all the dishes are served together.'

Nell quickly improvised. 'We will put large name cards on each buffet dish. Sir Thomas's mawmenee, Violet's junket or Lady Henrietta's apple flummery, for example.'

'I do believe,' Lady Clarice said excitedly, 'that they will enjoy that *very* much. What shall *we* eat, however?'

Nell silently groaned. She had been hoist with her own petard. She had no option but to take a risk. 'The same dishes,' she said, as if surprised that there could be any doubt.

Lady Clarice looked perplexed. 'But we can't take their food.'

'We shall share it, just as we share the gathering with them,' Nell explained. 'That will be the spirit of the occasion. Sharing.'

For a moment it hung in the balance. 'You are right,' Lady Clarice declared. 'How may I assist you?'

The worst was over. 'I wouldn't want any of the ghosts to be omitted by mistake. I have your earlier list but I would like another giving the ghosts' usual haunting locations and the dates of their deaths so that I can research what their favourite dishes would have been.'

'You shall have it. We'll need the equipment again, of course.'

Nell foresaw chaos. Rapid response required here. 'We need to record the evening for posterity, certainly,' she said with an authority she did not

272

feel. 'Cameras, phonograph and notepads. Your thermometers, if you wish. But only a few. If more than one or two people move around we might disturb the ghosts' consultations.'

At least she now had a plan for the buffet, although Nell still didn't know what Lady Clarice imagined would happen tomorrow, nor why Inspector Melbray was so eager to join in.

Apparently, others thought differently. All the world and his wife seemed to think she was the fount of all knowledge not only about the murder but now about the Gathering of the Ghosts. Guy was the first intruder into her chef's room, where she was busy studying recipes. Should these be completely true to the period the ghost lived in or just reflect their likely general tastes?

'They said I'd find you in here, Nell. Enjoy the ball, did you?' he greeted her.

'Immensely. I always enjoy my work. How about you?'

'Immensely. I enjoy mine too. Seriously, Nell, I'm hoping you can tell us what Inspector Melbray's up to.'

'You said "us". Your band?'

'No, they're going their own separate ways today and unless you change your mind about coming with me I shall do the same the day after tomorrow. The "us" is Foster and me. What's going on?'

'If you mean the murder cases, I don't know. If it's tomorrow night, I still don't know, apart from the menu.'

'Unusual for you, Nell. What happened to the Nell

273

I-know-exactly-what's-going-on-and-where-I'm-going?'

'She got lost,' Nell replied amiably.

'I don't believe you.' Guy sat down. 'Everyone's drawn to you for answers like flies to flypaper.'

'How elegant.'

'Including that inspector.'

Dangerous ground. 'I hear you're coming tomorrow night.'

'Yes, and also Foster. And, I gather, the general's coming as well as his lovely lady wife.'

'How kind General Warminster is,' Nell remarked innocently.

Guy grinned. 'He wouldn't let her come alone. Her Ladyship didn't want to come at all but it's Scotland Yard's order. Personally I think that fellow's gone doolally, relying on ghosts to point him in the right direction. What does he hope to get out of it?'

'It wasn't the inspector's idea,' Nell pointed out. 'It was Lady Clarice's.'

'Just humouring her, are we? I can't believe Scotland Yard would waste its time with ghost shows otherwise. Even if you are the main attraction.'

'My buffet, not me. I'm not one of the ghosts,' Nell said crossly. 'And nor do I see how the evening is going to help solve the case.'

'I can't wait to see if Charlie Parkyn-Wright appears to point the accusing finger.'

'He probably will. Murdered ghosts are supposed to come back when their cases remain unsolved. Like Banquo's ghost in *Macbeth*.'

'Eh?'

'The ghost appeared in the middle of the banquet to point the finger of guilt.'

'Quite nice little rooms, aren't they?' Lady Enid was the next visitor to the chef's room. 'I had no reason to visit this wing during my husband's reign at Wychbourne. No, I'm mistaken. My husband insisted on our opening the dancing in the servants' hall on New Year's Eve, before we returned to the ballroom for our own. The gesture was greatly appreciated.'

The dowager sat in state in the shabby armchair usually occupied by a large pile of cookery books, which were now heaped on the table in front of where Nell was sitting. She was amazed at Her Ladyship's presence but had no idea why she was here. More rose petal preserve? Mrs Fielding had duly delivered several to the Dower House with many a smirk at Nell.

'What is going to happen tomorrow night, Miss Drury?' Lady Enid enquired. 'All I hear from my son is that ghosts are to gather here and so are the police. It sounds most irregular to me. Is the information I have received correct?'

'Yes, although it isn't clear what will happen,' Nell tried to explain. 'There will be an excellent supper, however.'

'An incentive to attend. I have reluctantly agreed to take part, even though I understand a certain gentleman will be present. I trust I will be seated some distance away. Even a ghost would be a preferable neighbour.'

'Everyone can choose where they wish to sit when they arrive,' Nell told her.

Lady Enid frowned. 'Then I shall insist on distance. Why the inspector believes I should attend is beyond my comprehension but the law must be obeyed. Do the ghosts know that, I wonder?'

The next visitor was Miss Checkam.

'What's happening tomorrow, Miss Drury? Do you know?' she asked anxiously. 'Lady Ansley says the police are coming to this gathering. What do they want?'

'I don't know,' Nell said wearily. 'To solve the case, I hope.'

'But the ghosts. I'm going to hate being in the hall with all the same people as before.'

'You said you weren't in the hall itself,' Nell pointed out mildly. 'You were on your way to the grand staircase when you saw Mr Charles by the gallery stairs.' That was one of the cold areas where Lady Clarice was sure Sir Thomas was drawing energy from the atmosphere, so perhaps she would find Mr Charles back there, Nell thought fancifully.

'Yes.' Miss Checkam looked flurried. 'And he was so very unkind to me.'

Mr Peters and Lord Richard would then have been bringing in equipment from the boot room. Could Miss Checkam have returned later . . .? No, she couldn't cope with this again. Let the ghosts sort it out, Nell thought. She had a menu to create.

Even now, she wasn't to be left alone. The first visitor was more welcome. It was Jimmy with Lady Clarice's list. The second visitor was Mr Beringer. Gamekeeper's son or not, he was a

276

guest in the house and it was surprising to see him here in the east wing.

'I'm sorry, Miss Drury. I've come to disturb your peaceful dreams. Richard and Helen are asking for you. Sophy is there too. I'm just their messenger. Am I interrupting you?'

'It can wait,' Nell said valiantly, bidding a silent adieu to the ghost menu. Perhaps this afternoon she would get some time to work on it, now that she had all the details of the prospective emotional diners. The list was a long one. Apparently sixty-one ghosts had set up residency in Wychbourne Court over the years but Lady Clarice was sure of only nineteen that had stayed the course, plus Charles Parkyn-Wright if he appeared. Not to mention Miss Harlington. It was going to be quite a gathering tomorrow night and quite a menu if she ever managed to write it – and cook it.

She accompanied Mr Beringer past the main staircase and into the conservatory. 'Did you enjoy Lady Warminster's ball, Miss Drury?' he asked politely on the way. 'I saw you dancing with Inspector Melbray. Good fellow, isn't he?'

For the umpteenth time, or so it seemed, she agreed that Inspector Melbray was a fine man. 'Although that depends on whether one's a criminal or not,' she added.

Mr Beringer laughed but then said soberly, 'Someone here must be. Someone who will probably be here tomorrow night.'

'As a ghost?'

'I imagine a few of them have guilty consciences. No, I meant us, of course.'

Her heart sank. 'Is that what Lord Richard and Lady Helen want to talk about?'

'You may find,' Mr Beringer said carefully, 'that it's you whom they expect to talk.'

Oh, splendid, she thought savagely. When they reached the conservatory, Lord Richard and his sisters were apparently engrossed in a discussion on whether a few extra palm trees might improve the décor. They were certainly trying to look only casually interested in her arrival. Whatever they were planning, she wanted no part of it.

'Hello, Nell,' Lady Sophy said brightly. 'Looking forward to tomorrow?'

'Enormously,' Nell assured her warily.

'Someone probably isn't,' Mr Beringer commented.

'Rex means Charlie's murderer,' Lady Helen said – looking almost her old self, Nell thought. 'And Elise's too.'

'We all think they're the same person,' Lady Sophy chimed in. 'But does the inspector?'

'I'm not in his confidence,' Nell said firmly.

'You seem to be good chums,' Lord Richard said suspiciously.

'One dance does not constitute chumminess,' Nell countered.

'Come on, Nell, do tell,' Lady Sophy pleaded. 'Everything's in the open now so you won't be breaking confidences.'

Nell explained yet again. 'About the ghosts, you know as much as I do, probably more. On the murder cases, I'm as much at sea as—'

'The inspector, it seems,' Lord Richard drawled.

'Perhaps that's why he's so keen to see everyone

tomorrow night,' Lady Sophy suggested. 'It's not the ghosts that draw him, it's the idea of us all being together.'

'We obliged him with that awful reconstruction that got nowhere,' Lord Richard said.

'Nowhere for us,' Nell contributed, 'but it might have done for him.' Her audience fell strangely silent, she noticed.

'Tomorrow night's serious then?' Lady Helen asked presently.

'Very.'

'Ghosts and all? They could be the smoke-screen,' Lady Sophy pointed out.

'It'll be a riot,' Lord Richard said. 'Fun, eh?'

'Perhaps. But,' Nell said firmly, 'no jokes tomorrow night. They'll get in the way of finding out the truth about the murders.'

Four pairs of eyes stared at her. 'Absolutely no jokes?' Lady Sophy asked wistfully. 'But it's such a jokey evening.'

Time to speak out. 'It's no joke at all,' Nell replied. 'Wychbourne Court needs to be rid of this cloud hanging over it. If tomorrow night helps, jokes won't be appropriate. If it doesn't, they won't have helped and might have hindered.'

Silence. 'Fair enough,' said Lord Richard at last. 'No Pepper's Ghost.'

And that, Nell thought, as she set off in search of young Jimmy, went for him too. No jokes. All catapults to be impounded, with no more broken plates. Poltergeists, indeed!

Sixteen

The day had begun badly and it was becoming worse. Nell disciplined herself not to panic but it was hard. Here she was with only an hour before the guests arrived – did one call them guests at what was effectively a séance? The junket for the ghost of Violet Smith hadn't yet set; the Mutton Cake for the seventh marquess's dog ghost Napoleon had been thrown away by Mrs Fielding, genuinely under the impression that it was left over from the servants' shepherd's pie; Lady Clarice was still frenziedly debating whether Nell's choice of carp baked with lemons and oranges was too ornate for Brother Sebastian and Sister Edith, the lovelorn couple who reneged on their religious vows and took refuge in the old chapel in 1457; Nell herself had realized that Jeremiah's Jugged Hare was too alcoholic even for a smuggler in the cellar; and the sobbing baby's Sweet Rice Pudding à la Portugaise had burnt.

It was all the poltergeist's fault, Nell decided. Muriel had suffered yet another attack. The lid of Lady Ansley's favourite teapot had flown from the table, catching Muriel's shoulder just as the teapot itself toppled over and smashed on the scullery floor. This was too much and Nell had marched straight over to Jimmy who had just come in from the kitchen yard.

'I told you, young man, no more jokes. No catapults,' she had blazed at him.

'It wasn't me, Miss Drury,' he howled in fright. She hadn't believed him until he produced an alibi.

'He was with me in the yard,' Mr Peters had told her anxiously. 'I needed help with the electric generator.'

She had apologised to Jimmy and calmed down, but if he hadn't done it, who had? she wondered uneasily. It was a bad omen.

The next obstacle had been Lady Clarice – a recurrent problem throughout the day. One issue had been particularly difficult to handle. Lady Clarice had been in the great hall, studying the table in its middle that had been earmarked for the buffet. It had only the tablecloth upon it at that stage, plus several small table lamps and three large vases of flowers and greenery which looked far beneath Wychbourne's usual selections. 'Ghosts are drawn to rosemary and to wild garlic and nettles and so forth,' Lady Clarice explained when Nell expressed doubts.

The lamps, however, were the pivotal point of Nell's alarm, since Lady Clarice had been in the process of removing them. 'It has to be dark for the ghosts,' she had dictated.

'We can't eat in the dark, though,' Nell pointed out. 'The main lights in the hall could be out but these have to be on. We could leave the lamps here and eat before the ghosts arrive.'

'*Before* the ghosts?' Lady Clarice had been horrified. 'Eating their food before their arrival would be most impolite.'

Nell had struggled for a compromise. 'Suppose we serve canapés from the sideboard for guests to have with their drinks before the ghosts arrive and then they can enjoy the buffet after the ghosts have dined and we can have light again. When will that be?' she asked, with little hope of a decision.

Lady Clarice considered the query with care. 'They will enjoy watching us eat, but these oil lamps would be much too bright for them if they were suddenly turned up once more.'

'Not the small table lamps that we'll put on the guests' tables, surely?' Nell was becoming increasingly anxious.

'Yes, Miss Drury, they will object,' Lady Clarice had snapped, which was unusual for her and was a sign that this situation was getting out of hand. 'I may ask the ghosts to remain throughout the entire evening. It must remain dark. After all, the inspector will also be speaking.'

'To the ghosts?' What the floundering fishcakes was this world coming to if Scotland Yard had to have a word with the Other Side before every step of its investigation?

'Certainly to the ghosts, Miss Drury. He tells me the ghosts are assisting him in his enquiries.'

So that had been that. She had upset Lady Clarice. What should she do now? Nell wondered. There wouldn't be time to lay out the buffet after the ghosts had disappeared – and how the dickens would they know when that was anyway? No help for it. The buffet had to be eaten later but be on the table before the lights were turned off. She'd have to hope that much of it didn't disappear before the ghosts had their chance to devour it.

The next problem she was expected to solve had been the correct wardrobe for the event.

'What do you think, Nell?' Lady Sophy had suddenly appeared at her side in the kitchen clad in a passable imitation of a nun's habit. 'Is this going to make Sister Edith's phantom feel at home?'

'No.' Nell had laughed despite her rising tension. 'Set an example, Lady Sophy. The ghosts will appreciate some formality. You need to be worthy of the fine aristocratic name you bear – that's what Sir Thomas and jolly Sir William will relate to.' She was particularly fond of Sir William, the gentleman whose portrait hung in the great hall and who had later been elevated by Queen Elizabeth to becoming the Baron Ansley, which must have made him even jollier.

Lady Sophy had sighed. 'You mean it's powder and pearls time? Can I wear my tiara?'

'Have you got one?'

'Of course. It's only a tiddly one as I'm a younger sister. Personally I think it should be the biggest. I have more to put up with.'

What should she herself wear? Nell wondered. Once again she was part chef, part participant. Tonight, she decided, she would dress for the role of participant, even if she hadn't got a tiara. After all, the *nice* inspector would be present.

One hour to go – and then Kitty banged on her door to tell her Lady Clarice wanted to see her yet again. What on earth did she want this time? Nell was not yet ready, but pulled her dress

283

over her head at high speed, threw her beads round her neck, tidied her hair and ran. She'd chosen the grey one again in deference to the ghosts. So much for the elegant, poised figure she had hoped to present.

Lady Clarice was clad in sober black with jet jewellery also, presumably with the ghosts' feelings in mind, but the stark black didn't suit her. For some reason this made Nell regret her churlishness. This, after all, was Lady Clarice's big night, she thought with a rush of affection.

'Nell, the inspector has asked me to take him on the ghost hunt tour again,' Lady Clarice informed her with great excitement. 'He suggested I might need a companion and mentioned you. I would be glad of your company.'

Nell's heart plummeted. Thank goodness everything was mostly ready in the kitchens and Kitty and Michel were organizing the buffet in the hall. She had congratulated herself after her last inspection that everything there looked efficient and welcoming – both for ghosts and guests. The main oil lamps were still on and the table lamps remained to be lit, but Mr Peters would see that Jimmy dealt with that in due course. The small lamps could be turned down to their lowest point to which even a ghost would not object, she comforted herself. After all, hand torches were standard ghost hunting equipment, so they must tolerate some light.

'What's the purpose of this tour?' she asked Lady Clarice warily as they made their way down the staircase. 'Inspector Melbray must have done it before and also he held that reconstruction.'

284

'He told me it was to get to know the ghosts. He wasn't able to spend time on that during his previous tours. I'm not averse to his plan. I have a thermometer with me and have explained to the inspector the importance of the varying temperatures and the consequent cold areas as the ghosts draw their energy from what's around them.'

Lady Clarice might be happy about it but Nell wasn't convinced by this so-called plan. Inspector Melbray must have more in mind than that. As they entered the great hall, Nell could see him; he wasn't in evening dress but a smart grey suit and waistcoat, clearly underlining the fact that this was a working session. She wondered what he wore when he was off duty. Not one for the fashionable Oxford bags, she decided, but she could imagine him in flannels and blazer boating down the river.

Concentrate, Nell, she told herself. She was not here to have fantasies out of *The Wind in the Willows*. She needed her wits about her. At the moment the inspector was talking to Mr Peters who was busy at the sideboard. Lady Sophy was as usual poking her nose curiously into every corner as though the ghosts might be lurking in the wings and even Lady Helen was taking an interest. Automatically Nell craned her head to check if Kitty had put the canapés there – yes, and Michel was bringing through dishes for the buffet table.

'A splendid array of refreshments,' Inspector Melbray remarked to Lady Clarice as he came over to join them. 'If I were a ghost, I would be only too happy to dine here. As a mere policeman,

I consider myself most privileged. I'm told the lights are to be turned off here shortly. Will that be the case on our tour?'

'No.' Nell was conscious of her hurried dressing as his gaze flicked over her. 'It's electric lighting upstairs. We can turn it off or on as you wish.'

'But that's not good for the ghosts,' Lady Clarice said anxiously.

'I'm sure they could put up with it for a few brief moments as we pass,' Inspector Melbray stated politely.

'What do you want us to do, Inspector Melbray?' Nell asked hurriedly, seeing Lady Clarice's mutinous expression.

'I'll explain as we go round.'

'Only four of the ghosts haunt the great hall itself,' Lady Clarice told him somewhat stiffly. 'Alfred, who might bring his spade with him – he was an Anglo-Saxon farmer; poor Sir Ralph, murdered by his brother with whom he had quarrelled over the Norman Conquest; William, the favourite of Queen Elizabeth – he does laugh rather a lot; and the unfortunate Gilbert, the butler killed by the fifth marquess. He will keep getting in Peters' way as he tries to serve drinks to his previous master.'

'They sound most interesting,' the inspector told her gravely.

Lady Clarice looked pleased. 'I'll instruct you about the others as we go around. Some rarely manifest themselves, unfortunately. The first marquess, Philip, all too often secretes himself in the library by the seventeenth-century poets' section. Do you wish me to point out when the air pressure or temperature changes?'

The inspector gracefully declined and the tour began. Realizing she had to face that gallery again, Nell braced herself as Lady Clarice led the way up to it.

'To think of it,' Lady Clarice said excitedly, 'that poor Sir Thomas.' She retold the story in detail, concluding with a triumphant, 'and the minstrel boy, his wife's lover, dealt his fatal blow. It does make me think of Lady Warminster and her gardener.' She hesitated. 'Perhaps I should not have mentioned that.'

'I'm not easily shocked, Lady Clarice,' Inspector Melbray replied, straight-faced. 'Just tell me what you told your group that night.'

Lady Clarice took heart as they edged along the gallery in single file. 'Sir Thomas is waiting but Charlie's ghost seems to be very coy at present, as I explained to you, Inspector. He is waiting perhaps for Miss Elise to join him but she has not yet done so. She is probably hiding in the dairy.'

Nell was all too thankful for Mr Charles's reticence as she edged past the cupboard, her heart thumping. To her, at least, this gallery had a distinctly unpleasant atmosphere – one that all the lavender polish in the world would not smother, although there was no evidence of that smell that had pervaded the air that Saturday night.

The thumping reduced a little as, at the foot of the gallery stairs, Lady Clarice turned into the corridor and led them along the back of the gallery towards the gunroom. 'Don't disturb the dog,' she pleaded as Inspector Melbray strode too boldly into the room.

Startled, he jumped aside, looking round cautiously. 'I don't see one,' he said.

'Napoleon is around somewhere, I'm sure. He always waited for his master in the gunroom. That would be my father, the seventh marquess in the 1880s. And next door you'll find poor Violet in the boot room. A maid, but a maiden no longer. She was betrayed by the fourth marquess.'

It seemed to Nell that the inspector was having some difficulty with these two residents, as he rather speedily decided to bypass the breakfast room and asked where they would be going next. This was all very well, she thought uneasily, but where was it leading? His silence on the real reason for their being here was increasingly unnerving.

'Up the back stairs to the upper floors of the main house,' Lady Clarice replied to him. 'There you'll meet Henrietta, murdered for unfaithfulness to her lord; Dorcas, who waited in vain for her husband's return; and if you are lucky, Calliope will be singing in the corridor and it's even possible you'll hear the baby crying in the nursery.'

The inspector received this information with an impassive face as Lady Clarice led them past the cellar room where Mr Peters and Mrs Fielding had had their romantic interlude to a flight of stairs to the upper floor.

'Could the people in the group you were leading, Lady Clarice, have changed their positions in the group while climbing these stairs?' he asked. 'This staircase is wider than the corridor that brought us here, which suggests that is possible.'

'I suppose it is.' Lady Clarice showed little interest.

Nell realized with alarm what the inspector might be driving at. The family. 'Lord Richard and Lady Helen were bringing up the rear along the corridor,' she said, 'but at this point that might have changed. They had a plan' – careful here, Nell – 'that might have taken their attention off who was here and who wasn't.'

Lady Clarice looked mystified but the inspector's eyes rested on Nell thoughtfully. 'Miss Drury,' he asked, 'could you work out which would be the easiest route in terms of time for someone to leave the group, get hold of the dagger and the photographer's cloth in the relative darkness, slip up to the gallery, down again and then either catch up with the group by using these stairs, *or* go up the main staircase and hope to join it en route, *or* wait for the group to return to the great hall. Would you put yourself in the murderer's shoes please?' He paused. 'Do you wear a watch to time it by?'

'I do.' At least concentrating on this would ease her tension, stop these nightmarish guesses at what and whom he suspected. If her job was to be a Baker Street Irregular, so be it. Nell set off, leaving her companions to salute whatever ghosts they wished upstairs. Should she use the gallery stairs nearest to her where Mr Peters might see her, or the stairs at the other end? The latter. Off she went – no, she hadn't yet seized the dagger and cloth from the hall. Unless, she realized with

289

growing excitement, she had already snatched them in the chaos before the groups left. It was quite possible given the low lighting.

Now she must run up these gallery stairs then either go along the gallery passageway visible from below or squeeze along behind the screen to where Mr Charles would be hidden. Access from either end whether behind the screen or in front carried the risk of being seen or heard by Mr Peters. But then the murderer wouldn't have known that Mr Peters had planned to stay in the hall. *Yes*, that was it!

Sure she was on the right track now, she continued timing her movements and hurried back down the gallery stairs. Decision time: would she have chosen to catch up the group or wait? Much safer to remain here. If she stood in the well of the staircase, she would be in darkness and even if someone should pass she would escape notice. The murderer would have his own torch to time his departure and at twelve thirty he had emerged when he heard familiar voices.

'Excellent, Miss Drury,' the inspector greeted her as she joined them in the hall, where people were now gathering for the great event. 'How long to get to the gallery and back down again?' he asked.

'Ten minutes.'

'Including taking the dagger and cloth?'

'I'd already taken them.'

He looked at her. 'Thank you.'

He seemed pleased but not disposed to discuss it further – naturally enough, she supposed, although questions shot up in her mind like mushrooms.

Why was he pleased? Did her contribution point to someone in particular? And who was it? Stop this, Nell, she told herself. There's nothing more to be done. It's in his hands now. She tried instead to concentrate on the gathering now assembling. There was no sign of any ghosts, at least.

Lord and Lady Ansley had arrived and Lady Clarice went over to join them, as did the inspector. As far as Nell could see, everyone seemed to be present. Perhaps Lady Sophy had had a hand in the family wardrobe, for jewels and tiaras were flashing. Lady Helen was in bright green and Lady Sophy in red, so they clearly had no fears about frightening the ghosts. The dowager had chosen purple and Lady Ansley blue. Lady Warminster, clad in a muddy stone-coloured satin, looked positively dowdy, to Nell's pleasure. She saw Lady Enid walking with great determination to join Lord and Lady Ansley with her back firmly to Arthur, who came up to whisper to Nell.

'I may be wrong, Sherlock, but do I deduce that Inspector Melbray has something to tell us this evening?'

'Perhaps.' Nell swallowed. Even just putting the obvious into words made her stomach tense again.

'I'm all agog. I see General Warminster is here too, anxiously protecting his wife from the foul embraces of their gardener-cum-chauffeur.'

'Arthur!' Nell said warningly.

'Consider that unsaid. I shall join them with their permission. I see the gardener is present, sitting with Mr Ellimore. Dear me, is the inspector gathering us together for a grand dénouement?'

He must be right. She could see Mrs Fielding, Mr Peters, Miss Checkam and Mr Briggs all in their Sunday best and sitting at a table with Jimmy and Muriel, the latter looking terrified. She saw Mrs Fielding put a motherly arm round her, a side of her that Nell had never seen before. Perhaps she had a warm heart after all.

'Eerie,' Nell thought with a shiver. Everyone gathered, sipping Mr Peters' excellent cocktails, and yet there was a muted air, not just because of what had happened here just over a month ago but the probability that tonight might see its ending. It was as though they were all moving like ghosts themselves on a course directed by Inspector Melbray.

At that moment it was growing even eerier as the lights went out and it took a few moments for the table lamps to be lit. Where should she sit? Nell wondered. It was settled for her as Inspector Melbray touched her arm. 'Join me, Miss Drury. I noticed you shiver. We should shiver together. This champagne cocktail that the butler just brought me is excellent. Is he new to that job? It wasn't Peters or your footman.'

She sat down with him at a table at the back, half reluctantly, half gratefully. 'It must have been Mr Peters, because only he is serving. The footman is preparing the drinks. Should I be shivering at the ghosts or at what is to come?' she asked boldly.

'I'm sure your buffet will be scrumptious.'

Checkmated again. She hadn't meant the buffet.

'I hope the ghosts agree,' she managed to reply lightly.

'I'm sure they will. After all, you've kindly marked the dishes for each one's use. I would fear to fight Napoleon's for his, however. Your role seems to be that of politician as well as chef, Miss Drury. Two roles, not one.'

'Just as your investigations are two cases, not one,' she said. 'Is that why you're here tonight?' She'd said this on the spur of the moment but now she thought it through. *Were* they separate cases? She'd assumed that Mr Charles's killer had also killed Miss Harlington, but suppose there were two killers? That would dramatically alter the picture.

His eyes flickered but before he could answer – if he had intended to – Lady Clarice had risen to her feet to speak. Nell's sense of dread overcame her. It was about to begin and, regardless of any ghosts, would sweep on to its inevitable end masterminded by Inspector Melbray.

Lady Clarice performed in style. 'My lords, ladies and gentlemen, we are here to welcome some very special guests who have lived and dined in this house over the centuries. They will dine with us again tonight – if enough food remains for them, of course.'

There was a titter of nervous laughter, which Nell could see Lady Clarice had not intended. She, like Nell, must have seen premature small raids on the buffet table, and was truly anxious on the ghosts' behalf.

'I do plead with you to take care if you move about,' Lady Clarice continued. 'Remember each sound you hear, each sense, every touch, every sight. Even if there are no full materializations, there will be signs. We have equipment here to record and photograph what we can. I shall now summon my friends the ghosts, and please turn down the wicks on your tables to their lowest point or preferably out.'

Nell reached out to the wick on their table but the inspector was quicker, putting his hand over hers to stop her. 'A little light never hurt anyone, even ghosts,' he whispered.

Nell watched as the hall fell dark and Lady Clarice became a distant figure, arms outstretched to her precious ghosts. What if nothing happened? Or if it did, would somebody stop it? Yes, Inspector Melbray would. She grasped at that, thankful of his presence.

'Come forth, Alfred, son of Alefric,' Lady Clarice intoned as the lights went out. 'Come forth, Sir Ralph, come forth, Dorcas and Lord William. Come forth, Henrietta and Sir Thomas. Let us hear you, Violet, come forth, Hubert – and come forth, Charles Parkyn-Wright.'

Nell held her breath. And then it began.

Someone screamed, someone hushed whoever it was, and there were more cries, more gasps, even sobs, and the sound of chairs being scraped back. Fear took over and spread like a fog among them. Nell blinked. Was she imagining this? Were her eyes playing tricks on her? She could hear the inspector's deep breathing at her side; he was as glued as she was to the spectacle before them.

'What is it?' she half croaked to him.

Up on the gallery there were tiny pinpricks of

light and, very slowly, they were *moving*. A procession of ghosts, monks perhaps, like that haunted house at Bilsington. No, she thought fearfully, it was the Wychbourne ghosts coming to dine.

'They're here!' she heard Lady Clarice shriek. 'Dear Sir William, dear Sir Thomas – and Lady Adelaide. Oh, welcome!'

This was crazy. Some of the portraits hanging on the walls were illuminated by lights – cold, harsh lights as though to indicate those depicted in the portraits were alive, coming to join the feast. Only with difficulty did Nell hold back a shriek herself, clutching at the inspector's arm before she could stop herself.

Someone shrieked again – Lady Warminster, Nell thought. She even heard the dowager yelp.

'Silence,' Lady Clarice pleaded. 'Oh, please, silence. Our friends the ghosts must dine with us.'

This was madness. It couldn't really be a gathering of ghosts, could it? Nell was shivering. Those lights on the gallery screens were still slowly, slowly moving, one or two already coming down the panelling. She was still clutching the inspector's arm as he leaned closer to her.

'I have to stop this, Nell,' he whispered. 'Are you all right if I leave you?'

'Yes,' she managed to reply.

'Don't move, then.'

She watched him make his way through the gloom and as the room quietened down she could hear him talking to Lady Clarice. 'The ghosts have asked me to stop the gathering,' he told her firmly. 'It's far too noisy for them to dine here tonight.' Nell saw Lady Clarice make a gesture of dissent but thankfully it was too late. 'Lights, please!' he shouted to the room at large. 'Every one of them. And then,' he said, lightening the tension, 'I suggest we eat this superb buffet.'

His words were an anti-climax but seemed to calm the gathering down. To Nell, though, they made it worse. There had to be more. *Had* to be. The inspector wouldn't have come here just for this.

Mr Peters and Jimmy rushed to light the wall lamps, while the table lamps now revealed sheepish grins and strained faces. No one instantly moved to the buffet, though. There was still too much uncertainty and fear. Gradually a semblance of normality was restored and Nell saw the glories of food and drink gradually helping to calm the company. She had ceased to care whether the ghosts were lingering to admire her cuisine and their nameplates. There were other matters more important.

Something more must be about to happen. This lull must have been deliberately planned by the inspector, she realized. A glance at the door to the entrance hall, which had briefly opened, had told her that there were uniformed police in the entrance hall. Had she been right in thinking there were *two* cases, not one? How was this evening going to end? Not with her buffet, she was sure of that.

Arthur came over to her, beaming, with Lady Clarice at his side. 'My dear Nell, what a triumph.'

Nell stared at him, wondering what he meant. He must have seen her bewilderment and hastened to continue.

'Clarice and you have provided us with such a splendid show. I quite thought for a moment that Parkyn-Wright was going to appear in person. Or perhaps that phantom butler would serve me a drink. Even Napoleon would have satisfied me. But do tell me what will happen next. I have a feeling that the ghosts are going to be followed by something quite different.'

'I do too,' she said quietly. 'And it won't be long now.'

Lady Clarice was oblivious to everything but her ghosts. 'Had we waited longer,' she wailed, 'there might have been materializations.'

Nell soothed her and watched with relief as the buffet continued, although she could not bear to take anything for herself. Mr Peters was kept busy (without the help of any phantom butler) serving drinks. Whether or not he had met Jeremiah, the smuggler in the cellars, he was managing splendidly now. She was not, though. She would almost welcome the ghosts' appearance; it would be preferable to what the inspector might have in store.

She could see him with Lord and Lady Ansley and the dowager, and he beckoned her and Lady Clarice to join them. 'I have to thank you, Lady Clarice,' he announced loudly so that everyone present could hear. 'The ghosts have been most helpful to my investigation. You pointed out,' he continued, 'that Charles Parkyn-Wright's ghost fell silent after Miss Harlington's murder. You also told me that people often return as ghosts to the place in which they were murdered, but only as long as the case remains unsolved and justice remains to be done. When Miss Harlington died, however, Mr Parkyn-Wright's ghost was no longer active. That suggested to me that his mission was accomplished.'

'In what way, Inspector?' Lady Clarice asked, puzzled.

'Because Miss Harlington, his killer, was dead.'

'*She* killed Mr Charles?' Nell reeled in shock. Even as she grappled with this, though, she realized what it would mean: that there were indeed *two cases*, not one. And *that* would mean, if the inspector was right about Miss Harlington, that there was still worse to come. But *was* he right? Why would she want to kill him? Then she remembered that strange scent in the gallery – that could have been Miss Harlington's.

'There is no doubt of that,' the inspector replied. 'We've found plenty of evidence that would have enabled us to charge her, but one question remained to be answered. How did she manage it in the time? Thanks to you, Miss Drury, it has been answered. With your working out that she took the dagger and dark cloth before they began the ghost hunt and also where she could have hidden to await the rest of the group's return, the picture was complete.' A pause. 'That is, where Mr Parkyn-Wright's murder was concerned.'

'I can't believe that, Melbray,' Lord Ansley said. 'Why should Elise want to kill Charlie? She was his victim.'

'We proved, again thanks to Miss Drury's suggestion, that Miss Harlington was a black-mailer and the actual drug dealer. Parkyn-Wright worked for her, not the other way around. These are modern times, Lord Ansley. Women as well as men can take the wrong path in life.'

'But who killed Elise?' Lady Helen burst out as everyone began to gather round. 'Did the ghosts tell you that too?'

Nell couldn't think coherently. Mr Beringer? William Foster? Not Mr Peters, surely?

'Unfortunately the ghosts failed to help on that score,' the inspector replied, 'but we mere police are capable of finding our own evidence. Lady Warminster—'

'It wasn't me!' Lady Warminster screamed, leaping up from her chair. 'It wasn't. She was dead when I reached that awful place. I was late, you see. I was supposed to be there at nine fifteen but I wasn't and she was *dead*. It was horrible.'

'Kindly explain, Melbray,' the general said quietly, comforting his sobbing wife.

'Of course. You weren't at the dinner following the reconstruction, Lady Warminster, and no doubt Miss Harlington had promised you a full account of your gardener's light-hearted appearance at the ball. I expect she told you she had business to discuss with Miss Drury and Mr Fontenoy at the old dairy and she could talk to you there after that. You could hardly refuse as your gardener had placed you in such an impossible situation with Lord Ansley. Were it revealed, it would be most embarrassing for you socially to have to admit that your own gardener was accepting His Lordship's hospitality under an assumed name.'

Lady Warminster's mouth didn't so much fall open, Nell noticed, as grow rounder and rounder as she took this in. 'Darling,' she said to her husband in between sobs, 'the inspector is quite right. That's what happened. Isn't it awful?' The general's arm went round her.

'If you've finished with my wife,' he said firmly,' I will drive her home. *Now.*'

'Not yet, General,' Inspector Melbray said evenly.

What now? Longing for this ordeal of uncertainty to be over, Nell saw General Warminster stiffen. This was the police's battlefield, not his, and he would be far too disciplined to argue. But pottering pancakes, where on earth was this leading? Crank up the engine, Inspector, she muttered to herself, rigid with tension.

'When you were there at the dairy, Lady Warminster,' the inspector continued as calmly as ever, 'did you see anyone else, other than Miss Harlington?'

'No.'

The inspector did not press her. What did that imply? Nell thought feverishly. Was Lady Warminster her killer? Was that why Inspector Melbray was playing her like a fish on the line?

'There was obviously someone there with her before you arrived, Lady Warminster,' he pointed out, 'and perhaps he was still hiding nearby. We found evidence that some of the guests at the reconstruction earlier that day and at dinner that evening had recently been in the dairy. I take it that you did not ask anyone to accompany you there? Mr Beringer, for example, or Mr Fontenoy or Lord Richard?'

'No,' she wailed. 'I went alone.'

'Or Mr Foster, perhaps?'

'He's not a gentleman,' she snapped back.

There was a moment's appalled silence and Nell saw poor William flush bright red.

'Why was it important that it should be – in your words – "a gentleman"?' the inspector asked gravely.

Flustered, Lady Warminster looked in appeal at her husband, but he remained silent. Eventually she said sullenly, 'Elise had said I could bring along a gentleman friend if I liked, but I don't know who she meant.'

'What about Mr Ellimore?' Inspector Melbray asked quietly. 'He's your friend, isn't he? Was Miss Harlington threatening to make this public, perhaps to your husband and perhaps because she was placing a misleading interpretation on this friendship?'

Guy? Nell's head spun. How had the inspector got this ridiculous notion? Despite the way he had phrased it, the implication was obvious that Lady Warminster and Guy might be lovers. But that was sheer fiction. He couldn't stand the woman. True, Guy was very pale but that must be the shock.

'Nonsense, Inspector,' Guy replied. 'I worked for Her Ladyship, that's all. We discussed the music for the ball at Stalisbrook Place and we played there. Nothing more. You've been misinformed.'

He spoke so confidently that Nell was reassured – but not for long.

'Miss Harlington was blackmailing you too,' the inspector said to him matter-of-factly. 'That's why you went with her to the old dairy that night, although I suspect she also enticed you by saying

301

you might find Mr Fontenoy and Miss Drury there.'

'Now that really is nonsense,' Guy whipped back at him. 'I'm not married so how could she blackmail me on the grounds that Daisy and I were having a fling?'

Nell froze. Was he admitting the inspector was right with those ambiguous words and the deliberate use of Lady Warminster's Christian name, or was the pressure of the questioning flustering him? Surely the latter; it must be that.

'Miss Harlington didn't threaten to reveal just your relationship with Lady Warminster. She was blackmailing you over something quite different. She was threatening to unmask you as a pretender and spinner of fantasies.'

'How dare you, sir. In what way a pretender?' But there was less bravado in Guy's voice now.

Even Nell realized he was shaken at that and shuddered. Pretender? And what fantasies? This was Guy, whom she knew so well. And what would General Warminster be making of this? Most people here looked stunned and bewildered but the general was maintaining his impassive and stoical front.

She was wrong about the general, for it was he who rose to his feet and said in steely anger: 'Inspector Melbray is right, Ellimore, and Miss Harlington was incorrect if she referred to you as a gentleman. No gentleman would talk of a lady as you have of my wife. And you, Ellimore, are indeed a pretender. You claim to have been a squadron leader in the Royal Air Force. You rightly wear with pride the Distinguished Flying

Medal awarded to you, but that is an honour awarded only to non-commissioned men. You were no squadron leader – you were a ground mechanic at Vert Galand. Noble work and dangerous, but not what you aspire to be.'

Nell could not bear to watch while Guy attempted to rally.

'And if so,' he managed to reply, 'why would I care enough about Elise's threats to kill her? I only made that claim for the sake of the band so that we could move in high society. It gave us prestige and that meant more business.'

'No,' Inspector Melbray said, 'it gave *you* prestige. It inflated your view of yourself. Certainly it affected the band, but more importantly to you it affected how you appeared to other people. Especially—'

'To you, Nell,' Guy interrupted dispassionately, turning to her as she sat there aghast. *Was* that true? *Could* it be? 'Sorry, Nell,' he added, taking his time over lighting a cigarette. 'You never saw it. What a team we would have made if only you had.' He switched his attention briefly to Lady Warminster. 'At least you saw something in me, Kitty.' Lady Warminster gave a brief moan, although her husband's expression was again impassive.

Guy's eyes then fixed on Nell again. But they looked odd, far away, and there was a smile on his lips. 'I had to do it, Nell.'

'Do what?' she whispered in dread.

'I'll save you time, Inspector,' Guy quipped, drawing himself up, shoulders back, gazing neither at Inspector Melbray nor his stunned audience,

303

but perhaps, Nell thought, at some conjured-up image of himself as the heroic officer he still aspired to be, regardless of the fact that he had already proved himself a war hero.

'I'm sure you already have enough evidence to hang me anyway,' he continued. 'It was I who strangled Elise Harlington – and so I did a lot of people a favour.'

This was her Guy? Nell scrabbled for a foothold in a swirl of disbelief. It couldn't be. There was some mistake. The inspector was already beginning to move when Guy spoke again. He wasn't fighting back now. He seemed more amused than scared, even when the police entered the room.

'Elise was threatening to spread the word everywhere, not just to you, Kitty,' he said casually. 'After all, you wouldn't have spread it any further, would you? You wouldn't like it known that you screwed a mere ground mechanic.'

Amid the general gasps General Warminster reacted immediately, addressing not just Guy but the assembled company. 'A gentleman,' he said quietly, 'fails to hear anything to the detriment of a lady, particularly those he loves. Apart from Mr Ellimore we are *all* gentlemen in this room and the term bears no relation to our status in life.'

The general turned to his wife, now sobbing uncontrollably, and put his arm round her. 'Come, my dear, let us return to our home.'

'Are you all right, Miss Drury?'

'Yes, thank you,' Nell lied. It was the second time Inspector Melbray had asked her that this evening. He had led an unprotesting Guy to the

304

waiting uniformed police and she had returned to the table they had shared earlier. All right? she wondered. How could she feel all right? Should she just go back to the east wing or to the drawing room? The inspector had asked her to stay but she wasn't sure she wanted to. Or did she? What was done was done and the shock might wear off soon.

He sat down with her at the table. 'It has been a long evening,' he said, 'and there is much for me to do. But there is also much for us to talk about.' He hesitated. 'There is that pleasant spot by the pond where we would be unobserved tomorrow, if you would care to know more.'

She flinched. 'Not about Guy.'

He stiffened. 'I am truly sorry but how could I warn you?' Another awkward pause. 'He has been arrested and soon I'm sure he will be charged. It is a sad case, one of many that has its roots in the war.' He took her silence for a refusal of his suggestion about the morrow. 'I understand why you'd prefer not to know what happened.'

She roused herself. 'I was wrong, Inspector. I *do* want to know. Truly.'

She couldn't understand herself why she was so upset. It wasn't as if she had loved Guy – save perhaps for a few heady days seven years earlier. And yet the enormity of what he had done, his probable fate, seemed too much to bear.

She and Inspector Melbray walked in silence to the pond the next day. Never had anywhere looked so peaceful, the grass so green, the trees so softly comforting. This place was a refuge from all that had happened. It couldn't last, but she could take the healing balm it offered. The inspector had brought a rug with him and he placed it carefully on the ground.

'I've no picnic with me, I'm afraid. But one day we'll have another one,' he remarked.

To sit on his rug seemed an enormous step, a step that needed some decision to be made, but she made it. He took his place by her side and it was only then that she took in that the smart suit had been replaced by flannels, that he wore no hat, that the jacket he had flung down at his side, if not a blazer, was definitely not one to wear to Scotland Yard. He was intentionally sending a clear message that he was not on duty – even if it was undoubtedly Guy whom he wished to discuss.

'I'll talk, shall I?' he asked presently.

'Please do.'

'It was Miss Harlington's diary that gave us the clues we needed after you put forward that theory of blackmail. And she among our suspects was most certainly the one, apart from the family, who could have known about that access passage where Parkyn-Wright was hiding behind the screen.'

'How would she know?'

'He had been dancing with her. He would have told her about the joke. It gave her the opportunity she needed. What we lacked then was tangible evidence, which we've slowly been gathering.'

She couldn't bear to mention Guy yet. 'You said Miss Harlington killed Mr Charles because of that.'

'Yes. We concluded that he intended to take over her role, to control the money and perhaps

306

was beginning to threaten her. Peters was good enough to tell us she was blackmailing him and Rex Beringer also came forward. Short of pushing Parkyn-Wright under a Piccadilly bus, the Wychbourne Court ball provided an ideal opportunity for Miss Harlington to rid herself of him, as many of the people they were blackmailing were around that night.'

Nell felt more in command of herself now. 'Why did Miss Harlington go to the dairy, though?'

'It took me time to work that out, owing to your meagreness over parting with the truth.'

'What the blithering bloaters do you mean?' she asked indignantly.

He laughed. 'That ridiculous arrangement you had with Arthur Fontenoy. I can't believe Miss Harlington was under the impression you were having a fling with Mr Fontenoy but she might have thought you'd worked out that she had killed Parkyn-Wright and felt she had to find out what was going on in case it provided fodder for her blackmailing talents. She didn't like you, Nell, and so she decided to camouflage her curiosity by taking Guy there, assuring him, so he admitted, that he would indeed find you there indulging your passion with someone else. To find you with Arthur would be a great joke. Then there was Lady Warminster too. Miss Harlington had no intention of letting her get away without a touch of blackmail over William Foster as well as Ellimore and ordered her along to the dairy with him. It would no doubt have amused Miss Harlington to have both of Her Ladyship's beaux there.'

'I don't understand why Guy didn't resist her

307

charms, though. He often used to get women like her giving him the glad eye. He didn't even like her.' There was no heart in Nell's defence. She had thought she had known him but she hadn't.

'Liking doesn't always come into such matters.'

She licked dry lips. 'He killed Miss Harlington because of his fling with Lady Warminster?'

'No. I told you once we do a lot of work on records. Frederick Peters' war record proved to be his undoing as far as Parkyn-Wright was concerned, and so did Ellimore's. General Warminster had kindly pointed out to us the discrepancy between the DFM medal and his supposed officer rank and that led to our discovering more about his war career. He really didn't want you to find that out, Nell. He needs constant props for his self-esteem.'

Such as her, she realized. Guy's need to roam wasn't a sign of strength but of weakness. General Warminster had sensed something was wrong and it had been Guy, not William Foster, to whom he had referred as 'a rum fellow' that night at Stalisbrook Place.

'Poor Guy,' she managed to say. She had clung too hard to those memories of long ago instead of filing them where they belonged, in the dusty cabinet of youth.

'He's yet another casualty of the war. The kind of injury you never see.'

'Like Mr Briggs's.'

'Indeed. We've a lot of evidence against Ellimore. He may' – he hesitated – 'avoid the worst sentence if he gets a lenient judge. He saw a lot of death during his time at Vert Galand and on home leave he was caught up in the Tontine Street Gotha bombing raid on Folkestone. Not pleasant. It does things to people's minds. I was in the police during the war, in the Met. We suffered too through the bombing, coping with the wounded returning home. Nothing to compare to being in the trenches or in the air when death was one's constant neighbour twenty-four hours a day, but our lives were grim too. It makes one understand how the Ellimores of this world can surrender real life to dreams.'

Nell turned to look at him. 'I wasn't in love with Guy. I just – this sounds dotty – felt years ago that I was.'

'Maybe you were both living in a fantasy world like Lady Clarice,' he said, perhaps to lighten the tone.

'Ghosts!' That brought Nell to with a start. 'I'd forgotten them. They came, didn't they?' She quickly rethought this. '*Something* happened last night.'

'Impressive, wasn't it? Lady Sophy is rather proud of her entertainment, in which her brother and sister fully participated. But please don't tell Lady Clarice.'

'It was a joke, then.' Of course. How stupid of her to have been taken in. She remembered now – they'd only promised no Pepper's Ghost, not to avoid all jokes. 'I thought it was real for a moment,' she continued. 'What *was* it?'

'Glow-worms moving around on the gallery latticework.'

As simple as that. 'What about the portraits coming alive? Did they?'

'Not quite. Heard of radio luminescence paint? I found pieces of painted paper poked in at the side of the frames and whisked them off before the Ansley heirs beat me to it. Then I made them pick up every single glow-worm from the gallery with orders to return them forthwith to wherever they found them.'

'But what about the poltergeist? Jimmy could only have been responsible for two of the three episodes.'

'Add to that the unexplained appearance of a phantom butler.'

'It *must* have been Mr Peters who served you.'

'No, I saw both of them. Shall we forget that and your poltergeist?'

'Yes,' Nell agreed fervently.

'Are you happy working here? This seems a weird place to me.'

'Yes, again. It's my home, my dream, even though it's been a nightmare recently.'

'Your job, that's what Ellimore told me. Your job came between you both.'

'Not entirely true. Anyway, what about *his* job? Why just mine? I *am* my job.'

'I have a job too. Scotland Yard is like Wychbourne Court. Twenty-four hours either working or thinking about it in my sleep. Will you ever marry, Nell?'

She hesitated. 'I doubt it. Will you, Inspector Melbray?'

'Someday I will. And it's Alex,' he said. '*Alex*, for Pete's sake.'